D1260016

MAGICIAN'S WARD

BOOKS BY PATRICIA C. WREDE

The Seven Towers
Sorcery and Cecelia (with Caroline Stevermer)
*Snow White and Rose Red**
*Mairelon the Magician**
Book of Enchantments
*Magician's Ward**

THE LYRA BOOKS
Shadow Magic
Daughter of Witches
The Harp of Imach Thyssel
Caught in Crystal
*The Raven Ring**
*Shadows over Lyra**

THE CHRONICLES OF THE ENCHANTED FOREST
Dealing with Dragons
Searching for Dragons
Calling on Dragons
Talking to Dragons

*denotes a Tor book

MAGICIAN'S WARD

Patricia C. Wrede

TOR®

A TOM DOHERTY ASSOCIATES BOOK
NEW YORK

MAGICIAN'S WARD

Copyright © 1997 by Patricia C. Wrede

This book is printed on acid-free paper.

A Tor Book
Published by Tom Doherty Associates, Inc.
175 Fifth Avenue
New York, NY 10010

Tor Books on the World Wide Web:
http://www.tor.com

Tor® is a registered trademark of Tom Doherty Associates, Inc.

Library of Congress Cataloging-in-Publication Data

Wrede, Patricia C.
    Magician's ward / Patricia C. Wrede.—1st ed.
      p. cm.
    "A Tom Doherty Associates book."
    ISBN 0-312-85369-6
    I. Title.
    PS3573.R38M34   1997
    813'.54—dc21   97-14690
                                                        CIP

First Edition: December 1997

Printed in the United States of America

0 9 8 7 6 5 4 3 2 1

For Lois Bujold,
without whom this would still be stuck in Chapter 7.
Twice.

Acknowledgments

This book would not have been possible, let alone finished, without the aid and comfort of the following people:

Pamela Dean Dyer-Bennet, Beth Friedman, Raphael Carter, Sarah Withee, and Elise Matthesen, who helped with sundry accents and foreign languages, and James Bryant, who provided the answer to a tricky research question. Any errors are, of course, my own.

My critique group, The Usual Suspects past and present, who were amazingly good about sitting through the same scenes over and over until I got them right, and who performed prodigious feats during the final days of production: Lois McMaster Bujold, Peg Kerr Ihinger, Elise Matthesen, Bruce Bethke, and Joel Rosenberg.

My editors, Delia Sherman and Patrick Nielsen Hayden, who were supernaturally patient when patience was most required, and who somehow knew exactly when it was necessary to crank up the heat.

Caroline Stevermer, Rosemary Ighel, Lois Bujold, and Pamela Dyer-Bennet, who provided much appreciated moral support, encouragement, lunches, and a careful eye to period detail.

My family, who were exceedingly understanding as regards late Christmas presents and last-minute cancellations.

MAGICIAN'S WARD

ONE

Cold rain drizzled on the dark London streets—at least, it *looked* cold. Kim peered out her bedroom window at the deserted square two stories below and pulled her shawl closer around her shoulders, though the fire in the grate was almost too warm for comfort. She hadn't had to shelter, shivering, in a doorway for nearly a year, but the memories lingered.

Still no sign of Mairelon. Is he going to stay out all night? Kim thought resentfully. *He gets to jaw with Lord Shoreham and eat at the Royal College of Wizards, and I'm stuck here with a great thick square book and that poker-backed aunt of his.* She shook her head. It was not what she had expected, a year ago when she had agreed to become Mairelon's ward and learn reading and magic. Then, she had thought it would be a great adventure.

" 'Anything might happen,' I thought," Kim said aloud to her reflection in the rain-dark window. " 'Anything at all.' I must have been touched in the head." She crossed her eyes and stuck out her tongue at her mirror image.

"Dicked in the nob, that's what I was," she muttered.

The bedroom door opened. "What did you say, Kim?" Mrs. Lowe asked in a mildly disapproving tone.

With a faint sigh, Kim slid off the window seat and turned. The relentless respectability of Mairelon's paternal aunt was very wearing. It seemed much longer than a week since they'd found her ensconced in the townhouse on their arrival in London. And since they were all technically guests of Mairelon's brother Andrew, who as elder son had inherited the townhouse, there was nothing to be done about Mrs. Lowe except spend time elsewhere. Which Mairelon had been doing rather a lot. Kim wished she had that option. "I didn't say anything," she told Mrs. Lowe in as mild a tone as she could manage.

"I was sure I heard your voice." Mrs. Lowe hesitated. "It wasn't any of that . . . that thieves' cant, was it?"

"Flash lingo," Kim said helpfully.

Mrs. Lowe frowned. "After all my nephew has done for you, the least you could do is to be more careful of your language."

"Mairelon doesn't mind the way I talk."

"My nephew is not always as conscious of the social niceties as he should be," Mrs. Lowe said. "Nonetheless, they must be observed. And you really should refer to him as 'Mr. Merrill.' He is your guardian, and it would show a proper respect."

"Did you want me for something?" Kim asked, hoping to dodge the discussion. "I have studying to do." She waved at the fat, leatherbound book on the nightstand beside the bed, and suppressed a grimace. Three more volumes were waiting for her in the library below. *Why he keeps shoving them at me when he knows I'm no great hand at reading. . . .*

"More magic, I suppose." Mrs. Lowe shook her head. "I'll speak to Richard about that in the morning."

"Speak to him?" Kim said, beginning to be alarmed. For the past week, Mrs. Lowe had made Kim's life a respectable misery. She had insisted that Kim accompany her to pay interminable morning calls on dull but acceptable acquaintances, forbidden all walks alone, and made it quite clear that, in the unlikely event of Kim's encountering any of her former friends, Kim was to cut them dead. Thus far, however, she had not attempted to interfere with Kim's magic lessons.

"I am sure you will have plenty of opportunity to study when you are back in Kent," Mrs. Lowe said. "Magic is all very well, but it is hardly a necessary branch of knowledge for a young woman in your situation. While you are in London, we must make the most of your chances. I cannot say I have any great hope of success, given your . . . circumstances, but there are one or two possibilities—That is why I wished to talk to you tonight."

"I don't understand," Kim said warily.

"Mrs. Hardcastle knows a gentleman who sounds as if he will do very nicely. Well, perhaps not a *gentleman*, but respectable enough. She has arranged for us to meet him tomorrow afternoon, and I wished to warn you to be on your best behavior."

"Best behavior—You can't be thinking of getting me legshackled to some gentry cull!"

"If what you just said was some sort of reference to arranging a suitable marriage for you, yes, that is precisely what I was referring to," Mrs. Lowe replied stiffly.

Kim didn't know whether to be amused or appalled. Her, married to a toff? In her wildest notions, she had never thought of such a thing. She looked at Mrs. Lowe, and her amusement died. The woman was serious. "It'd never work."

"It certainly won't if you burst out with a remark like that over Mrs. Hardcastle's tea table. Consider carefully what I have said, and be prepared tomorrow, if you please. I am afraid that your . . . interesting background means that you are unlikely to have many opportunities of this nature; you would be ill advised to waste this one. Good night."

Kim stared at the closing door, then flung herself back into the window seat. *Marriage!* She's *the one who's dicked in the nob. There isn't a toff in London who would marry a penniless, nameless sharper, even if I have gone all respectable.* She shifted restlessly in the window seat. Respectability did not sit comfortably with her, but what other choices did she have?

She couldn't go back to the streets, even if she were mad enough to want to. What with all the regular eating, she'd filled out more than she'd have thought possible; posing as a boy now would be out of the question. She hadn't the training to be a housemaid or take up a trade, even if she could find someone to hire her. Mrs. Lowe's "respectable gentleman" wasn't a serious possibility, but sooner or later Kim would have to think of something. She couldn't stay Mairelon's ward forever.

Though that doesn't seem to have occurred to him.

But Richard Merrill—whom she still could not think of as anything but Mairelon the Magician—didn't look at things the way other people did. *Well, if he did, he'd never have got himself made my guardian.* For all the awareness he showed, you'd think he was perfectly willing to go on feeding, clothing, and housing Kim until they both died of old age.

Maybe she should ask him about it. Maybe she would, if she could figure out what "it" was, exactly—or at least well enough to explain. "I'm bored" would only get her a larger stack of books to study; "I'm not happy" sounded ungrateful; and "Your aunt is a Friday-faced noodle" was insulting. But there had to be some way to put it.

Meanwhile, she had three more pages of Shepherd's *Elementary Invocations* to decipher before morning. She didn't want Mairelon to think that she wasn't working at her lessons, not if that Mrs. Lowe was going to ask him to stop them. Sighing, Kim climbed out of the window seat.

The text on magic occupied Kim for several hours, but when she finally laid it aside and went to bed, she found it impossible to sleep. She lay in darkness, staring up at the plaster ceiling and listening for the clatter of Mairelon's carriage on the cobblestones outside. Around her, the household quieted as the housemaids and sculleys finished their days' work and climbed the narrow servants' stair to their beds under the eaves. The watchman's cry, muffled and perfunctory, came faintly through the window. *Poor old cull,* Kim thought as a gust of wind sent raindrops rattling like gunfire across the panes. *I'm glad I'm not out in this.*

Suddenly she sat bolt upright in the bed. *That sounded like . . .* The noise came again, soft but clear. *Someone's downstairs. Someone who's got no business being there.*

Kim slid out of bed. Her eyes slid past the bellpull without pausing. If she summoned a maid, she'd only have to send the girl for a footman, and by the time all the running around was done, the cull downstairs would have gotten away. And if she was wrong, if there wasn't anyone, she'd have to endure endless lectures from Mrs. Lowe. She could call someone when she was sure.

She started for the door, then stopped. Her white nightdress stood out in the darkness; she didn't want the cracksman to spot her and pike off before she got a footman or two to help catch him. Her dressing gown was a dark, rich blue that would blend with the shadows; she picked it up and struggled into it. Then she eased the door open and slipped into the darkened hallway.

Moving lightly, she made for the stairs. Another soft, scuffing sound came from below, followed by a distinct creak; hadn't *anyone* else noticed? *Probably a novice, on his first crack lay. Somebody should have told him to stick by the walls. Mother Tibb wouldn't have sent anybody out that didn't know at least that much.*

Suiting her own actions to her thoughts, Kim plastered herself against one wall and started down the stairs, setting her bare feet as near the wall as she could. No creaks betrayed her. Halfway down, she caught the flash of a dark lantern and froze. The light flickered past. A moment later, a figure skulked down the hallway, opening doors and peering through them. The strong smell of a cheap lard candle and the scent of wet wool preceded him; he must have been standing in the rain for some time to be so drenched. Finally, with a grunt of satisfaction, the man let the last door swing fully open and disappeared into the library.

The *library?* What could a thief want from the library? The silver was downstairs, on the ground floor, and Mairelon's brother didn't keep valuables on display in his townhouse. The whole thing had more of a rum look by the minute. Kim frowned, considering; then a hastily stifled expletive decided her. There was no knowing what this cove was up to. She'd just make sure he couldn't pike off, and then she'd call the footmen.

Silently, she crept down the remaining steps. A cautious look showed the cracksman bent over the end table, peering at the shelves behind it by the light of the dark lantern. Kim smiled grimly and, holding the handle to prevent the betraying click of the latch snapping into place, carefully closed the library door. Now, if she could just lock it in place somehow . . . But the door had no lock, and there was nothing nearby she could use to jam it. Magic, perhaps? She ran over in her mind the short list of spells she could cast with some reliability. There was one that might do the trick, if she could get it right.

She took a deep breath, then focused her eyes on the handle. In her mind she pictured it as it was, staying as it was, motionless, frozen, immovable, and in a voice barely above a whisper began the spell that would make the image real.

An outraged bellow and a loud crash from inside the library rattled her concentration. "—*sta, atque*—" she continued, and then the door burst open, knocking her sprawling. An instant later, the escaping housebreaker stumbled over her and went down. Kim shouted and grabbed at him. Her hands slid against silk, then tightened around thick, damp wool. The burglar twisted and something tore; the man scrambled away from her, leaving her holding a scrap of cloth.

Kim tried to roll to her feet and ended up tangled in her dressing gown. The man regained his feet and pelted down the hall, just as a sleepy-eyed footman appeared on the far stairs. The burglar shoved the hapless footman against the wall and dashed down the stairs and out of sight. Crashing noises and yells marked his continued progress. The footman recovered himself and plunged after his assailant. More shouts drifted upward.

As Kim, muttering curses, struggled to a standing position at last, she heard footsteps on the stairs behind her. She turned and found Mrs. Lowe, lamp in hand, staring at her with shock and disapproval.

"Kim! Whatever have you been doing? And in such a state!"

Kim glanced down. Her dressing gown had come undone,

and she showed distinct traces, even in the lamplight, of having rolled about on the floor. A torn and ragged bit of lace trailed off the hem of her nightdress, and her hair was probably every-which-way, too. Mrs. Lowe, of course, was turned out in more proper style—not a wisp of gray hair escaped from under her dainty lace cap, and her dressing gown was crisper and neater than Kim's had been even before her encounter with the burglar. Kim pulled her dressing gown closed and discovered that several of the buttons were missing.

"I heard someone in the library," Kim said as she scanned the floor for the buttons. One of them lay next to the baseboard, beside a piece of wood with a splintered end. Kim bent toward it.

"Nonsense. You were dreaming, I'm sure."

"I wasn't asleep." Kim reached for the button, and her fingers brushed the splintered wood. A light tingling ran up her arm, and she jerked her hand back in surprise. *Magic?* She touched it again. *Not a strong spell, but recent. Mairelon'll want a look at this.* Frowning, she picked up wood and button together and shoved them in the pocket of her dressing gown.

"If you *did* hear something, it was probably one of the maids. They keep different hours in town, and I expect you are not yet accustomed—"

Kim tucked another button in the pocket of her dressing gown and looked back at Mrs. Lowe. "It wasn't one of the maids. They wouldn't be carrying on like that if it had been," she added, waving at the stairs. The shouts and crashing noises had ceased, but it was nonetheless obvious that there was far more activity on the ground floor than was normal at this time of night.

"At least you had the good sense to put on your dressing gown before you came down," Mrs. Lowe said, tacitly conceding the point. "Still, wandering about the house *en désha-*

billé at this hour is most irregular, no matter what your reasons."

"I bet Mairelon won't think so." The injudicious words slipped out before Kim thought.

Mrs. Lowe's thin lips pressed together in a hard line. Then, in deceptively soft tones, she said, "Mr. Merrill, Kim, not Mairelon. Showing proper respect is—Where do you think you are going?"

"To find out whether they've caught the flash cull that was turning out the library."

"Indeed you shall not," Mrs. Lowe said. "You will return to your room at once, and we will discuss matters further in the morning."

"What matters?" said a new voice from the lower stairs.

"Mairelon!" Kim said, turning toward the voice with a sigh of relief.

TWO

Richard Merrill climbed the last few steps and stood eyeing Kim and Mrs. Lowe with a quizzical expression on his round, cheerful face. His dark hair looked damp and a little disheveled, but his coat and pantaloons were immaculate. Kim wondered what he had done with his cloak. *Probably left it in a heap in the front hall because the footmen were too busy chasing burglars to take it.*

"What matters?" he asked again. "And why wait to discuss them? From the look of things, no one's going to get any sleep for hours. Kim, Harry says he rescued you from someone, or possibly several someones, who from his description were apparently seven feet tall and more indestructible than the strong man down at Astley's Amphitheatre. Ought I to congratulate him, or should he merely be sent to the kitchen to sleep it off?"

Before Kim could answer, Mrs. Lowe frowned and said in tones that promised dire retribution for someone, "Who is Harry?"

"One of the footmen. He's on his way to the pantry to receive a hero's due, on the strength of a bruised shin and a knock on the head. The question is, does he deserve it?"

"He got banged up against the wall when that cracksman piked off, that's all," Kim said. "Unless they had a run-in later."

"No, the fellow got clean away. Still, I think we'll leave Harry to his laurels, well-earned or not. What I want now is the rest of the story." He looked at Kim expectantly.

"I was upstairs when I heard—"

"Not tonight, Kim," Mrs. Lowe broke in. "You have had quite enough excitement for one evening, and tomorrow is going to be a busy day. I'm sure that if Richard thinks about it, he'll agree that you ought to be in bed. You'll have plenty of time to talk in the morning. Come along."

Mairelon put out a restraining hand. "I appreciate your concern, Aunt, but I wish to speak to Kim now, if she's agreeable. It won't take long."

"Of course I'm agreeable," Kim said.

"That's settled, then." Turning his head, he called down the stairs, "Hunch! Bring a lamp when you come up."

Mrs. Lowe looked startled. "Kim is not the best judge of what is most appropriate, Richard. If you will stop for a moment and think, you will see that."

"What? No, no, Kim is quite good at this sort of thing. Go on, Kim—you were upstairs, and you heard something."

"She will catch a chill, running about half dressed at this hour," Mrs. Lowe said firmly. "She belongs upstairs in her bed."

"Half dressed?" Mairelon said with mild interest. He looked at Kim and shook his head. "Nonsense. She's wearing a dressing gown. Now, I'll grant you, it wouldn't be quite the thing if she were going to go walking in Grosvenor Square in the rain, but I promise you I won't let her. We'll stay right here in the library."

"Kim needs her rest, Richard."

"She's more likely to get it if she has a chance to talk first," Mairelon said, frowning slightly.

"I'm not sleepy," Kim put in.

Mrs. Lowe sighed. "If you insist, Richard. I shall join you as chaperone, of course."

"I think not." Mairelon's attention was firmly fixed on his aunt at last, and his expression had gone bland and unfathomable, the way it did when he was about to be particularly stubborn about something. Mrs. Lowe did not seem to realize it.

"Richard, Kim's reputation—"

"—is quite safe. I'm her guardian, remember." His tone was polite and gentle, but brooked no contradiction.

Mrs. Lowe hesitated, then acquiesced. "Very well, Richard. No doubt you have your reasons. I must tell you, however, that it is most irregular, and the possible consequences—"

"In the morning, Aunt," Mairelon said. He glanced at Kim and gave a tiny nod in the direction of the library. Turning back to Mrs. Lowe, he went on in a soothing tone, "As you said, it is late, and I'm sure this has been a strain on your nerves. Things will look different when you've had a good night's sleep."

Kim slipped quietly around behind him and into the darkened library. The murmur of voices in the hall continued; then she heard heavy footsteps on the stairs, and Mairelon's voice: "The library, Hunch." She stepped back as Mairelon's manservant came through the door, carrying a candle. He was tall and thin, and everything about him drooped: his shoulders, his mustache, the baggy trousers he insisted on wearing.

" 'Ere now, Kim, where—oh, there you are. Stay still; I'll 'ave these 'ere lamps lit in no time."

Light flared, then steadied as Hunch adjusted the lamp-wick. "There. Now—'Struth! That 'Arry wasn't 'alf right, by the look of it. What 'appened?"

The burglar's dark lantern lay on its side next to an over-turned end table; it was a good thing the candle had gone out. A dozen books were scattered across the floor, some looking as if they had fallen when the table went over, others as if they had been dropped or thrown.

"An excellent question, Hunch." Mairelon entered, closing the door firmly behind him. "We've heard Harry's tale; I trust yours will be somewhat . . . less imaginative, Kim."

"I thought I heard something, so I came down to have a look," Kim said. "A man with a dark lantern was in the hall, looking in all the rooms. He went into the library. I was going to lock him in and call a footman, except he must of heard me working the spell or something, because he came charging out while I was still in the middle of it. He tripped over me, and I yelled, and he got away from me. The footman—Harry?—was coming up to see what the noise was, and the rum cove ran slap into him before he piked off down the stairs. That's all."

"Brief and to the point," Mairelon said. "Though not, per-haps, up to Aunt Agatha's standards of elocution. What a good thing we sent her off to bed."

"I found this in the hallway after the turn-up," Kim said, pulling the scrap of wood from her pocket and laying it on top of the books. "I don't know what it is, but it's been mag-icked."

Mairelon picked up the scrap and turned it over in his hands. It looked like a piece of a wooden rod, about four inches long and as big around as Kim's little finger. "Techni-cally, the term is 'infused,' not 'magicked,' but in a general sort of way you're quite right."

"What's the difference?"

"Something that's been enchanted, or 'magicked,' as you put it, has had a spell cast *on* it. Something that's been infused has had a spell stored *in* it." Mairelon frowned at the piece of rod.

"What kind of spell?" Kim asked.

Mairelon blinked, then smiled. "That *is* the next question. One of them, anyway. Normally, once the spell has been invoked, it's used up—there's no way to tell what it was."

"That's normally," Kim said, recognizing the tone. "What's weird about this?"

Mairelon's smile broadened. "Whoever made it was exceedingly clumsy; it's as if he put the spell together from bits and pieces. And not all the bits and pieces went off when the wizard invoked it."

" 'E's a beginner, then?" Hunch said.

"Mmm. Possibly. But Kim's a beginner, and she could do a better job than this."

"Well, are there enough bits left that you can tell what it was supposed to do?" Kim said, trying to decide whether she should be pleased or insulted by the comparison.

"Let's find out, shall we?" Mairelon pointed the piece of rod at the nearest bookcase and muttered something under his breath.

Nothing happened. Mairelon frowned and said something longer that sounded like Latin to Kim. As he spoke, he waved the rod in a slow circle.

Several of the books began to glow with a soft, golden light. Mairelon gave an exclamation of satisfaction, then began muttering rapidly, moving the rod in a rapid, complex pattern. The glow dimmed, then steadied. After a moment, Mairelon relaxed and set the rod on the table.

Kim looked down. The books that lay scattered about

the floor were all glowing as well. "This is crazy! He couldn't of sherried off with all those."

"If it were that simple, we wouldn't have books all over the library floor," Mairelon said. "I'll wager he was looking for one or two particular volumes. The question is, which ones?"

"If you was to clean up a bit o' this 'ere mess, you might 'ave an easier time figuring it out," Hunch said.

"An excellent notion." Mairelon stepped forward and lifted the little table back onto its crocodile paws. "Put the books here, and we'll have a look."

Hunch picked up the scattered volumes, while Kim rather gingerly helped Mairelon pull glowing books from the shelves. When they were all piled on the end table, they made an impressive heap.

"Now, what have we here?" Mairelon murmured. "*The Mountains of Doubt, Collegium Sorceria, Discoverer, Après Cinq Cents Ans, Fire Keepers Vol. VI*—I wonder why he didn't want the first five?—*A Pottery Pigeon, Reflecting Quadrille, Maturing Without Heaviness* . . . Our housebreaker appears to have excellent taste."

"Well, 'e can just taste things somewheres else next time," Hunch muttered.

"I am inclined to agree with your recommendation, Hunch," Mairelon said. "I don't suppose you got a look at his face during all the excitement, Kim?"

"No," Kim said with regret. "I got a piece of his coat, though. He's a toff, or someone as wants to be."

"Really?" Mairelon looked at Kim with interest. "How did you deduce that?"

"He was wearing a silk waistcoat. I felt it. And this isn't homespun." Kim pulled the torn piece of wool from her pocket. Two buttons came with it, and bounced off under the settee.

"Ripped his coat, did he?" Mairelon said. "How lucky for us."

"Lucky?" Kim said, mystified.

"Yes, of course." He crossed to the heavy table in the middle of the library and studied it a moment, frowning. "Help me move this closer to the center of the room. Hunch, get me the blue chalk and a pot of ink. Oh, and an unused candle for Kim."

"You ain't doing nothin' dreadful now, Master Richard," Hunch said in a stern tone. "Not in Master Andrew's 'ouse."

"Hmm? Oh, not at all, Hunch," Mairelon said as he and Kim shifted the table. "It's only a spell Shoreham's been working on for a while—an adaptation of the standard scrying spell. He showed it to me the day before yesterday; it's quite clever. You'll see."

"All right, then," Hunch said, though he continued to frown. "Lord Shore'am is a proper gentleman."

Mairelon shot his servant an amused glance and pulled a handkerchief from his pocket. Carefully, he spread it over the tabletop, smoothing the creases with his fingertip. The corners of the handkerchief hung over the center of the table's sides, so that a triangle of bare wood was left in each corner.

"Yes, but what is this spell supposed to *do?*" Kim said.

"Help us catch our burglar, with luck," Mairelon replied. "Hunch, where's that ink? Thank you. Give Kim the chalk." He set a small ink bottle on one of the bare corners of the tabletop.

"*Mairelon—*"

"You'll see in a minute. Now, what can I use—ah, yes, this will do nicely." He plucked a small silver salver from a shelf beside the door and positioned it carefully in the exact center of the handkerchief. "There. Hand me that scrap of cloth you found."

"Mairelon, I'm never going to learn any magic if you don't give me any explanations," Kim said in exasperation as she gave him the piece of wool.

"And you'll never be a great magician if you can't make half an understanding do for a start," Mairelon said, dropping the scrap into the salver. "A competent one, perhaps, but not a great one. The chalk, if you please."

Sighing, Kim handed him the chalk. He sketched three careful crosses in the remaining corners of the table, then drew an unsteady circle around the salver on the handkerchief. Absently, he stuck the chalk in his coat pocket as he surveyed the setup. Then he looked up at Kim. "Now you may demonstrate the results of your studies for me. I want you to set the ward."

"Me?" Kim stared at the candle in her hand, suddenly appalled. The warding spell was nearly always set when a complex or dangerous enchantment was being attempted; in theory, it protected the mage from outside interference, and any bystanders from the consequences of a spell gone wrong. In practice, the degree of protection such a spell afforded was directly related to the skill of the spellcaster. An apprentice's ward was unlikely to stand up to more than an apprentice-level mistake. And Mairelon wanted Kim to set a ward while he worked a new spell.

"Don't worry," Mairelon said. "This is a relatively simple enchantment. Normally, I wouldn't bother with a ward at all, even though this is the first time I've ever cast it. But you can use the practice, and it will keep our work from disturbing anyone. Or from attracting attention outside the house," he added as an afterthought.

Only partially reassured, Kim nodded. She thought for a moment, to make sure she had the steps of the warding spell clear in her mind. Then she took a deep breath. *"Fiat lux,"* she said, concentrating on the candle.

The candlewick burst into flame. Kim held it still for a moment, until the smell of melted beeswax reached her and the tingly pressure of a spell in progress ran up and down her arms. Then, keeping her eyes fixed on the candle, Kim turned and walked in a slow, clockwise circle around Mairelon and the table. As she walked, she recited the words of the warding spell four times, once for each side of the table. She had more difficulty than she had expected in judging her speed correctly so that the words came out even, but she managed it. When she reached the spot where she had begun, she turned to face Mairelon and said the final *"fiat."* With considerable relief, she felt the ward rise around them like an invisible curtain.

"Very good," Mairelon said softly. "I couldn't have done better myself. Now, watch carefully, and try to split your concentration so that you can still hold the ward while you watch. You may not always have someone handy to cast a ward for you when it's needed, so you'll need to learn to hold it without even thinking about it."

"Sort of like picking a lock and listening for the nabbing culls at the same time," Kim said, nodding carefully. She felt the ward shift as she spoke, and hastily returned her attention to it. When it was steady again, she whispered, "Only trickier."

Mairelon laughed. "Yes, I imagine it would be. Very well; it's my turn."

He picked up the scrap of cloth and concentrated for a moment, then crumpled it and dropped it into the salver. The springy wool flattened out immediately, but the scrap was too small to cover much of the salver. Uncorking the bottle of ink, Mairelon poured it slowly over the cloth. The ink soaked quickly into the wool, then rose around it in a flat black pool. Mairelon studied it a moment, then picked up the salver and tilted it this way and that until the ink coated the bottom with shiny blackness.

When he was satisfied at last, he set the salver on the handkerchief once more. Holding his left hand over it, he began speaking, too rapidly for Kim to follow. The tingling sensation of a spell in process struck her with renewed force, and she had to concentrate to keep control of the ward. Mindful of his instructions, she tried to pay attention to Mairelon's spellcasting, but her Latin and Greek were still rudimentary. She recognized perhaps one word in twenty, but even the unintelligible phrases had the hard-edged feel that only came with magic. They hung in the air around Mairelon's hand, building the invisible, dangerous structure of the spell.

Kim suppressed a shiver. She did not want to distract Mairelon; even a small mistake would send razor-edged words flying like shards of shattered glass. She wondered whether she would ever be sure enough of her control to risk building a spell around her own hand. It seemed unlikely, but a year ago the thought of learning magic at all had seemed not merely unlikely, but impossible.

Mairelon finished speaking and, without moving his arm, folded his outstretched fingers in toward his palm. The hovering spell slid past his hand onto the ink-covered salver. "Now, we look," he said.

Puzzled, Kim stared at him; then she realized that he meant for her to look at the salver. She lowered her gaze, and saw that a picture had formed on the surface of the ink, like a reflection in a mirror or a puddle of water.

A man muffled in a scarf, top hat, and long cloak hurried along a narrow street. The shop windows behind him were dark and shuttered, and the wind whipped his cloak out behind him. "Well, well," Mairelon murmured. "It looks as if you were right, Kim. Our housebreaker is a gentleman. Let's see. . . ."

The picture in the ink wobbled, then shifted so that the man was hurrying directly toward them. His head was down, and one hand gripped the brim of his hat; between that and the scarf, little of his face was visible. Gold gleamed on his middle finger, and Kim leaned forward to look more closely.

"Blast!" said Mairelon. "I wanted a look at his face. Perhaps if we try another angle—"

The image wobbled and distorted, like a reflection in water when a pebble drops into it. Kim got a brief impression of blue eyes and a damp wisp of hair plastered wetly to a high forehead, and then the picture was gone. The shiny surface of the ink reflected only a glimmer of light from Kim's candle.

Mairelon scowled at the salver, then reached for the ink-soaked wool. As he lifted the cloth, the ink slid off like hot oil running out of a pan, leaving the threads clean. "You can drop the ward now, Kim," he said as he pocketed the scrap.

Obediently, Kim recited the closing phrase and blew out the candle. Hunch collected it and the empty ink bottle and carried them off. Mairelon continued to frown at the salver. "That was not nearly as useful as I'd hoped," he said. "Perhaps I should have waited; we might have gotten a glimpse of his rooms. But I was hoping to see his face, and I didn't want him to have a chance to change his coat."

"Well, if you'd waited much longer, he wouldn't of had the coat at all, I'll bet," Kim said.

"Why do you say that?"

"Why else would a toff be on Petticoat Lane at this time of night, unless he had something for the togs-men?"

Mairelon blinked. "Petticoat Lane? You're sure?"

Kim snorted. "I spent enough time there. He was just down from Flash Annie's, by where Willie Bast used to lay up. It's a good job for him that it's a mucky night out, or he'd be rid of more than his coat."

Hunch returned and picked up the salver with a disapproving look. "Are you done with this, Master Richard?"

"What? Yes, of course. Did you notice anything else, Kim?"

"He has blue eyes," Kim offered. "And he wears a gold ring with a flower on it and a ruby in the center."

"And he has his boots from Hoby," Mairelon said. "It's not much to go on, but it's a help. Now, let's make a list of these books and see what we can tell from it."

The pile of books on the table had stopped glowing sometime during Mairelon's scrying spell. Mairelon sat down and began sorting through them, while Hunch brought him a pen, paper, and a fresh bottle of ink. As Mairelon wrote titles, Kim shifted books so he could see the ones he hadn't written down yet, and in ten minutes the list was complete.

"There," Mairelon said, and glanced around the library. "I believe that's all we can do tonight." He picked up his list and, in the absence of a blotter, blew gently on the ink to hasten its drying.

"What about tomorrow?" Kim said.

"Tomorrow, I'll take this over to the Royal College and see whether Kerring has any thoughts on it."

"Who's Kerring?"

"Lord Kerring is head archivist at the Royal College of Wizards," Mairelon replied. "If there's a connection among all these titles, he'll spot it. He might even have some idea which wizards would be likely to know a bit about burglary."

"That cove didn't know the first thing about the crack lay," Kim said. "I wouldn't of heard him at all, if he had."

Mairelon looked thoughtful. "Possibly he's more of a magician than I'd been thinking. If he was depending on magic to pull off his theft—"

"He was still a clunker," Kim said firmly. "And I didn't notice any spellcasting."

"He invoked the spell he had stored in this," Mairelon said, holding up the broken rod.

"Then why didn't I notice it?"

"Because it was *invoked*, not *cast*," Mairelon replied. "The spellcasting took place when the spell was originally stored in the rod, which could have been hours ago, or even days. When the spell is invoked, you wouldn't notice anything unless you were touching either the storage container or the object the spell was intended to affect."

"I think I see," Kim said.

"If our burglar had another trick or two like this, he could have used them without alerting you," Mairelon went on, fingering the rod. "Rather a good precaution to take if you're going to burgle a wizard's house, now that I think of it. I believe we should set a few wards around the house tomorrow, just in case he comes back."

"What if that there burglar comes back *tonight?*" Hunch said.

"Then the library will no doubt be a wreck when we come down in the morning, Harry will probably collect another lump on his head, Aunt Agatha will be prostrate with the vapours, and I shall have to apologize to everyone for my carelessness." Mairelon smiled sweetly at Hunch. "Unless, of course, you spend the night here, on watch."

"I might 'ave known you'd think of that," Hunch muttered. "Well, as long as you don't go 'aring off after 'im while I'm busy elsewhere."

"Hunch! Would I do such a thing?"

"You 'ave before."

"I'm a reformed character."

Kim choked back a snort of laughter. Mairelon turned and looked at her with mock disapproval.

"I seem to recall telling Aunt Agatha that I'd send you up before you took a chill. As we appear to be finished here, for the time being—"

"As long as you don't go haring off after that burglar without me," Kim echoed.

"You're getting to be as bad as Hunch," Mairelon said, and Kim laughed and left him.

THREE

When Kim came down to breakfast the following morning, Mairelon was there before her. Mrs. Lowe was fortunately not in evidence, and Kim bolted her meal in hopes of getting away before she turned up. After five minutes, Mairelon looked up and said mildly, "What's the rush?"

"Mrs. Lowe," Kim replied, then flushed as she realized how it must sound. Well, she'd wanted to talk to Mairelon about his aunt, hadn't she? She just hadn't planned on blurting it out over breakfast. She must be more tired than she'd thought.

"Ah." Mairelon looked suddenly thoughtful. "Has Aunt Agatha been so much of a problem?"

"Nothing I can't manage," Kim said. Then honesty forced her to add, "Yet."

Mairelon glanced at Kim's almost empty plate. "I see."

Gathering her courage, Kim said, "Yesterday, she said something about—"

The far door opened, and Mrs. Lowe entered. "Good morning, Richard. You're up early. Good morning, Kim."

"I've a busy day ahead of me," Mairelon said, rising politely to greet her.

Mrs. Lowe helped herself to eggs and herring from the platters on the sideboard, then joined them at the table. Much to Kim's relief, she took the chair beside Mairelon. "I hope all this running about will not go on indefinitely," she said, picking up her fork.

"Some things are difficult to be definite about," Mairelon said.

"Your levity is unbecoming, Richard, and not at all to the point," Mrs. Lowe said, giving him a stern look. "In another week, the Season will be upon us, and as you have chosen to come to Town for once, I shall expect you to find a little more time for your social and family obligations."

"Oh, you may expect whatever you like, Aunt." Mairelon's tone was careless, but there was a set to his shoulders that told Kim he was not pleased.

"People are already arriving, and I fear there are still quite a few who are . . . confused about your proper standing."

"I can't imagine why. I'm the least confusing person I know."

Kim choked on her toast. Mrs. Lowe frowned, but it was impossible to tell whether it was at Kim or at Mairelon.

"I think you are being deliberately dense, Richard," Mrs. Lowe said after a moment. "I am of course referring to your role in the theft of the Saltash Set from the Royal College of Wizards seven years ago."

"I had no role whatever in the *theft* of the Saltash Set," Mairelon said, frowning. "I had a role in its *recovery.* Rather a large one."

"Yes, of course, Richard, but still . . . Your innocence may have been established in a legal sense—"

"Not 'may have been,'" Mairelon put in, his frown deepening. "Has been."

"—but there are those in Society who still have doubts. Your . . . eccentricities since your return have done nothing to reassure the *ton*."

"Eccentricities?" Mairelon raised his eyebrows.

"As you chose not to appear socially during last year's Season, you perhaps do not realize just how much talk there has been." The muscles in Mrs. Lowe's neck tightened, and Kim realized that she was carefully not looking in Kim's direction.

Kim tensed angrily, then forced herself to relax. It wasn't exactly a surprise that Mrs. Lowe disapproved of her, and it might be true that the existence of Mairelon's unusual ward had somehow tarnished his reputation. Toffs were odd that way; even after a year of life among the gentry, Kim knew she didn't understand them.

"Gossip drives the Season," Mairelon said, and there was a faint edge beneath the outward blandness of his tone. "I'm glad to have been of service."

"It is no service to yourself or your family," Mrs. Lowe said severely. "If you do not exert yourself a little this year, I shall have to wash my hands of you."

Kim looked up hopefully, but managed to bite her tongue before anything untoward slipped out. Mairelon, however, caught her expression and laughed. His reaction drew his aunt's attention to Kim, and, after giving them both a quelling look, Mrs. Lowe said, "There is another thing I have been meaning to speak to you about, Richard."

"And what is that?"

"Your ward's education," Mrs. Lowe replied, and Kim's stomach clenched.

"Kim has been doing very well," Mairelon said. "She's learned to read, and her magic skills are coming along nicely. It will be a while before she has the necessary Latin and Greek, of course, but she has a remarkable memory for chants and invocations, and an eye for detail that will be very useful when she gets to more advanced work."

Pleased and a little surprised by the unexpected compliment, Kim looked down at her plate.

Mrs. Lowe coughed. "I was referring to her *social* education, Richard. It has been sadly neglected. No doubt you had your reasons, and it could not matter much while she was safely in Kent, but now that you have brought her to London it is imperative that she learn how to go on."

"Why?" Kim demanded, looking up. "It's not as if I'm going to balls or anything."

"So long as you are my nephew's ward, you will undoubtedly meet persons of consequence from time to time," Mrs. Lowe said. "Your behavior toward them will reflect on your guardian, and on the rest of his family. And while the Merrill family is undeniably well-connected and well-off—"

Forty thousand pounds in the Funds is only "well-off"? Kim barely managed to stop herself from shaking her head in disbelief.

"—connections are no protection from scandal." She turned to Mairelon. "So long as her time is so completely occupied by her magic studies, Kim is unlikely to learn what she needs to know in order to cope with Society."

"But does Society know how to cope with Kim?" Mairelon murmured. "Still, perhaps you're right." He looked at Kim. "How would you like to come along to the Royal College of Wizards with me this morning? It's time you had a look at it, and I'm sure you'll like Kerring."

Kim, caught with her mouth full, could only nod emphatically. Mrs. Lowe frowned. "Richard! That is not at all what I meant."

"No? Well, I'm sure it will work out."

"Furthermore, Kim and I have an important engagement this afternoon for tea," Mrs. Lowe said. "She can't possibly spend the day at the Royal College."

"Oh, it won't take all day," Mairelon assured her. "Kim, if you're finished lingering over your breakfast, we should be going."

Kim dropped her cutlery at once and stood up. Mrs. Lowe frowned. "Richard, you can't take that girl out in—I mean, her conduct is not always to be depended upon."

Mairelon smiled seraphically. "According to you, neither is mine. We'll make a splendid pair. But don't worry; Hunch will keep us on the near side of acceptable behavior. Kim?"

Choking back laughter, Kim followed him to the door, while Mairelon's aunt sputtered in annoyance behind them.

The Royal College of Wizards occupied a long, rectangular building on the Thames, across from Westminster Abbey. The central section dated back almost to the Conquest; the rest was the work of latter-day heads of the college who had maintained their privileged position against subsequent kings and bishops alike. Westminster Hall, where Parliament met, had had to expand into a palace upriver, instead of onto the desirable land already occupied by the wizards.

Kim did not have much chance to study the outside of the building. As soon as their coach pulled up at the entrance, Mairelon jumped down before the footman could reach the carriage door. He headed briskly for the weathered oak doors of the college, leaving Kim no choice but to hurry after. Inside, they whisked past the main hall, allowing Kim only a glimpse of threadbare banners and stone pillars, and a brief whiff of musty air. They climbed a narrow flight of stone stairs, whose centers had been worn down a good two inches by centuries of magicians hurrying up and down. At last, they emerged in a small, bare entrance room with two other doors. Without hesitation, Mairelon crossed to the far door and tugged sharply on the faded bellpull beside it.

"Now, if Marchmain hasn't got all the apprentices busy hunting out historical documents for some project or other— Ah, here we are."

The right-hand door opened, and a slender, brown-haired young man entered and peered at them nearsightedly. "May I be of assistance?"

"I'm Richard Merrill, and this is my apprentice, Kim. We need to see Lord Kerring, if he's here. Is he?"

"I believe so," said the young man, "but he's busy."

"Kerring's always busy. We'll see him anyway. Come along, Kim."

"I don't think that's a good—" The young man broke off. Mairelon had already brushed past him and disappeared through the doorway.

"Don't worry," Kim told him as she followed Mairelon. "If this Lord Kerring cove knows Mairelon—I mean, Mr. Merrill—then he'll know who to blame for interrupting him. And it won't be you."

With the apprentice trailing after, they made their way through a maze of narrow corridors. Finally, Mairelon stopped before a door that, to Kim, looked exactly like all the others they had just passed. He waited just long enough for Kim and the apprentice to catch up, then opened the door and went in.

The room on the other side was much larger than Kim had expected, but there was very little space to walk in. Bookcases not only lined the walls but poked out at right angles to them, leaving only narrow aisles which were further choked by occasional precarious stacks of books on the floor. A narrow table beside the door was piled shoulder-high with books, and there were more books under it. The room smelled of musty paper, old leather, and dust. Kim sneezed.

From one of the alcoves, a deep voice boomed, "What's that? Who's there? Never mind, just go away. I'm working."

"You're always working, Kerring," Mairelon said. "We'll leave as soon as we've gotten a couple of answers."

A very hairy head poked around the side of one of the bookcases. "You're not going to get them that—Richard Merrill! Why didn't you say it was you? What have you gotten into this time?"

As he spoke, Lord Kerring emerged from behind the bookcase, and Kim could not help staring. At first, she thought he was short, but as he came toward them she realized that he was actually of average height; he only looked short because he was so round. He was of middle age, and his clothes looked like something out of one of the ragbags on Threadneedle Street—they had clearly been of excellent quality when they were new, but now they were so rumpled and dusty that they would not have looked out of place on a costermonger in the Hungerford Market. A tuft of cat hair clung to the back of one sleeve. He had dark, curly hair and a bushy beard, both much in need of trimming.

Kim stared. *He's a lord? And a wizard to boot?*

"Come in, sit down," Lord Kerring said, waving the relieved apprentice out the door. "Is this that young wizard you found last year? Introduce me."

"I'll be happy to, when you give me a moment's breathing

room," Mairelon said. "Kerring, my ward and apprentice, Kim. Kim, this is Lord Kerring, one of the senior wizards of the college."

"Enchanted," Kerring said, and bowed with unexpected grace. His eyes twinkled as he added, "Though not in the literal sense. Why haven't you brought her before? Will you be coming out this year, Miss Merrill?"

"Just Kim. I don't think so." *Or rather, when hell freezes over.* She had a momentary, dazzling vision of herself whirling across the dance floor at an elaborate ball, then shook her head. *Even if I got an invitation, I'd end up sitting out. The Society toffs agree with Mrs. Lowe.* "Mr. Merrill has been very kind, but I don't really belong in Society."

Kerring gave her a sharp look, as if he knew exactly what she had been thinking. "Nonsense, my dear. A wizard is the social equal of anyone."

The beginnings of a frown vanished from Mairelon's face. "You're quite right, Kerring, and it's a solution I hadn't thought of. Thank you."

"You're welcome. I think." Kerring looked at Mairelon blankly; when this was not enough to produce an explanation, he opened his mouth to continue. Mairelon forestalled him.

"Now, if you'll just give me a hand with this other matter, we'll leave you to your books." Mairelon drew a piece of paper from his pocket and handed it to Kerring. "Can you tell us anything about these books? What they might have in common, or why anyone might want them?"

Kerring studied the list, frowning. "It's an odd assortment. What is it, someone's collection that you're thinking of buying?"

"Part of my brother's library, actually," Mairelon said.

"They don't seem much like his kind of thing," Kerring

said. "I wonder . . . Wait here for a minute." He disappeared behind one of the bookshelves, and Kim heard the sounds of drawers opening and closing, and paper rustling. Finally Kerring reappeared, carrying Mairelon's list and a little sheaf of documents.

"Found it!" he said triumphantly. "I thought these were familiar. They're part of a collection your father had me assess about, oh, fifteen years ago."

"Only part?" Mairelon said.

"The part I recommended he buy." Kerring waved the sheaf of documents. "The whole collection was much more extensive. It belonged to a Frenchman, an *émigré* who ended up in debtor's prison. De Cambriol, that was his name. His wife was a French wizard, one of the group they called *Les Griffonais;* she was just beginning to make a name for herself when she died. That's why your father was interested in her books."

"Her books?" Kim said. "I thought you said they belonged to her husband."

"He inherited them," Kerring said. "It was quite a nice little collection, actually, but he wasn't a wizard himself and had no interest in magic, so when he fell on hard times, he sold them off. Didn't do him much good, I'm afraid. Too many gambling debts; the proceeds from the sale didn't even begin to buy him out."

"And my father bought them," Mairelon said in a thoughtful tone.

"Some of them," Kerring corrected him. "Madame de Cambriol's magic collection, to be precise, plus one or two others he thought looked interesting. I thought he'd bought her *livre de mémoire*, too, but I don't see it on your list. Pity; there's a deal of interest in the *Griffonais* these days. Your brother could have gotten a nice price for it."

"What's a . . . a *livre de* thingumy?" Kim asked, at the same moment that Mairelon said, "Interest?"

Kerring's beard split in a grin. "One at a time. A *livre de mémoire* is a sort of book of notes that a lot of French wizards keep. A memory book, we'd call it."

"Just who is interested in *Les Griffonais?*" Mairelon said. "And why?"

"Everybody," Kerring replied, gesturing expansively. "Because of the restoration of the French monarchy, you see. Now that they've finally gotten rid of that pushy little Corsican they let take over the country, there's a lot of curiosity about things under the old regime."

"I believe there was rather more to Napoleon than that," Mairelon murmured. "Thank you very much for the information, and if you hear of anyone asking specifically about *Les Griffonais* or Madame de Cambriol, do let me know. Andrew might be interested in selling off some of the books."

Lord Kerring gave Mairelon a sharp look. "You're up to something, Merrill, and don't think I don't know it. I expect a full account for the archives once it's over, whatever it is."

"If you insist," Mairelon said. "I believe we have what we came for. Good day; perhaps I'll see you at the club next week."

"No doubt. Good day, Miss Merrill. I expect I'll see more of you when you start your journeyman's work. And I assure you that it will be a pleasure." Kerring bowed.

"Thank you, my lord," Kim stammered, and managed to curtsey without losing her balance. Kerring gave her an avuncular smile, and a moment later she and Mairelon were outside the library once more.

Mairelon was frowning slightly as they started down the hall. *Thinking again,* Kim told herself. *Well, he can just think out loud where I can hear it.* "Now what?" she asked him.

"Mmm? Kerring is an old reprobate at times, but he's a sound man and there's no denying he knows his work."

"Fine for him," Kim said. "But what do *we* do now?"

"We go back to the house and see whether we can turn up Madame de Cambriol's memory book. If it's not there, we'll know our burglar got what he was after."

"But you don't even know whether it was in the library to begin with," Kim said.

"If Kerring thinks my father bought it, I'm willing to wager he did," Mairelon said. "There might even be an inventory around somewhere. We'll have to check. Come along; we haven't time to waste."

FOUR

Mairelon was extremely cheerful all the way home, but he refused to tell her anything more and she could not think of a way of questioning him that was likely to get a useful response. Not when he was in such a fey mood, anyway. When they reached Grosvenor Square, the opportunity was lost; Mrs. Lowe was hovering by the door, and took Kim in hand at once.

"You'll have to hurry, or we'll be late," she said as she bustled Kim up the stairs. "I've sent for Sally to do what she can with your hair. It ought to have been in papers all morning, but that can't be helped now."

"It wouldn't have helped then," Kim muttered.

"What did you say?"

"Nothing."

"I hope you don't intend to be difficult about this," Mrs. Lowe said. "Mrs. Hardcastle has gone to a good deal of trouble to arrange this meeting, and it is probably the best opportunity you will have to settle yourself comfortably."

As if that's the reason I came back to London, Kim thought, frowning. Fortunately, Mrs. Lowe had stepped forward to open the bedroom door, and did not see Kim's expression. Mrs. Lowe's maid, Sally, bobbed a curtsey as they entered. A pair of curling tongs lay heating in the fire, and a pale yellow walking dress waited on the bed. Kim rolled her eyes. "You mean I have to change clothes, too, as well as having my hair fussed with? What's wrong with what I have on?"

"Mrs. Hardcastle informs me that Mr. Fulton is partial to yellow," Mrs. Lowe said coldly. "Now, sit down and let Sally fix your hair. We have barely half an hour before we must leave."

Kim considered briefly, then sat. She could, she supposed, delay their departure if she worked at it, but delaying or avoiding this call would only make Mrs. Lowe more determined to arrange another. She had to think of a way to put an end to the matter once and for all, or she'd fall in the soup sooner or later.

"You have lovely hair, Miss, though it's a bit short," Sally ventured as she wound the first strand around a curl-paper. "I dare say it'll look that nice when it's all done up proper."

"That will do, Sally." Mrs. Lowe studied Kim for a moment, and then she and Sally went to work. With considerable effort and ingenuity, they produced a passable arrangement of curls from Kim's dark, unruly hair. At least, Mrs. Lowe said it was passable, but even to Kim's unpracticed eye the coiffure bore no resemblance to the elegant styles worn by real ladies. *I look like a fishmonger's daughter trying to ape Quality,* she thought gloomily. *I bet it'll be all straggly before we've gone three blocks. If it stays up that long.* She shook her head experimentally, and Mrs. Lowe clucked at her.

Getting into the gown without disarranging her hair was an effort, and Kim was glad that Sally was there to do most of the work. When Mrs. Lowe was satisfied with Kim's appearance at last, they descended the stairs once more.

Mairelon was waiting in the hall. "There you are at last! I thought you were in a hurry. I've had the coach waiting for half an hour." He picked up his gloves. "Shall we go?"

Mrs. Lowe stared at him, for once bereft of speech.

"You're coming, too?" Kim said with relief.

"Oh, yes." Mairelon smiled seraphically at his dumbfounded aunt. "After all, Aunt Agatha said only this morning that she expects me to pay more attention to my social duties. I thought I had best begin at once, before I forgot." He signaled the footman, who opened the door wide, and offered his arm to his aunt. By the time Mrs. Lowe recovered from her shock, they were in the carriage and on their way. Mrs. Lowe could hardly rip up at Mairelon as long as Kim was present, so the journey was accomplished in silence.

They emerged from the carriage in front of a sturdy brick townhouse of modest proportions. Two of the lower windows had been bricked over. An iron railing enclosed a yard or so of space in front of the house, where an extremely ugly pottery urn stood empty. Three slate steps, freshly scrubbed, led up to the wooden door. An impeccably correct butler opened the door and led them up the staircase inside. Kim, noting the empty candle sconces on the wall and the half-hidden darns in the linen drape covering a table in the upstairs hall, was not impressed. *Mrs. Hardcastle may be bosom-bows with Mrs. Lowe, but she's not as full of juice. This place wouldn't be worth the time—let alone the risk—to a decent cracksman.*

They found Mrs. Hardcastle in the saloon, a dark and austerely furnished room whose narrow windows did little to lighten the atmosphere. Mrs. Lowe checked briefly in the doorway, and when Kim entered close on her heels, she saw why.

Mrs. Hardcastle had more guests than they had expected. Not only that, the young woman shaking her golden-guinea curls at the offer of a slice of cake was a diamond of the first water. From the top of her high-crowned hat to her heart-shaped face and perfect complexion, to her slender figure, to the elegantly turned ankles and dainty feet set off by neat kid boots, she was everything that current fashion demanded of a Beauty. *No wonder old poker-back's nose is out of joint,* Kim thought with satisfaction. *She didn't bargain for any competition, let alone a regular out-and-outer.*

Beside the Beauty sat an undistinguished girl, also turned out in expensive (though in her case, unbecoming) fashion. A sober-looking gentleman and their middle-aged hostess completed the company.

Though Mrs. Lowe must have been annoyed, she gave no sign of it beyond that initial hesitation. She greeted Mrs. Hardcastle with the warmth due an old friend, and acknowledged the necessary introductions with perfect aplomb. The Beauty was a Miss Letitia Tarnower; her companion, Miss Annabel Matthews. The sober gentleman was, of course, Mr. Henry Fulton.

As the newcomers seated themselves, Kim studied Mr. Fulton. He looked to be in his mid-thirties, which was considerably younger than she had expected. His morning-dress was neat and correct, but lacked a certain elegance. *He's a Cit, and well enough off for Mrs. Lowe to think he's "reasonably respectable," but he doesn't follow Society fashion. Well, most Cits don't.* She wondered whether he had been informed of the purpose of their meeting.

Then Mr. Fulton caught her eye, reddened slightly, and looked away. *He knows.* And if he had come intending to inspect a potential bride, then she could no longer simply dismiss Mrs. Lowe's maunderings about marriage and her opportunities in London.

She glanced at Mr. Fulton again. His face was pleasant enough. *I ought to jump at him. There can't be very many well-to-do Cits willing to take up with a girl off the streets, even if I am the ward of a gentleman now. So why is the idea so . . . repellent?*

"Tea, Miss Merrill?" Mrs. Hardcastle said.

"Yes, thank you."

Mrs. Hardcastle beamed as if Kim had said something clever. Kim blinked, then accepted the teacup with a noncommittal murmur. This earned her an encouraging nod and a not-too-subtle significant look in Mr. Fulton's direction.

Kim chose to ignore the hint. She sat sipping at her tea, in the faint hope that a polite lack of interest would discourage any more attempts to draw her into conversation with Mr. Fulton. There was also a slim chance that sitting quietly might keep her from committing any of the social solecisms that would earn her a trimming from Mrs. Lowe once they returned home.

"I am pleased to find you here, Mr. Fulton," Mrs. Lowe said. "My nephew's ward was particularly eager to make your acquaintance."

"Yes, it is so nice to meet new people," Miss Tarnower said with a dazzling smile before Mr. Fulton could respond. "Mrs. Hardcastle's acquaintance is so very *varied* that one never knows who will turn up. I would not be astonished to find the Prince of Wales himself at one of her saloons."

Mrs. Hardcastle looked quite struck for a moment, then shook her head. "It is kind of you to say so, but I fear that His Highness is considerably above my touch."

"Oh, pooh! You are too modest. Everyone knows you, and you know everyone. I'll wager that if I gave you a name, you could tell us all about that person, no matter who it is! There now, you cannot say it is untrue."

"Ah, but it would be inhospitable of her to correct a guest," Mairelon said.

"That was not what I meant at all," Miss Tarnower said with a puzzled frown. "Oh! I see. You are bamming me."

"Letitia!" Miss Matthews said in an urgent undertone that carried rather better than she intended it to.

Miss Tarnower glanced at her companion, then turned back to Mairelon. "Is your acquaintance as wide as Mrs. Hardcastle's, sir?" she asked with another dazzling smile.

"Oh, at least," Mairelon murmured.

"Richard," Mrs. Lowe said softly, in the same warning tone that Miss Matthews had used. Being more experienced, her pitch was better-chosen; if Kim had not been sitting next to her, she would not have heard a thing.

"Mr. Merrill is well known in France, I believe," Mrs. Hardcastle told Miss Tarnower.

"Too well known," Mairelon said. "Even under the new king."

"But I am not interested in the king of France." Miss Tarnower frowned, as if suddenly struck by a thought. "Unless he is to be in London this Season?"

"I believe that to be unlikely," Mrs. Hardcastle said.

Mr. Fulton leaned forward. "I take it you were in France during the war, then, Mr. Merrill?"

"Some of the time," Mairelon acknowledged with a faint smile.

"I thought your name was familiar," Mr. Fulton said with some satisfaction.

"It is of no consequence," Mrs. Lowe said hastily. "It was a . . . personal matter."

"What, still?" Mr. Fulton looked from Mrs. Lowe to

Mairelon and said apologetically, "I am very sorry if I have been indiscreet, but since my brother saw no harm in relating the story to me, I thought—"

"Tommy Fulton!" Mairelon said, snapping his fingers. "Last time I saw him was in that little French town where Old Hooky set up his, er, coin exchange. St. Jean de Luz, that was it. Good heavens, are you his brother? How is he?"

"He was badly wounded at Waterloo, and I fear his health has not been the same since," Mr. Fulton replied. "Still, he does tolerably well."

"I'm glad he made it through." Mairelon's face clouded. "Too many didn't."

Mrs. Lowe was frowning in a mixture of relief and mystification that Kim found puzzling. Didn't she know or care what Mairelon had really been doing during those years when London Society thought he had run off with the Saltash Set?

"Tom speaks very highly of your . . . work," Mr. Fulton said to Mairelon.

"No need to mince words," Mairelon said. "Not now, anyway." He smiled at the puzzled expressions of the two young ladies opposite him. "I met Tommy Fulton while I was on the Peninsula, spying on the French. He was one of the pickets who made it possible for me to cross back and forth across the lines when I needed to. Very solid."

Mr. Fulton inclined his head. "He will be pleased to know you remember him so kindly."

"Remember him? I could hardly forget him. Did he tell you about the incident with the chickens?"

Seeing that the conversation was about to degenerate into military reminiscence, Mrs. Lowe and Mrs. Hardcastle both hurried into speech.

"I am sure you have many fascinating tales, but—"

"Perhaps Richard can visit your brother some other—"

The two ladies both stopped short and waited politely for each other to continue. Since Mr. Fulton was also waiting for one of them to finish her speech, this gave Letitia Tarnower the opportunity to reenter the conversation.

"I dislike chickens," she announced. "They are stupid birds, and they have nothing whatever to do with who one knows, which is what we were discussing."

"Yes, and I quite agree that it is pleasant to meet new people," Mrs. Lowe said, though her tone was at odds with her words. She managed a stiff smile at Miss Tarnower, then turned to Mr. Fulton with a warmer expression. "It is, for instance, very pleasant to make your acquaintance at last, Mr. Fulton. We have heard so much about you."

"I, too, have heard much about you, Miss Merrill," Mr. Fulton said, and smiled. "I must say, it did not do you justice."

Beside Mrs. Hardcastle, Mairelon frowned suddenly. Mrs. Lowe nudged Kim and gave her a pointed look. Annoyed, Kim raised her teacup and sipped again. *Old fusspot. It would serve her right if I did disgrace her in public.* Then she blinked and began to grin. *And I bet it'll send Fulton to the rightabout in a hurry, too.*

Mairelon was watching her, and his frown deepened. Before he could queer her pitch, she looked at Mr. Fulton and said very deliberately, "Don't go pitching me no gammon. You ain't heard near enough, acos I'll lay you a monkey the gentry-mort ain't told you I was on the sharping lay afore Mairelon took a fancy to adopt me."

Mrs. Lowe's breath hissed faintly between her teeth in anger; Mrs. Hardcastle looked shocked, and the two younger ladies, merely puzzled. Mr. Fulton seemed taken aback, but he rallied enough to say, "No, I don't believe she did."

"Well, I ain't no mace cove, and I don't hold with bubbling a flash cull, not when it comes to getting priest-linked, anyways."

"Kim!" Mrs. Lowe had recovered from her surprise-induced paralysis; it was a tribute to her good breeding that she kept her voice low despite her anger and chagrin. "Hold your tongue, at once."

Kim set her teacup on the table. Looking up, she met Mr. Fulton's eyes. "And I'll tell you straight, this ain't been my lay, right from the beginning," she continued, as if Mrs. Lowe had never interrupted. "I ain't never been no Madam Ran. So I ain't going to get in a pucker if you was to shab off."

"I . . . see," Mr. Fulton said in a dazed voice.

"Well, I do not," Letitia Tarnower said crossly.

"I should hope not!" Mrs. Hardcastle groped in her reticule and produced a bottle of smelling salts, which she at once made use of. "I have never heard anything so vulgar in my life! Not that I understood the half of it myself."

"Really?" Miss Matthews's wide eyes were fixed on Kim. "Was it so very bad?"

"It was certainly intended to be," Mairelon said. His eyes, full of amusement, met Kim's, and she felt light-headed with relief. As long as he hadn't taken her antics in bad part, she didn't give a farthing for Mrs. Lowe.

Unexpectedly, Henry Fulton laughed. "Miss Merrill, I think we are both correct. I had not heard nearly enough about you, and what I did hear *certainly* did not do you justice."

Kim blinked and said cautiously, "Well, that ain't my lookout."

"Kim!" Mrs. Lowe said. "Be *still!*"

"It is much too late for that," Mrs. Hardcastle said acidly. "Really, Agatha, you might have told me."

"Told you what?" Mairelon said. "That my ward was once a street thief? I didn't think it was a secret."

"A street thief?" Letitia wrinkled her nose and looked at Kim with disfavor. "How horrid."

"I think it is the most romantic story I have ever heard," Miss Matthews said with conviction.

Mr. Fulton gave her an approving look, which caused Miss Matthews to blush in confusion.

Kim shook her head. Abandoning cant language, she said soberly, "It may sound romantic, but living on the street isn't very pleasant. Horrid describes it much better."

"I do not believe that was what Miss Tarnower was referring to," Mrs. Hardcastle said. She seemed even more upset by Kim's reversion to standard English than she had been by the string of thieves' cant.

Mrs. Lowe rose to her feet. "We must be going," she said stiffly. "At once."

"But you have only just arrived," Letitia objected. "And I *particularly* wished to ask Mr. Merrill something, because he has been on the continent."

Kim had not thought it possible for Mrs. Lowe to get any stiffer, but she did. "Another time, perhaps."

"Nonsense, Aunt," Mairelon said, leaning back in his chair. "We can spare another few minutes to gratify the young lady's curiosity."

"Richard . . ."

"What was it you wanted to ask, Miss Tarnower?" Mairelon asked.

"Why, only if you had ever heard of a Prince Alexei Nicholaiovitch Durmontov," Letitia said.

"Durmontov?" Mairelon said in a thoughtful tone. "No, I can't say that I met anyone of that name while I was in France, though there were a number of respectable Russians there from time to time. Of course, most of the people I dealt with there were not respectable at all."

"That appears to continue true." Mrs. Hardcastle sniffed and looked pointedly in Kim's direction.

"Well, it's only to be expected," Mairelon said consolingly. "London Society isn't what it once was."

Both Mr. Fulton and Miss Matthews experienced sudden fits of coughing. Kim found herself entirely in sympathy with them; she was having trouble choking back her own laughter at Mairelon's deliberate outrageousness.

Mrs. Hardcastle, however, was neither amused nor misled. "I was speaking, sir, of your so-called ward."

Mrs. Lowe bristled and began to say something, but Mairelon held up a restraining hand. "Were you, indeed?" he said in a deceptively gentle tone to Mrs. Hardcastle. "Then you will certainly not wish to attend her come-out ball. I must remember not to send you a card."

Kim's stomach did a sudden flip-flop. *Come-out ball? He's got windmills in his head. Doesn't he?*

"Richard!" Mrs. Lowe gasped.

"Ah, yes, you wanted to be going," Mairelon said, ignoring the reddening Mrs. Hardcastle. "I find that for once I am in agreement with you, Aunt." He rose and nodded to Mr. Fulton. "Give my regards to your brother. If you'll send me his direction, I shall stop in to see him. Your servant, ladies." He made an elegant bow that managed to include Miss Matthews and Miss Tarnower while excluding Mrs. Hardcastle, and ushered Kim and his thunderstruck aunt from the room.

FIVE

They were hardly out of Mrs. Hardcastle's house before Mrs. Lowe turned to Mairelon. "Richard, I fear that your unfortunate impulses have landed you in difficulties once again."

Mairelon raised an eyebrow. "I do hope that you are not referring to my ward. I thought I was finished with that subject for today."

"Not at all," Mrs. Lowe said with a look at Kim that spoke volumes, none of them pleasant. "But *that* I intend to discuss with you privately, at a later time." She climbed into the carriage and waited for Kim and Mairelon to find their own seats. Then, as the carriage began to move, she said, "No, I was referring to your invention of a come-out ball for Kim. While I fully understand your desire to give Mrs. Hardcastle a set-down, I must tell you that it will certainly have precisely the opposite effect, once she realizes that no such party is being planned."

"I'm sure she feels just as you do," Mairelon murmured.

"But think of her chagrin when she discovers that it will, in fact, be held."

"Richard, your flights of fancy take you too far," Mrs. Lowe said severely. "You can't possibly introduce a girl of dubious antecedents into Polite Society." She gave Kim another look. "Particularly a girl whose behavior cannot be depended upon."

"That's three," Mairelon said with apparent interest.

"Three what?" Mrs. Lowe asked, clearly at a loss.

"Three mistakes in one speech. First, Kim's, er, antecedents aren't dubious, they're completely unknown. That is, if you're referring to her parents. Second, her behavior is entirely dependable and shows a great deal of good sense."

"If you call using vulgar cant phrases in Mrs. Hardcastle's drawing room *showing good sense*—"

"And third," Mairelon went on implacably, "I am quite capable of introducing my ward to Polite Society—though judging by this afternoon, I'd say the adjective is extremely ill-chosen."

Kim found her voice at last. "Mairelon—"

"Kim, I have told you a dozen times: Refer to your guardian as Mr. Merrill, if you please," Mrs. Lowe snapped.

"I don't please," Kim said. "And I'm no good at wrapping it up in clean linen, so there's no use my trying. Mairelon—"

"You are being deliberately impudent and unmannerly," Mrs. Lowe said crossly. "I don't know which of you is worse."

"Yes, it's why Kim and I deal so well together," Mairelon said.

Before Mrs. Lowe could respond to this provoking remark, the carriage came to a halt and the footman sprang to open the door, putting a stop to further conversation. As they descended, a ragged boy of nine or ten materialized next to the front stoop, and stood staring up at Mairelon. Automatically, Kim moved her reticule to her far hand and backed off a step.

The boy ignored her. "You that Merrill cove?" he demanded of Mairelon. "The frogmaker?"

"I'm a magician, and my name is Merrill."

"Got something for you to give to a chap named Kim," the boy said. "A bob cull up by Threadneedle told me you'd give me a bender for delivering it."

Mairelon studied the boy for a moment, then reached into his pocket and pulled out a coin. "There's your sixpence. What have you got?"

"Here you go, governor." The boy dropped something into Mairelon's outstretched palm, snatched the sixpence from his other hand, and ran off down the street.

"Fascinating," Mairelon murmured, looking after him. "Now, who do we know who would use such an . . . unusual method of communication? And what does it mean?"

Kim leaned over to see what Mairelon was holding. It was a cheap wooden button, scratched deeply from one side to the other. "It's from Tom Correy," she said. "He's got a secondhand shop on Petticoat Lane, off Threadneedle. This is how he always used to let me know he wanted to see me. How did he know to send it to you? I never told anyone where I was going."

"I did," Mairelon said, handing her the button. "In a general sort of way. I wonder what he wants? Somehow, I doubt that the timing is coincidental."

"Tom didn't have nothing to do with that filching cove last night!"

"Kim!" Mrs. Lowe said. "Mind your language."

" '*Anything* to do with,' " Mairelon said calmly. "And I didn't claim he had. If he's heard something about the business, though, that might account for his summons." He frowned suddenly. "Or our mysterious burglar may be hoping to hire you to complete his work."

"As if I would!"

"Yes, well, he doesn't know that, does he?"

"*Need* we discuss this in the street?" Mrs. Lowe said with a significant look in the direction of the interested footmen.

"A reasonable enough point," Mairelon said, and they proceeded into the house.

Inside, Mrs. Lowe looked at Mairelon and said, "I wish to speak further with you about all this, Richard. I will expect you in the drawing room. Immediately." Without waiting for an answer, she swept up the stairs, leaving Mairelon and Kim standing just inside the door.

"I have a few questions, too," Kim said.

"Aunt Agatha got in before you, I'm afraid," Mairelon said. "You'll have to wait. Unless you want to join us?"

"No," Kim said hastily. "I'll talk to you after."

"In the library. You can study your orisons and invocations while you wait," Mairelon said, and disappeared down the back hall before Kim could say anything more.

Fuming, Kim went up to the library and flopped into a chair. *Introduce me to Polite Society! He's dicked in the nob. And anyway, the last thing I want is to spend more time having tea with widgeons like that Tarnower gentry-mort.* She glared at the book of invocations, but didn't bother picking it up. Even if she could calm down enough to puzzle out the letters, nothing she read while she was in this state would stick. *And what in thunder does Tom Correy want? He can't have a job for me; if he knows about Mairelon, he knows I don't need to go on the sharping lay any more. And how am I going to sneak down to Petticoat Lane in skirts?*

Tom wouldn't have sent for her if it wasn't urgent, but he didn't know that Kim was a girl. She'd dressed and acted as a boy for all her years on the London streets, and only Mother Tibb had known the truth. The back alleys of London were dangerous places at the best of times, and doubly dangerous for girls. Petticoat Lane wasn't quite as bad as the rookeries of St. Giles, or the stews around Vauxhall and Covent Gardens, but it was still far from safe.

If I go well after dark, in boy's clothes, I might still be able to pass. But she had no idea what had become of her old garments, and even if she had, they wouldn't fit her now. Mrs. Lowe would never countenance a shopping expedition for an appropriate jacket and breeches, let alone Kim's actually wearing them anywhere. Mairelon . . . Mairelon wouldn't mind the boy's clothes, but Kim felt oddly reluctant to ask him for help in this. She owed Tom a lot, from the bad times before she'd met Mairelon, and the debt was one she had to pay herself.

When Mairelon arrived fifteen minutes later, Kim was no nearer a solution to her problem. She looked up as he came in, and with a particularly cheerful grin he said, "Well, that's settled, more or less. Now, what was it you wanted to ask?"

All thoughts of Tom Correy fled from Kim's mind at once. "Settled?" she croaked. "What's settled?"

"The business of presenting you to Society," Mairelon said. "Aunt Agatha doesn't like it, of course, but it's clear enough that she'll agree to sponsor you eventually."

"Eventually?" Kim grasped at the slim hope.

Mairelon's grin widened even more. "Right now, she's too furious with me to agree to anything, but she'll come around as soon as I propose letting Renée D'Auber sponsor you instead. She's far too conventional to let my ward be presented by someone who's not a member of the family."

"You *enjoy* annoying her," Kim said in surprise.

"Nonsense. It's much too easy—everything annoys Aunt Agatha. Now, you had some questions, I think?"

"Not exactly. It's just that you forgot to ask me."

Mairelon blinked, then looked a little sheepish. "I'm sorry about springing it on you, but I wanted it to be clear to Aunt Agatha that you hadn't been scheming for a come-out all along. It worked, too."

"That's not what I meant," Kim said. "That just explains why you didn't *tell* me what you were planning. I'm talking about *asking* me whether I wanted to be launched into Society."

"I didn't think I had to," Mairelon said. "It's obvious that you haven't been happy since we got back to London. I thought you wanted a change."

So he did *notice,* Kim thought, but the knowledge only added to her growing annoyance with him. "Well, I haven't been, and I did want a change, but that's not the point. A year ago, I wanted to get off the streets, but I didn't want it badly enough to go to the stews."

"I should hope not," Mairelon said, and for an instant he sounded exactly like his aunt. Then he gave her a worried look, and the resemblance vanished. "It's not just a matter of presenting you, you know. I'm hoping that if we circulate a bit during the Season, we'll run across our mysterious toff burglar."

"That's *not the point*," Kim repeated. "A year ago, you *asked* me if I wanted to be your ward, when it was a lot plainer that I'd jump at the chance. But you didn't ask me about coming out in Society, and you didn't ask me about 'circulating during the Season.' You're as bad as Mrs. Lowe."

"What?" Mairelon looked startled, and for the first time, Kim felt as if she might have gotten through to him.

"Mrs. Lowe didn't ask me whether I came to London to catch a husband, she just decided that's what I wanted. Or that it would be best for me. And you didn't ask about this. You both act like I'm some fog-headed mort who ain't got sense enough to make up her own mind about anything."

"I'm sorry."

"*I'm sorry* don't fix it."

"What would? Do you want me to tell Aunt Agatha you refuse to be presented?"

"Yes," Kim said. "That's exactly what I want."

Mairelon looked startled. "Why? It's not because of that Hardcastle woman's remarks this afternoon, or the Tarnower girl's attitude, is it? Their opinions really don't matter in the slightest."

"Not to you. But I ain't been out with your poker-backed aunt every day for a week without noticing that the opinions of bubble-brains like those two matter a lot to some people. Your aunt, for one."

Mairelon frowned. "And do they matter to you? Is that why you're so . . . overset?"

"*No.*" Kim flung her hands up in exasperation. "Not the way you mean, not now. But if I was to get launched into Society, their opinions would *have* to matter, wouldn't they? Because that's what Society is, mostly."

"What an unfortunately truthful observation," Mairelon said. "I take your point. I shouldn't have sprung this on you in front of them."

"You shouldn't of sprung it on me at all! You ought to of asked me about it first, and not just because you thought I'd give you a trimming if you didn't." Kim stopped and took a deep breath. Then she said quietly, "It's *my* life. And I ain't— I'm not a noodle."

"No one said you were."

"You act like it." She shook her head. "Maybe it's just how you toffs are, deciding what other people should do. But I wasn't born and bred to it. I don't like it. And I ain't never going to get used to it."

There was a brief silence. Then Mairelon shook his head.

"Very well, if you really don't wish to have a come-out, I'll talk to Aunt Agatha again. Tomorrow, I think; that will give her time to calm down, and I can probably convince her that her excellent arguments persuaded us to reconsider, which might even put her in charity with both of us."

"Good," Kim said, trying to convince herself that she meant it. After all she'd never have thought of it herself, the fairy-tale images of being presented at a real Society ball were hard to dismiss now that they'd been offered to her. *Just like the ash-girl in the stories Red Sal used to tell. But it ain't a story. Cut line,* she told herself severely.

The library door opened, and Hunch came in. " 'Ere's that list of books you wanted."

"The inventory? Excellent." Mairelon took the papers that Hunch held out to him and scanned the first page. After a moment, he shuffled it to the bottom of the stack and began on the next. Kim watched, feeling an odd mixture of relief, curiosity, and regret. Halfway down the fourth page, Mairelon paused. His frown deepened momentarily; then he smiled. "Found it at last!"

"Found what?" Kim said. "That liver book Lord Kerring was talking about?"

"*Livre de mémoire,*" Mairelon corrected, "and yes, I have. *Le Livre de Sept Sorciers: un livre de mémoire* by Madame Marie de Cambriol. It was in this library, all right; now let's find out whether it still is. According to this, it should be a smallish volume with a blue leather binding."

Kim took a quick look at the page in Mairelon's hand, to make sure she would recognize the title when she saw it, then started going through the shelves on one side of the room. Mairelon took the other side, and Hunch, muttering under his breath and chewing on his mustache, began on the cabinets under the windows.

Three-quarters of the way down the second set of shelves, Kim found it—a short, slim volume sandwiched between two much larger ones. "Is this it?" she called, holding it up.

Mairelon joined her. "It certainly is," he said, scowling at it.

"What's the matter?" Kim said. "I thought you'd be pleased that it hasn't gone missing."

"Oh, I am, I am," Mairelon said. "But you must admit, this confuses things considerably."

Hunch look up. " 'Ow's that, Master Richard?"

"Well, if it had been missing, we'd have had a good idea that this was what our burglar was after," Mairelon replied. "Now, we can't be sure, especially since that spell we used last night didn't make it glow like the other books he'd pulled off the shelves."

"It was in between two big books," Kim said. "They might have hidden it enough that the glow didn't show."

"Or Madame de Cambriol might have done something rather special to safeguard her notes," Mairelon said in a thoughtful tone.

"Or that there cracksman might 'ave piked off with something else," Hunch put in. " 'Ow would you know if 'e 'ad?"

"You're starting to pick up thieves' cant from Kim," Mairelon observed. "I'll have a look at this tomorrow; perhaps it will give me some ideas. Oh, and that reminds me—Kim, what do you intend to do about that button?"

"Button?" Kim stared, wondering why Mairelon would care about the buttons she'd ripped from her dressing gown during her row with the burglar; then her mind made another connection, and she said, "You mean, the one Tom Correy sent?"

"Yes, of course. You said it was a sort of summons. Do you want to go?"

Kim looked at him in mild surprise. "Tom wouldn't ask me

to come if it wasn't important. Of course I'm going, if I can figure out how."

"We'll take the coach. Aunt Agatha won't need it; when I left, she was talking about having a spasm, and that generally occupies her for at least a day. Up High Holborn to Thread-needle, isn't it?"

"That's not what I meant," Kim said, but she couldn't help smiling. *All that fretting about whether to ask him, and he just barges into the middle of things without a second thought.* "I meant . . ." She gestured, taking in her yellow walking dress, kid boots, and painstakingly curled hair.

Mairelon's eyes focused on her. A startled expression crossed his face; then he nodded. "Yes, I see. You can't very well go wandering about the London back streets dressed like that, no matter what time of day it is. Particularly if Correy still thinks you're a boy."

"That's it," Kim said, relieved that he had understood without more explicit explanation.

"Hunch," Mairelon went on, "do you think you can find a suitable set of boy's clothes? Something a bit better than what she had when we met, but not fine enough to attract attention."

"And loose," Kim put in, then sighed. "I hope it works. I wouldn't fool a blind man in broad daylight, but I might still be able to pass for a boy at night."

"Nonsense. You won't have any trouble at all," Mairelon said.

Kim stared at him. It was so like Mairelon to have overlooked the inconvenient physical changes in his ward that she could not help being amused, but she was a little hurt as well. Hadn't he looked at her even *once* in the past six months?

"She's right, Master Richard," Hunch said unexpectedly. "Look at 'er. She ain't skinny enough no more."

Mairelon gave Hunch a startled glance, then looked at Kim for a long, considering moment. Slowly, he nodded. "I . . . see. I apologize, Kim." Kim felt herself beginning to flush; fortunately, Mairelon turned toward Hunch and did not see. "Do as well as you can, Hunch."

"Cook might 'ave somethin' from the last errand boy," Hunch said. "I'll check."

"Don't forget something suitably disreputable for me," Mairelon called after him as he left the library.

Kim looked at Mairelon. "You expect to come with me?"

"I *am* your guardian," Mairelon said.

All Kim's annoyance with his high-handed ways boiled over once again. "If that means that I get no say in anything I do, I'd rather go back to the streets."

There was a brief, stunned silence. Then Mairelon said, "You don't mean that."

"Not yet," Kim admitted. "But even Mother Tibb *asked* what we thought of a job before she sent us out."

The silence stretched again. Finally, Mairelon said, "You said you wanted to go."

"I do." Kim took a deep breath. "But I don't think you should come with me."

Mairelon tensed. "Why not?"

"I'll have a harder time with Tom if you do. He won't be expecting no toffs, just me. If you show up, even dressed like a dustman, he'll muffle his clapper and I won't find out a thing."

"You can't go to that end of town alone."

"Why not? I *lived* there alone, for five years after Mother Tibb swung."

"But you haven't been on the streets for a year," Mairelon came back swiftly. "You're out of practice."

"You're more out of practice than I am," Kim retorted.

"Especially seeing as you weren't ever *in* practice. I've got a better chance of not getting noticed if I go alone."

The library door swung open, and Hunch entered, carrying a large bundle. Mairelon waved him toward the table and raised his eyebrows at Kim. "Not in practice? While you were living on the back streets, I was nosing about in France, if you recall."

"Huh." Kim sniffed. "France ain't London."

Hunch choked. Kim eyed him with disfavor. "Well, it ain't," she said.

"*Isn't*, Kim," Mairelon said.

"Ain't," Kim said firmly. "I got to talk to Tom tonight; if I sound too flash, he ain't going to be comfortable."

"Very well. Just don't slip in front of Aunt Agatha, for I won't be responsible for the consequences."

Kim nodded. "I won't. But you still ain't coming with me."

Hunch frowned and began nibbling on the left end of his mustache. Mairelon sighed. "Kim—"

"If you try, I won't go. And Tom won't talk to you alone, whatever he's got to say. If he'd meant for you to come, he'd have let us know somehow."

Mairelon studied her for a moment, frowning slightly. Finally, reluctantly, he nodded. "If you're determined. But I still don't like the idea of you crossing half of London on your own at that hour. Hunch and I will take you up High Holborn in the carriage."

"That's going to be inconspicuous for sure," Kim said scornfully. "Me, pulling up at Tom's door in a coach at midnight."

"Much as I'd like to do just that, I hadn't planned on it. I *have* done this sort of thing before, you know. We'll wait at the bottom of Threadneedle Street, or somewhere else nearby if you can think of a better place."

It was Kim's turn to nod reluctantly. She had, for a few wild minutes, hoped for a night run through the back streets of London, an opportunity to visit some of her old haunts besides Tom Correy's place. But Mairelon's points were well-taken. The London rookeries were a dangerous place even for the experienced, and her experiences were a year out of date. The less time she spent on the streets, the better her chance of avoiding robbery or murder. Memories were no good to the dead.

"That's settled, then," Mairelon said briskly, and handed Kim a stack of wrinkled clothing. "Now, do go and try these on while there's still time for Hunch to find more if they don't fit. And for heaven's sake, don't let Aunt Agatha see you, or we'll both be in the suds."

SIX

A heavy London fog had settled over the dark streets by the time Kim approached Tom Correy's shop in Petticoat Lane. Here there were no streetlamps to mark the road with flickering yellow light, and Kim was grateful. In the dark and the fog, she was only a shadow moving among shadows. This close to the St. Giles rookery, anyone who was noticing enough to spot her would likely be knowing enough to pretend he hadn't.

Even so, the thought of Mairelon and Hunch, waiting in the carriage a few streets away, was more comforting than she had expected. The smells of coal smoke and uncollected horse dung, the sounds of drunken revelry from the public house on the corner, and most of all the penetrating chill of the fog brought back the constant undercurrent of fear that she had lived with for so long. She had almost forgotten the fear, in her year of safety and security with Mairelon.

A church clock chimed the quarter hour. Kim jumped, then shook herself. *Past midnight already. I'll be home as late as a fashionable lady coming back from a ball.* She frowned at the thought, then dismissed it. Pulling her jacket firmly into place, she knocked at Tom's door.

An unfamiliar dark-haired youth opened it and looked at her suspiciously. "Who are you and what d'you want?"

"I come to see Tom Correy," Kim said.

"And I'm a valet to His Majesty," the youth sneered. "You're lookin' to unload something you pinched from your betters."

"What if I am?" Kim said. "You ain't one of 'em, so it ain't no lookout of yours."

"Ho!" The doorkeeper made an awful grimace and raised his fists. "See if I ain't!"

"I can see it just by looking at you," Kim said. He was sturdy enough, but his movements were too slow; even out of practice, she had little to fear from a scrap with him, unless he landed a lucky punch. She shook her head. *I'm not here to pick fights.* "You're wasting time. Tom's expecting me."

"No, he ain't," the youth retorted. "He ain't expecting nobody what would come sneaking around the back. He—"

"Here, Matt, what's the racket?" Tom's voice drifted out of one of the inner rooms, followed by Tom himself. His face split in a broad grin when he saw Kim. "Kim, lad! You got my message, then. Come in, come in, and tell me how you're keeping."

"Hellfire!" said the doorkeeper in obvious chagrin. "You told me you was expecting some flash frogmaker!"

"Well, so I am," Kim said in her best Grosvenor Square tones. If Tom had already said that much, there was no point in pretending. "But I didn't want to be noticed, and walking the alleys in pantaloons and a silk cravat would have gotten me noticed for sure."

"Garn!" said Matt, obviously impressed in spite of himself. "You ain't no frogmaker."

"Oh, ain't I?" Kim glanced quickly around. The door was closed, and the windows shuttered; no one but Tom and Matt was likely to see. Raising her right hand, palm upward, she focused all her attention on it and said, *"Fiat lux!"*

The tingling sensation of magic at work swept across her hand and arm. An instant later, a ball of light flared into being in the air above her palm. It was brighter than she'd intended; either she really was getting better at spellcasting, or annoyance had given her spell a boost. She rather suspected it was the annoyance. However it had happened, the effect was impressive. She heard Tom's breath hiss against his teeth in surprise, and Matt's startled exclamation, but she was concentrating too hard to respond.

Kim let the light float above her hand for several seconds. Then, one by one, she folded her fingers inward. The light dimmed, and as the last finger touched her palm, it vanished. The tingling sensation vanished as well, leaving her hand feeling unusually sensitive. She let it fall to her side, resisting the temptation to flex her fingers; it would spoil the effect.

"Coo," said Matt, his eyes bulging. "Ain't that a sight! What else can you do?"

"Get along with you," Tom said, cuffing Matt's shoulder. "Do you think a real magician has nothing better to do than show off tricks like a Captain Podd with his puppets? Kim's got things to do, and so have you."

With a resigned nod, Matt started for the inner door. Tom stood aside to let him pass, then called after him, "And if you say one word about this to anyone, I'll have Kim's master turn you into a frog!"

Kim couldn't make out the words of the muffled response, but it was apparently an affirmative, for Tom nodded in satisfaction and pulled the door to. Looking gravely at Kim, he said, "You hadn't ought to have done that."

"It was just light," Kim said uncomfortably.

"That's not the point, but it's too late to mend matters now." Tom sighed. "I just hope Matt has the sense to keep his jaw shut. If his uncle hears about this, we're grassed."

"What are you talking about?"

"I forget, you don't know what's been going on." Tom studied Kim for a moment, and forced a smile. "You're looking well. I guess that Mairelon cove wasn't gammoning me about feeding you up and teaching you magic and all."

"No, he's done all that, right enough," Kim said.

Tom gave her a sharp look. "So? And what hasn't he done?"

"Nothing. It's just . . . different. Toffs take a bit of getting used to, that's all. I'm fine."

"You're a sight better off than you'd have been if you'd stayed here, and don't you forget it," Tom said emphatically.

"I ain't likely to, what with regular meals and all," Kim said. "Why did you want to see me? And what was that about Matt's uncle? Who is he, anyway? You never used to have anybody to help out."

"Matt is one of my Jenny's nephews," Tom said, and Kim grinned at the possessive fondness in his tone when he spoke of his wife, even in passing. Some things hadn't changed. Oblivious, Tom continued, "Her sister's eldest boy, come to London to learn a trade."

"So? Ain't he working out?"

"He was working out fine, until somebody talked Jack Stower off the transports. That's why I wanted to talk to you."

"Stower's loose? When did that happen?" Kim was surprised, but not unduly alarmed. Jack Stower was Tom's brother-at-law, and a bad lot if there ever was one. Kim had never had much use for him, but she'd never feared him as she had his boss, Dan Laverham. And both Jack and Dan had been arrested a year ago, when she'd first hooked up with Mairelon. A twinge of uneasiness shook her. "Laverham ain't loose as well, is he?"

"No, he danced on air last November. It's just Jack."

Kim blew out a long, noisy breath. "Then I don't see what you're nattered about. Jack will have it in for me, but I can handle Jack now."

"I thought that's what you'd say," Tom said gloomily. "And if it was just Jack Stower, I wouldn't have sent for you to come here. But he's hooked up with Mannering, and if that don't worry you, it ought to."

"Why? Jack may think he can borrow enough to turn himself into a toff, but it ain't going to happen. And if he's in over his head with Mannering and the other cent-per-cents, he'll have more to worry about than me."

Tom stared at her for a moment, then shook his head. "I forget how much has changed since you've been gone. Mannering ain't just a moneylender, these days. He's got ambitions."

"Like what?"

"Like rounding up anyone with a hint of magic to 'em, and persuading them to work for him."

Kim snorted. "Laverham tried that once, and Ma Yanger gave him a week's rash, and Sam Nicks pitched him out a window, and George and Jemmy and Wags gave him an earful in the middle of Hungerford Market. You're telling me a creaky old moneylender's had better luck?"

"A lot better luck, one way and another, and nobody knows why. George and Jemmy and Wags turned him down when he first tried, right enough, but two weeks later they were working for him. Sam was stubborner, and he woke up one morning in an alley with his throat slit. Ma Yanger ain't working for Mannering, but she ain't working for nobody else, neither."

— 73 —

"Ma Yanger's given up witching people?" Kim said incredulously.

Tom nodded. "She's holed up in her rooms, and she won't see nobody. Been that way for two months now. And that's how it is with everyone else—they're working for Mannering, or they ain't working at all. And since Stower came back, Mannering's lads have been asking about you."

"Me?"

"Stower told him you can do magic, *and* that you were getting training from some fancy toff wizard. I think Mannering would like to get his hands on both of you. I figured the toff could look out for himself, but I thought somebody ought to tell you what was up afore you found out the hard way."

"Thanks, Tom." With a shiver, Kim remembered that Jack was one of the few people from her old life who knew of her masquerade. *It doesn't matter any more if people know I'm a girl*, she told herself, but the old habits and fears kept her tongue locked.

"So you see why you hadn't ought to have been showing off in front of Matt," Tom went on. "Jack Stower is his uncle, and they've been thick as treacle since Jack turned up again. Jenny's after me to keep Matt away from him, but how she expects me to do that I don't know," he added gloomily. "It ain't like I can put leg-irons on the boy."

"I wish I could help," Kim said, but Tom shook his head.

"That ain't why I asked you to come. Matt's my business, and I'll deal with him. But I don't know that I can keep him from talking to Jack about this, and if he does, Mannering will be after you like a shot."

"Maybe he already has been," Kim said thoughtfully. "You wouldn't know something about a green cracksman who bungled a job in Grosvenor Square last night?"

Tom considered for a moment. "No, but I can ask around if you like."

"Let it go," Kim said, shaking her head. "If Mannering's got you that nattered, you hadn't ought to get any more mixed up in this than you are already. I'll find out about it some other way."

"Kim, if Mannering has already made a try for you—"

"It wasn't anything like that," Kim said hastily. "Somebody tried to nobble a book from Mairelon's library, near as we can tell, and botched the job. It probably didn't have anything to do with Mannering. He's a deep old file; he wouldn't send an amateur on a crack lay like that."

"You're sure it wasn't bungled apurpose?"

Kim snorted. "The cull didn't know the first thing about housebreaking. Mairelon thinks he was depending on a spell to keep from getting nabbed, and even that didn't work."

"I still don't like it," Tom said. "He's a sneaking one, Mannering is."

"All the more reason he'd know better than to send a green 'un to mill a ken in Grosvenor Square. It's pure luck the cull wasn't laid by the heels right then." Seeing that Tom still looked unconvinced, Kim shook her head. "I'm sorry I mentioned it. And I really am glad of your warning."

"I don't know what good it'll do you," Tom said in a gloomy tone. "Jemmy and Sam and the others knew what was up, and knowing didn't help them none."

"Jemmy and Sam ain't proper wizards from the Royal College," Kim said. "I ain't, neither, but Mairelon is. And Mairelon won't take kindly to nobody messing with his ward. If Mannering knows anything about toffs, he'll twig to that as soon as he finds out where I am. If he finds out at all."

"Maybe you're right," Tom said thoughtfully. "Mannering deals with toffs all the time, what with his business and all. He ain't like Laverham, passing off sham gentility."

"It wasn't no sham with Laverham," Kim said. "He was

born on the wrong side of the blanket, but he was a toff, sure enough."

"No! Laverham? You're bamming me."

Thankful to have found a neutral topic to take Tom's mind off fretting, Kim allowed herself to be drawn into gossip about old acquaintances. Tom reciprocated as well as he was able. Many of her former fellows were in Newgate Prison, "polishing the King's iron with their eyebrows" as they looked out through the barred windows. Some had been transported; a few, like Laverham, had been hung. On the whole, it was a depressing catalog, and Kim was almost glad when time came to give Tom a final "Thank you" and slip away at last.

The shadows on the streets and alleys seemed darker and more threatening as she made her way down Threadneedle toward the Thames. Even at this hour, the street was not quite deserted, and she kept a wary eye on the bingo boy staggering from one public house to the next and the tired coster-monger pushing his barrow home from Covent Garden.

Mairelon's carriage waited at the end of the street, just where she had left it. Hunch sat in the coachman's seat, chewing on the ends of his mustache. When he saw Kim, his gloomy expression lightened in relief, and he thumped on the carriage roof. "She's 'ere, Master Richard."

There was a muffled noise from inside, then Mairelon's head poked out of the carriage window. "There you are, Kim! I was just about to come and fetch you."

"It hasn't been that long," Kim said. "Tom and I had things to talk about."

"You can tell me about it on the way home," Mairelon said. He sounded somewhat disgruntled, and when Kim climbed into the carriage, she saw that he had changed into a workingman's wrinkled shirt, vest, and breeches.

He's disappointed because he couldn't go larking about the alleys,

Kim thought, and shook her head. He ought to have better sense. She smiled suddenly, remembering her own eager response to the thought of a night out. *Seems like neither of us is strong on good sense.*

"Well, what happened?" Mairelon said as the coach began to roll. "Did Correy just want to talk over old times?"

"Not exactly," Kim said. "Jack Stower's loose, and Tom thinks he's trying to make trouble." She repeated what Tom had said about Mannering, his ambitions, and his apparent interest in Mairelon and Kim.

When she finished, Mairelon rubbed his chin, frowning. "What else do you know about this Mannering fellow?"

Kim shrugged. "He's a moneylender. He never had much to do with the canting crew, that I heard, but he wasn't above laying out a bit of the ready to folks like Laverham, that had some security to offer. It don't—doesn't—make sense that he'd want to take Laverham's place. He's more of a gent already than Laverham ever was."

"Perhaps he's not interested in climbing the social ladder. Or perhaps he has . . . unusual methods in mind." Mairelon smiled suddenly. "Perhaps I should drop in at his office one day soon."

"There ain't no call for that," Kim said, alarmed. "We got enough on our plates already, what with that cove poking around after that book and all. There's no reason to go *looking* for trouble."

"Of course not," Mairelon said, but the impish smile still hovered around the corners of his mouth. Kim resolved to have a talk with Hunch. Maybe the manservant could get some sense into Mairelon's head, or at least keep him from going off half-cocked and stirring up a pot of problems. Maybe. Not that anyone seemed to be able to check Mairelon's queer starts when he got the bit between his teeth.

"I wish I hadn't said anything about it at all," Kim muttered as the coach drew up behind the townhouse.

"What?" Mairelon said.

"I said I wish I hadn't told you about Mannering," Kim repeated.

"Why?" Mairelon studied her face for a moment. "You're really worried about this, aren't you?"

"Tom doesn't get all nattered over nothing. And he's nattered about Mannering and Stower, right enough."

"I see." Mairelon hesitated, then nodded slowly. "Very well. I won't pursue the matter until we've dealt with our literary housebreaker, unless we get some further indication that pursuing it would be advisable. And I'll speak to you beforehand."

"Fair enough," Kim said, slightly dazed. *He wouldn't say it if he didn't mean it. Don't that beat everything?*

"Then if that's settled, I suggest you turn your attention to sneaking inside without waking Aunt Agatha. I see no reason to precipitate another scene if we can avoid it."

"Right," said Kim, and slid out of the carriage.

SEVEN

Kim woke late the following morning, to sunlight and the clatter of carriage wheels on the cobbles below her window. As she dressed, she considered what to do with the little heap of boy's clothes in the corner of the wardrobe. If a housemaid found them, she'd report to Mrs. Lowe and there was sure to be a row. Finally, Kim stuffed them in a hatbox, tucking them around the hat as best she could, and shoved the box back onto the top shelf of her wardrobe. With luck, she could think of some excuse to give the box to Hunch later in the day, and he could dispose of the clothes without causing comment.

Feeling unreasonably cheerful, Kim left her bedroom and started downstairs. Halfway down the first flight of stairs, she heard muffled thumps and shouts drifting up from the lower floors. She quickened her pace, wondering what was going on now. It couldn't be the cracksman again, not in broad daylight.

As she turned onto the last landing, she heard an unfamiliar feminine voice below shriek, "Darby! Close that door at once!"

"He's headed for the stairs!" a second voice cried. "Catch him!"

An instant later, a small, yellow-brown monkey leaped onto the banister railing just in front of Kim and directed a high-pitched shriek of defiance at his pursuers. Kim, momentarily unnoticed, reached out and collected him in a firm hold. The monkey shrieked again, this time in surprise. Then, wrapping his long tail firmly around Kim's wrist, he relieved himself on her skirt.

"Don't think you're getting out of it that easily," Kim told him. Maintaining her hold with some care, so as to be sure that she would neither hurt the monkey nor be bitten herself, she rounded the corner and looked down.

The entry hall was full of people, boxes, and trunks. At the bottom of one of the piles of luggage, a large wicker cage lay on its side, its door open wide. Several disheveled footmen and an elderly, bright-eyed man in a coachman's many-caped cloak were scrambling over boxes and trunks toward the stairs; in the far corner, one of the housemaids was having hysterics. In the center of the commotion stood a tiny doll of a woman, looking upward with anxious hazel eyes. Her brown hair, where it curled out from under an exceedingly elegant wide-brimmed hat, was liberally streaked with gray. When she saw the monkey in Kim's arms, her worried expression broke into a cheerful smile that was the mirror of Mairelon's.

"Ah, you have captured Maximillian! Thank you very much. Would you be so kind as to bring him here and restore him to his cage? It is by far the simplest thing, when he is so nervous and upset. I am afraid he dislikes traveling."

Willingly, Kim made her way to the foot of the stairs and

deposited the monkey in the wicker cage, which one of the footmen had hastily righted. The woman secured the latch with a small padlock and said to the footman, "Now, take him up to the library, and be sure to put the cage in a corner where it will not be overturned again. I will bring him water and a bit of fruit presently, when he is more settled." She turned to Kim. "You must be my son's ward, Kim. I am so pleased to meet you at last. I am Lady Wendall."

Kim stared, her brain scrambling in several directions at once. *Lady? Her son's ward? This is Mairelon's mother, and she's a Lady Wendall?* Feeling a strong sense of ill-usage, she belatedly bobbed a curtsey. *Somebody ought to have warned me!*

As she straightened, she found herself being critically examined by the diminutive new arrival. "I thought so," Lady Wendall said cryptically after a moment. "My dear, who has—"

A door down the hall opened. "Whatever is going on?" Mrs. Lowe said as she came out into the hall, and then, in thunderstruck tones, *"Elizabeth?"*

"Good morning, Agatha," Lady Wendall said. "I should think that what is going on is obvious; the footmen are moving my trunks in."

"What . . . how . . . why wasn't I informed?"

"I told them not to disturb your breakfast." Lady Wendall nodded at the footmen, then favored Mrs. Lowe with a charming smile. "Speaking of breakfast, I am positively famished; these early hours are not what I am accustomed to. Do join me, and we shall talk while we eat."

With that, Lady Wendall swept past Mrs. Lowe into the dining room. Mrs. Lowe pursed her lips as if she had bitten into a bad orange, glared at the footmen, and went after Lady Wendall. Kim hesitated; they might not want her to join them. But neither of them had said anything, and the temptation was irresistible. She followed them in.

Lady Wendall had gone straight to the sideboard and was shaking her head over the dishes as she lifted the covers. Mrs. Lowe watched for a moment, her face a politely frozen mask, then took her seat. As she picked up her fork, she saw Kim in the doorway, and her eyebrows twitched together. "Whatever have you done to your dress, Kim?"

"It was the monkey," Kim said.

"Monkey?" Mrs. Lowe blinked, for once at a complete loss.

"Yes, and quite unpleasant for you, I'm sure," Lady Wendall said, turning toward the table with her hands full of loaded dishes. "Use one of the napkins to clean it off for the time being."

"She can't sit down to breakfast like that!" Mrs. Lowe protested as Kim set to work with the cloth. "She must go and change at once."

"I'm sure Kim is just as hungry as I am," Lady Wendall said with a smile. "It wouldn't be kind to make her wait. Unless you'd rather change first, Kim? We can all wait for you, if you'd prefer."

Kim shrugged. "It's no matter to me." Having food at all had always been far more important to her than the condition of the clothes she wore to eat it. She set the napkin on a side chair and began filling her plate.

"The stain will set and ruin the dress," Mrs. Lowe said.

"So much the better," Lady Wendall responded with unimpaired calm. "It's not a good color for her at all, and I intend to have it disposed of as soon as possible."

Mrs. Lowe stared, and her chin lifted. "Disposed of?" she said in ominous tones.

Lady Wendall nodded. "Unless you're particularly fond of it, Kim. It's well enough to wear about the house in Kent, but not for your first Season in London."

"It is entirely appropriate for a girl in her situation," Mrs. Lowe said firmly.

"I didn't say it was inappropriate," Lady Wendall said gently. "I said it was unbecoming. And Kim will want to look her best during her come-out."

"Elizabeth, I do hope you are not going to encourage Richard in this notion he has taken of having the girl presented."

Kim's half-formed protest stuck in her throat. She wasn't going to have a come-out, she'd settled that with Mairelon, but she couldn't quite say so if it meant agreeing with Mrs. Lowe in public. She coughed, trying to clear away the obstruction, but before she could find a good way to phrase her comment, the door opened and Mairelon entered.

"Good morning, Mother," he said. "I thought it must be you when I heard the commotion in the hall, and I was sure of it when I found a monkey in the library. Why a monkey, of all things?"

"Yes, isn't he charming?" Lady Wendall said. "Pahari Singh sent him to me. Actually, he sent three of them, but I'm afraid the other two didn't survive the voyage from India."

"*Three* monkeys?" Mrs. Lowe said.

"Who is Pahari Singh, and why on earth would he send you one monkey, let alone three?" Mairelon demanded.

"He was a good friend of your father's, from his days in India, though that, of course, was before you and Andrew were born. He was in London a few years ago on business, and he made a point of renewing the acquaintance."

"That explains who he is," Mairelon said, "but not why he should choose to send you a batch of monkeys."

"I believe he wanted to make sure I would have more than one serving," Lady Wendall replied. "Though his note was not exactly specific on the subject."

"Serving?" Mrs. Lowe said faintly. She set her fork carefully beside her unfinished breakfast. "Elizabeth . . ."

Mairelon looked at Lady Wendall with considerable misgiving. "Mother, are you saying that Mr. Singh sent you this creature as a . . . an addition to your dinner menu?"

"In a way. Monkey brains are considered a delicacy in India, and—"

"You're going to eat a *monkey brain?*" Kim broke in, thoroughly taken aback.

Lady Wendall gave a regretful sigh. "Not any time soon, I am afraid. I simply couldn't bear to have Maximillian slaughtered. It will just have to wait until the next time I visit India."

"Thank goodness for that," Mairelon said. "You know, monkeys are filthy creatures. You're lucky he doesn't have lice. Or fleas."

"Oh, he had both, when he arrived," Lady Wendall said imperturbably. "I had him bathed, naturally."

"I should hope so," Mrs. Lowe put in. She appeared to have recovered her equanimity, though she had not yet returned to her breakfast. "That does not explain, however, why you have chosen to introduce him into this household."

"Well, Lord Wendall couldn't very well take Maximillian to Suffolk with him, and I couldn't very well leave him in Russell Square with the renovations going on. So of course I brought him with me."

"Renovations?" Mairelon frowned. "Mother . . ."

"Renovations?" Mrs. Lowe stared. "Elizabeth, do you mean to say that you intend to stay *here* for the entire Season?"

"Yes, of course," Lady Wendall said. "Lord Wendall and Andrew are going to be in Suffolk discussing canals for the greater part of it, so Andrew offered to let me use the townhouse. He did warn me that Richard and Kim—and you, of course, Agatha—would be here, and I was of two minds about it until I heard that Richard was planning to give Kim a formal come-out."

"And when did you hear that?" Mrs. Lowe said, with a look at Mairelon that would have set fire to a heap of coal.

"Yesterday, at Lady Weydon's saloon," Lady Wendall replied. "Sally Jersey told me; she had it from someone who had been having tea with Richard. And I can already see that I was quite right to come." She turned to Mairelon. "Really, Richard, I thought you'd have had better sense. You've got her rigged out like a greengrocer's daughter."

"Kim's clothes are entirely suitable for her situation," Mrs. Lowe said, bristling.

Kim shifted uncomfortably. "It's not slap up to the nines, but neither am I."

"Nonsense," Mairelon said. "You look perfectly all right to me."

"That is precisely the problem," Lady Wendall told him. "Why on earth didn't you ask your friend Mademoiselle D'Auber to help you? If there's one thing the French know how to do, it's dress."

"She offered," Mairelon admitted, looking a little guilty, "but we didn't have time before Kim and I went down to Kent, and since we've been back, there have been other things. . . ."

"Well, you had better send her a note today," Lady Wendall said. "I shall be occupied in going through Kim's clothes, to see which of them are suitable, and in engaging an abigail for her."

Mrs. Lowe frowned. "Surely one of the housemaids will do well enough."

"I don't want an abigail," Kim said. "And—"

"I don't blame you in the least," Lady Wendall told her,

"but an abigail you must have if we are to launch you into Society." She studied Kim for a moment, her expression disconcertingly like Mairelon's when he was concentrating all his attention on something. "Someone young and flexible, I think, who will know when to make allowances for the eccentricities of wizards."

"Kim is hardly eccentric, Mother," Mairelon said.

"Nor is she the only wizard in this household," Lady Wendall replied. "Though if you can think of a more socially acceptable description of her background than 'eccentric,' I will be delighted."

"I am relieved to see that you are aware of the problem," Mrs. Lowe said stiffly.

"Perhaps Renée can recommend a suitable abigail," Lady Wendall went on. "You must remember to ask her when you speak to her about Kim's clothes."

"Mairelon—" Kim said, feeling desperate. The whole conversation was getting out of hand. If one of them didn't say something soon, she was going to find herself presented whether she wanted to be or not. And Mairelon had promised to speak with Mrs. Lowe about it. . . .

But Mairelon's face had the peculiar expression he wore when he had just had an idea, and he was oblivious to anything else. "Renée. Of course; I should have thought of that myself. You haven't anything planned this morning, have you, Kim? Good; finish your breakfast, and we'll go see Renée."

"I'm finished," Kim said. "But—"

"Change your clothes first," Mrs. Lowe said. "You positively cannot be seen on the street like that."

Lady Wendall nodded. "*Just* what I have been saying. I'll send a note to Madame Chandelaine this afternoon; there's no better dressmaker in London."

There was no use talking to any of them now. Maybe Renée D'Auber would have some advice; she was a lot more sensible than most toffs. Kim rolled her eyes and left.

When Kim and Mairelon arrived at Renée D'Auber's townhouse, a formidably correct butler showed them up to the drawing room at once. There they found Mademoiselle D'Auber busy at a small writing table. Her auburn hair was braided close to her head, and there was a smudge of dust or ink on the point of her chin; she resembled neither an elegant lady of fashion nor a wizard of power and skill, though she was both. A stack of books stood on a side table next to her. A faint scent of incense lingered in the air; Mademoiselle D'Auber must have been spellcasting recently. As the butler announced them, she looked up and smiled.

"Monsieur Merrill! And Mademoiselle Kim. It is of all things good to see you."

"And it is always good to see you, Renée," Mairelon said with a warm smile.

"You are kind, but it is not often that you come so early," Renée said, returning Mairelon's smile. "Sit down, and tell me what it is that brings you."

As she took a chair covered in wine-red silk, Kim watched her two companions with curiosity bordering on bafflement. Though she had known both Mairelon and Renée D'Auber for a year now, she could not begin to pretend that she understood their relationship. There seemed to be no element of romance between them, and she had observed them closely enough to stake her position as Mairelon's ward that there was no physical intimacy, either. Yet there was an undeniable warmth and familiarity in their conversation that, if

Mrs. Lowe were to be believed, was not fitting between an unattached man and a respectable young woman of quality. Maybe it was because they were both wizards, or perhaps it had something to do with the years Mairelon had spent gathering intelligence in France.

"Two things," Mairelon said. "First, can you tell me anything about a group of French wizards called *Les Griffonais*? They apparently had something of a name in France before the Terror."

Renée looked at him with considerable amusement. "And you expect that I will know something of them? The Terror was nearly thirty years ago, and me, I was not yet born." She held up a hand to forestall Mairelon's next comment and continued, "I do not say I have not heard of them, but I wish to know why you have this interest before I say any more. Otherwise you will not tell me anything, and I shall perish of the curiosity."

"My father bought part of a library collection that once belonged to a Madame Marie de Cambriol. Lord Kerring down at the Royal College says she was one of the group."

"And?"

Mairelon sighed. "And somebody seems a little too interested in Madame's collection for my peace of mind."

Mlle. D'Auber looked at him with disfavor. "You, my friend, are entirely English, which is a thing impossible to understand. And you are even more impossible to get answers from than other English persons. Kim! What is it that he means by this 'too interested for his peace of mind'?"

"Some toff wizard broke into the house night before last," Kim said. "He was looking for something in the library, and he had a spell with him that lit up all the books from the Cambriol mort's collection."

"We think he only wanted one of the books," Mairelon said, "but Kim ran him off before he could take it."

"You are sure?"

Mairelon shrugged. "Andrew had an inventory done when my father died; everything on the list is still there."

Renée nodded. "Very good. Now I will tell you what I know, which is not much. I never met this Marie de Cambriol, but the Sieur Jacques de Cambriol was a friend of my father's. His wife died very suddenly, a year or two after they emigrated, and when I was very little he used to come to dinner with my parents."

"Was the Sieur de Cambriol a wizard?"

"No. I do not know what he was in France, before the Terror, but afterward he was a gambler. Papa spoke of him often, and tried to help when he could. He died nearly ten years ago, I think, in the debtors' prison."

"So they escaped the Terror and came to England—"

"No," Renée corrected. "They left France before the Terror began, the Sieur Jacques and his wife and their friends." She frowned. "The Sieur used to tell me the story, with much waving of hands. I am afraid I do not recollect the details at all clearly—it was not a daring escape, you see, but simply prudent. And the prudence, it did not at all interest me when I was a child."

Mairelon straightened. "The de Cambriols *and their friends* left France before the terror? That wouldn't by any chance be the rest of the group of wizards?"

"I think it was," Renée said after some thought. "But I am not positive, you understand."

"Do you know who the others were?" Kim asked.

"*Les Griffonais?* Let me think. Madame de Cambriol, of course, and the Comte du Franchard and his wife, the

Comtesse de Beauvoix. The duchesse Delagardie. The Hungarian, M. László Karolyi. M. Henri d'Armand. And Mademoiselle Jeannette Lepain, who as a child I thought was of all things most romantic because she married a Russian prince."

"Do you know whether any of them are in England now?" Mairelon said.

"No, I do not know," Renée said. "They were not, you understand, friends of mine; I do not think even Papa knew any of them except Sieur de Cambriol."

"Well, at least now I have some names," Mairelon said. "Thank you, Renée. I wonder whether Shoreham is still keeping track of the *émigrés;* I believe I'll stop in and ask him tomorrow."

"And your other reason for coming to visit me?" Mlle. D'Auber said. "You said there were two."

"What? Oh, yes, well, that's Kim's, actually. Mother arrived this morning and says she's not dressed properly; she thought you might be interested in helping out."

"*Mairelon,*" Kim said, thoroughly exasperated.

"Yes, he is of all persons the most excessively trying," Renée said, nodding. "Now you will tell me what it is he is trying to say."

"He said, it, but—Lady Wendall only wants me to dress better because she thinks Mairelon's going to present me to Society. And he isn't."

Renée's eyebrows rose expressively. "Not?"

"Kim doesn't wish it," Mairelon said shortly.

The eyebrows twitched, then rose even higher. "Indeed. Then how is it your so-estimable mother is of the idea that you will do so?"

"Gossip," Mairelon said.

"It ain't just gossip!" Kim said. "It's what you said at that tea. Your mother believes it, and the way she's going on, I'm like to be presented tomorrow whether I want it or not."

"I'll explain to Mother as soon as we get back," Mairelon said. "She'll understand. Though she would certainly enjoy managing it."

"One moment," Renée said, looking from one to the other. "I wish first to know why it is that Mademoiselle Kim does not wish to be presented."

"I—" Kim swallowed hard. "Look, this ain't—isn't going to sound right, but I just don't like it. Making up to a bunch of old cats just because they say who gets invited to a lot of boring teas and balls . . . Doing the wizard stuff is hard enough. And I'm not good at watching what I say." She gestured helplessly. "It just wouldn't work."

"But of course it would work!" Renée shook her head reprovingly. "You are a wizard. It is expected that you will be entirely original. And there are many advantages, you know."

"Like what?" Kim said, half wanting to be convinced but not really believing it was possible.

"M. Merrill's Mama is exceedingly well known; if it is she who introduces you to Society, you will be accepted by everyone. And it is often useful for a wizard to know a great many persons. Also, if you are not presented, there will always be persons who wonder why. Some will think that you cannot truly be a wizard."

"I hadn't thought of that," Mairelon said slowly, "but you're right. They would."

"Why?" Kim said. "That doesn't make sense!"

Renée shrugged. "To them, it does. They cannot conceive that anyone would not wish to be presented. If you are not, they will say it is because you *cannot* be, and since a wizard can always be presented, you must not be one. It is very foolish."

"Well . . ."

"There is also M. Merrill to consider," Renée went on. "A great many people thought he had stolen the Saltash Set, and now they do not think he is enough respectable even though the set is returned and milord Shoreham has arrested the real thieves."

"That is ridiculous!" Mairelon said.

Renée waved his objection aside. "I say only what people think. And since you do not often go to balls or parties, a great many persons of no intellect whatever think that it is because you are not invited and not because, like Mademoiselle Kim, you do not find it interesting. It would have been altogether better if you had spent the Season in London last year, as we talked of then."

"I did," Mairelon objected.

"You spent it with milord Shoreham, and not at the balls and parties," Renée said. "It is not at all the same. But if Mademoiselle Kim is presented, you will *have* to go to balls, and people will see that you are quite enough respectable after all. Or at least, that you are not so unrespectable as they had thought."

Kim stared at Mlle. D'Auber, speechless. This was an aspect of the matter that she had never considered. From the look on his face, neither had Mairelon, though she couldn't tell whether his look of chagrin came from the realization that some of Society thought he was not "enough respectable," or from the realization that if his ward were to come out properly, he, too, would be required to attend balls and parties. Knowing Mairelon, she suspected the latter.

"I do not think it will be nearly so boring as you fear," Renée said to Kim, smiling. "Not with M. Merrill's Mama in charge. And once you have been presented, it is done, and you may attend the balls or not, as it pleases you."

"And if you do it, Aunt Agatha will turn positively purple," Mairelon murmured, recovering quickly.

The silence that followed stretched on for what seemed forever. Finally, Kim sighed. "All right, then. I'll try it. But I still think you all have windmills in your heads."

"Of a certainty," Mlle. D'Auber said. "How else is one to deal with M. Merrill?"

EIGHT

After leaving Mlle. D'Auber's, Mairelon ordered the coach to stop at the Horse Guards, where Lord Shoreham had his office. Unfortunately, Lord Shoreham was unable to give him any more information regarding the French wizards, though he promised to have his records checked for anything that Mairelon might find useful. They arrived home early in the afternoon, and Kim was immediately swept up by Lady Wendall.

"Is there anything in your wardrobe of which you are particularly fond?" she demanded of Kim almost as soon as Kim entered the house.

"I don't think so," Kim said, considerably startled.

"Good. Then I will have one of the footmen take all of it to the used clothing shops tomorrow," Lady Wendall said. "Except of course for the outfit you have stored in the hatbox; that clearly has uses other than fashion to recommend it. Did you speak to Mlle. D'Auber about shopping tomorrow?"

"I forgot," Kim said. "Mairelon had other things he wanted to talk about."

"Richard always does. Well, I'll send a note around this afternoon. I suggest you spend the time on your magical studies; tomorrow, you will be quite thoroughly occupied."

Nothing loath, Kim escaped to the library, where she alternated between watching the monkey's antics in its wicker cage and trying to puzzle out a few more of Mairelon's assigned texts. Since all of them included occasional examples in foreign languages that were quite beyond Kim's comprehension, she had a long list of questions ready for Mairelon by the time he came to check on her progress. Mairelon readily agreed to translate and explain the questionable bits, but his answers only frustrated Kim more.

"Don't these coves know how to say anything straight out in English?" Kim demanded after Mairelon had finished explaining a particularly convoluted paragraph written in Greek, which boiled down to *Don't try this; it doesn't work.*

Mairelon laughed. "It wouldn't sound nearly as impressive in plain English."

"I thought the point was to tell wizards how to do magic," Kim said crossly. "Not to sound impressive."

"Wizards are at least as vain as anyone else," Mairelon said. "Possibly more so."

"Well, I don't see why I have to learn all this foreign talk just so some cull who's been dead since before I was born can sound flash when he says, 'Wiggle all the fingers on your right hand.' "

"You'll just have to trust me when I tell you it's worth the effort," Mairelon told her. "You could probably learn quite a few of the simple spells by rote, but it would be very difficult for you to get much beyond that."

"Why? I have a good memory."

"Yes, but magic isn't just a matter of memory. It takes understanding, too. Here, I'll show you." Mairelon set the book aside and went over to his mother's desk. After a moment of rummaging and a few more of scribbling, he returned with a sheet of paper bearing a peculiar diagram and four words.

"This is a spell," he said, thrusting the paper into her hand. "You ought to be able to handle it at your level. You cast it by drawing this diagram, starting with this—" he pointed "—and ending with these. As you draw each of these points, you say one of these words, in order."

"How do I say them?" Kim said, staring at the unfamiliar jumble of consonants and vowels.

Mairelon obligingly pronounced each word in turn. "Now cast it."

Kim gave him a startled look, then lowered her eyes to study the paper. The drawing was of a circle quartered by two double-headed arrows, the heads of which protruded on all four sides. *Draw the circle first, then the cross, and then the arrowheads, and say one word at each arrowhead. Fine.* She took the pen and ink Mairelon handed her, and bent to her task.

As she spoke the first word, she felt a faint tingling. It strengthened a trifle with each additional command, and when she looked up, she thought she saw a faint greenish haze around several of the bookcases, and a brief shower of green sparkles near Mairelon's coat. The effect faded almost at once. Mairelon nodded in approval.

"Not bad. But look here. The circle represents magic; the four arrows are four directions. *Epistamai* is Greek for 'to know,' *videre* is Latin for 'to see,' *l'herah* is Hebrew for 'to show,' and *revelare* is Latin again, meaning 'to reveal.' Put it all together, and you have a spell that lets a magician find out what things around him have been enchanted."

"You can tell that most of the time just by touching them," Kim objected.

"You can't go around touching everything you suspect of

being magical," Mairelon said. "Quite apart from the attention you'd attract, it's not always wise."

"Trap spells, you mean."

"Among other things. Now, cast it again."

Frowning slightly, Kim did so. This time, two of the bookcases glowed a steady green, the third button on Mairelon's coat was a shower of green sparks, and one of the candlesticks was briefly surrounded by a faint green mist.

The effect took longer to fade, too. A greenish haze still remained around his button when he finally said, "It was clearer that time, wasn't it?"

Kim gave him a startled look. "Couldn't you tell?"

"It's not a general spell to show *everyone* what's enchanted. It's only supposed to show *you.*"

"Oh. Yes, everything was brighter."

"That's the difference between knowing a spell by rote and actually understanding what you are saying."

"But—" Kim paused, frowning. Then she dipped the pen once more and began to draw the figure. "To know," she said as she completed the first arrow. "To see. To show. To reveal . . . Ow!" An instant too late, she flung a hand over her eyes to shut out the blinding light that flared from the bookcases and the searing flashes from Mairelon's button.

"And *that* is why you can't just learn spells in English in the first place," Mairelon said in a tone of smug satisfaction.

"You might of warned me!" Kim said, keeping her eyes closed.

"Some things take better if you aren't told about them first," Mairelon said. "Besides, I wanted to see whether you'd think of it on your own."

"You still could of warned me." Cautiously, Kim opened her eyes. Green spots still danced in front of them, but the light had weakened to a bearable level.

"If it's any comfort, you're doing rather well. I didn't think of trying a spell in English until my third year of formal study, and I was fool enough to pick a translation spell to try it on. For the next week, everything I said or wrote came out in a garble of French, Spanish, Italian, Russian, and some outlandish tongue I didn't even recognize. I couldn't explain to anyone what had happened, and with everything I said coming out in a muddle, I couldn't use magic to correct matters."

"What did you do?"

Mairelon grimaced. "There wasn't much of anything I *could* do. Fortunately, Mother knows a bit of the Art herself, and when I came in sounding like all the workmen at the Tower of Babel rolled into one, she could tell there was magic involved. She sent for my tutor, and of course once he did the spell properly, he understood me. He told the family, which settled things down considerably. There was nothing to be done about me, though, except wait for the enchantment to wear off. I had to make do with sign language for a week."

"Are you trying to say that if I'd waited until next year to try that, it would have been even worse than it was?" Kim demanded.

"Much worse," Mairelon said cheerfully. "The further you get in your study of magic, the more power you use without thinking about it. Using a foreign tongue keeps it all from spewing into a spell uncontrollably. And the reason most spells are in ancient Greek and Latin is that nobody grows up speaking those languages any more, so every wizard can use spells written in them without having to translate them first."

"So if I was to say this spell in French, it would work just as well as it does in Latin?" Kim asked.

"Yes, exactly. Of course, the more complex the spell, the more important the precise shades of meaning become. When we get to advanced work, you'll find that some spells have completely different effects, depending on whether you say them in Latin or Greek or Hebrew."

"And Mlle. D'Auber could do spells in English if she wanted, but I can't."

Mairelon beamed. "Yes. As far as the Royal College can determine, mere fluency in a foreign language does not cause the same problems as growing up speaking it. English is a foreign language to Renée, so she could certainly cast spells in it." He paused, then added absently, "I sometimes wonder how the Jewish wizards manage. Hebrew is used in quite a lot of spells, and one would think— But then, if they *have* found a way around the language problem, one can't blame them for keeping it secret. Not after the way they've been treated over the centuries."

Ignoring this novel viewpoint, Kim frowned. "All right, but why do I have to learn *three kinds* of foreign talk? Isn't one enough?"

"It is an unfortunate side effect of history," Mairelon said. "The ancient Romans couldn't cast their spells in Latin, so they used Greek. The Greeks couldn't cast spells in Greek, so they used Latin. And mixing in a little Hebrew kept spells from being quite so easy to steal, because the spellcaster had to know at least two languages."

"I still say it's too tangled," Kim grumbled. "And what do all those spells *do*, anyway? The ones I saw—on the bookcases and your waistcoat button and the candlestick."

"Finding that out is a different spell," Mairelon said. "And we're not through with the theory of this one, yet. Now, if you alter the order, like this, nothing happens, but if you change the arrowheads to triangles . . ."

An hour and a half later, Kim's head was buzzing. She was amazed by the number of changes that could be wrung out of the simple spell merely by changing the order of the words or the way in which the diagram was drawn, and she had a new respect for the reasons behind Mairelon's emphasis on accuracy in spellcasting.

The following morning, Lady Wendall appeared at Kim's room, accompanied by a plump, middle-aged woman whose sharp eyes belied her outward appearance of placid respectability.

"Wilson will be your abigail," Lady Wendall informed Kim. "If you must go out without Richard or myself, take her with you."

"Even to St. Giles?" Kim said, nettled.

"Not at all, miss," the plump woman responded. "St. Giles ain't no place for a respectable woman, let alone a young lady of Quality. So if you go there, it'll be for wizardly doings, and you won't be needing me. My lady meant more usual places. Shopping and such."

Kim made a face, and Lady Wendall laughed. "Wilson is quite right. Wizards do not require an abigail when they are on magical business, though of course it is wise to bring one with you even for most of that. You will become accustomed in time, I am sure."

"That doesn't make any sense," Kim objected. She didn't feel up to explaining that it was the thought of shopping, and not of being shadowed by a respectable abigail, that had made her grimace.

"Of course it doesn't make sense," Lady Wendall said. "The rules of Society seldom do. One must simply learn them, no matter how little sense they make."

"Oh. It's exactly the opposite of magic, then."

Lady Wendall laughed. "Yes, I am afraid so. But if you transgress the rules of Society, you may well find yourself an outcast. Wizardry cannot protect one from everything." She paused. "I do hope you will try not to err, my dear. You may not find social ostracism much of a threat, but it would be so uncomfortable for Richard."

Kim frowned. "You mean that Mrs. Lowe was right?"

"I doubt it," Lady Wendall murmured. "Right about what?"

"About how me being his ward makes him look bad to the nobs."

"Not at all. It is a minor eccentricity on his part, but wizards are allowed considerably more freedom in some regards than most people. Were you to create a great scandal—if you eloped to Gretna Green or attempted to turn His Highness into a toad—that would certainly reflect on Richard, the same as if his brother or I were to do such a thing. I don't think you need to worry too much, however. A little common sense is really all that is needed."

Maybe that's all it takes for you, Kim thought, but she held her peace. Lady Wendall was trying to be reassuring, but Kim could not help feeling that she would be facing less obvious pitfalls than a runaway marriage or a misdirected spell.

Lady Wendall smiled. "Now, if you will put on your green walking dress, we will proceed to Madame Chandelaine's to procure you a proper wardrobe."

With a sigh, Kim nodded. She let Wilson dress her and arrange her hair, then joined Lady Wendall. She was still considering Lady Wendall's comments, and wondering whether the whole come-out business wasn't really a mistake after all, and so they had almost reached Madame Chandelaine's before she thought to ask whether Renée would be accompanying them.

"Mlle. D'Auber is to meet us at Madame's," Lady Wendall told Kim. "We will have a certain amount of time to talk while you are being fitted, but I warn you that Madame is an inveterate gossip. If you do not wish to find the whole of London discussing your affairs, you will have to watch what you say."

When they arrived, they were ushered immediately into a private room at the back of the establishment. Renée was already there, engaged in a spirited conversation with a black-haired woman of formidable proportions. Unfortunately, the conversation was in French, so Kim did not understand a word. Lady Wendall greeted the two in the same language, and for a moment Kim was afraid that all three of them would speak French for the entire afternoon. After her greeting, however, Lady Wendall returned to English and said, "Has Mlle. D'Auber explained our requirements, Madame?"

"A wardrobe for the young lady, I believe?" The formidable Frenchwoman studied Kim with a critical eye.

Lady Wendall nodded. "Garments suitable for my son's ward, whom I shall be presenting this Season. And also suitable for an apprentice wizard, recognized by the Royal College, who is having her first Season."

"A wizard in her first Season?" Madame's gaze sharpened with curiosity and interest.

"It is not at all uncommon for wizards to enjoy the Season," Mlle. D'Auber pointed out gently.

"It is, however, uncommon for the young ladies to admit that they are wizards—especially in their first Season," Madame said. "It is not a thing the Mamas believe is of help in catching a husband. Last Season, I had the dressing of only two such; this Season, none at all."

"My son's ward is uncommon," Lady Wendall said. "In fact, her antecedents are somewhat . . . unusual."

"Wizards are always unusual." Madame waved dismissively. "But of a certainty, they do not always admit it. I will find it a pleasure to have the dressing of one who does. Turn around, Mademoiselle, if you please."

Kim complied.

"Charming," Madame said. "Entirely charming. It will be well, I think. Elspeth! The green-figured muslin, and the yellow silk. And the China blue crêpe."

"Not yellow," Renée put in firmly. "For Kim, it is a color entirely unbecoming."

"So?" Madame studied Kim a moment, frowning. "Yes, yes, I see. The white sarcenet, then, and the lilac. What will she be doing for her display? Roses?"

"We have not yet decided," Lady Wendall said. "I can assure you, however, it will not be anything so usual."

"Display?" Kim said, her head already spinning from the talk of so many colors and fabrics. "What display?"

"If you wish me to design a dress for her presentation ball, I must know what illusion she is to perform," Madame said. "Something in peach would be well with Mademoiselle's coloring, but not if she is to perform red roses or a fire."

"Perform?" Kim said, now thoroughly alarmed. "What do you mean, perform?"

"We will leave the dress for her ball until later," Lady Wendall informed Madame. "There are still three weeks before it will be needed." She turned to Kim. "It is customary, on those occasions when a wizard is being presented, for her to perform some magical illusion with her magic tutor before she opens the dancing. Climbing roses have been very popular in the last few years, though in the Season following Waterloo a Miss Taldworth attempted an image of Napoleon surrendering his sword. She did a very bad job of it, quite apart from the fundamental inaccuracy of the image, and it was an *on dit* for weeks. Since then everyone has kept to things that are simpler."

"Or they avoid it entirely," Renée said. "The Mamas, they

presented last year more than two young ladies who were wizards, I think."

"You mean I'm going to have to do a spell in front of a bunch of *toffs?*" Kim said, outraged that no one had mentioned this before she had agreed to this come-out.

"Yes, exactly," Lady Wendall said serenely. "You and Richard have plenty of time to design something that will reflect your unique background, as well as demonstrating your abilities as a wizard. I am looking forward to seeing what you decide upon."

"I could pick everyone's pockets at once with magic," Kim said, still disgruntled. "That'd 'reflect my unique background,' all right."

Lady Wendall considered. "I don't think so. Unless Richard has been pushing you far harder than he ought, spells of that magnitude and scope are still beyond your abilities. An illusion along those lines, however, would be just the thing. You must discuss it with him when we get home."

A teetering pile of fabric bolts, supported by Madame's young assistant, staggered into the room. "Ah, Elspeth!" Madame said. "On the table, if you please. Now, Mademoiselle. . . ."

Kim spent the next several hours being measured, draped, fitted, and paraded before the critical eyes of Lady Wendall, Renée D'Auber, and Madame Chandelaine in a variety of dresses. Lady Wendall began by ordering a cream walking dress that needed only to be shortened and a morning dress in the green-figured muslin, both to be delivered on the morrow. After that, she became more particular, choosing a sleeve from this dress and a flounce from that one, to be combined with a different bodice and a fuller skirt. Renée added advice and suggestions of her own, and Madame also put in a word from time to time. No one asked for Kim's opinion.

The number and cost of the dresses appalled Kim. Lady Wendall's idea of an acceptable wardrobe was considerably more lavish than Mairelon's or Mrs. Lowe's; in her days on the street, Kim could have lived comfortably for two years on the price of a single walking dress. The ball gowns were naturally much worse, and there were far more of them than Kim could imagine ever needing. But both Lady Wendall and Renée D'Auber looked at her in complete incomprehension when she tried to explain her objections, so eventually she gave up and let them do as they wished.

When they had finished negotiating with Madame, there were more things to be purchased elsewhere: gloves, bonnets, stockings, slippers, and all manner of other small items. By the time they returned to Grosvenor Square at last, they were laden with packages and Kim was exhausted. Even Mrs. Lowe's disapproving comments over dinner failed to penetrate her fatigue. She fell into bed that night, thankful that at least the shopping part was done with.

NINE

Kim discovered her mistake over the course of the next week. Not only was the shopping not done with, there were an enormous number of preparations necessary for the ball Lady Wendall proposed to hold. Everything, it seemed, had to be done immediately, beginning with writing out and sending invitations to some four hundred persons of Lady Wendall's acquaintance. Kim's poor handwriting kept her from helping with that chore, but plenty of other things needed to be done.

Her magic lessons were a welcome break from the sudden plunge into social arrangements. Mairelon had begun focusing more on specific spells, which Kim found far more interesting than the dry tomes full of jaw-breaking foreign languages that she had been studying earlier. When she thought about it, she realized that she was learning a great deal of magical theory along with the practical specifics of the spells they reviewed together, but working with Mairelon made theory intriguing instead of dull.

In the evenings, Mairelon gave her dancing lessons, while

Lady Wendall played the pianoforte. Kim picked up the patterns of the country dances very quickly, but waltzing made her nervous. For too many years, she had carefully avoided getting near people, for fear they would discover that she was not the boy she had pretended to be. Allowing anyone, even Mairelon, not only to come close, but to circle her waist with his arm brought back old fears, though she had to admit that the sensation was pleasurable on those rare occasions when she could relax enough to enjoy it.

The mysterious burglar did not reappear, for which Kim could only be thankful. Between shopping, preparations for the ball, and lessons in magic, dancing, and etiquette, her days were too full to admit any additional activities. It was almost a relief when Lady Wendall announced over dinner that they would be spending the following evening at the opera.

"Most of your gowns have arrived, so you will be sure of making a good appearance," Lady Wendall said.

Mrs. Lowe looked up. "You will understand, I am sure, if I do not choose to join you."

"Of course," Lady Wendall said. "Though I think you refine too much on Kim's misadventure at Mrs. Hardcastle's."

"Nonetheless, I prefer a peaceful evening at home to the . . . uncertainties of a public appearance at this time."

"Nonsense, Aunt!" Mairelon said. "What can happen at the opera? You go, you sit in a box and listen to a lot of caterwauling, you wave at other people during the interval, and you come home."

"I sincerely hope that your evening will be as unexceptionable as you say," Mrs. Lowe said. "But I remain at home."

"In that case, I shall invite Renée D'Auber to accompany us," Lady Wendall said.

The whole thing sounded less than appealing to Kim, but she had agreed to this come-out business, and she would see it through. Her misgivings increased when Wilson, the abigail, helped her get ready. Apart from fittings, it was the first time Kim had worn formal evening dress. The apricot crêpe hung smoothly over the matching satin slip, but she was not at all sure she could walk without stepping on the deep flounce of blond lace that trimmed the hem. The bodice was fashionably tight and low cut—too low cut, Kim thought. Her shoulders and breasts felt decidedly exposed. It hadn't seemed nearly as skimpy during the fittings. A thin scarf woven with gold threads did little to mend matters. Feeling nervous, Kim went down to join the others.

"Excellent," Lady Wendall said as Kim came down the stairs. "That color is perfect."

"I'm sorry I kept you waiting," Kim said. Lady Wendall's dress was at least as low cut as hers, and the drape of lace trim that fell over the dark green silk of the bodice made it look even more precarious.

"It's only to be expected," Mairelon said. "It always takes longer to put on a costume the first time."

"Richard!" said his mother. "You are talking as if we were going to a masquerade instead of the opera."

"Am I?" Mairelon said vaguely. "Ah, well. Hadn't we better be going?"

Lady Wendall rolled her eyes and took Mairelon's arm. *But Mairelon is right,* thought Kim as she followed them out to the carriage. *It is a costume, and I am only playing a part, the same way I played the part of a boy for so long.* The thought was depressing; it made her wonder whether she would have to play at being something other than what she was for all her life. *But what am I, if I stop playing parts?* She shivered and thrust the thought away. *This* part was what mattered tonight, dispiriting as it might be. And on top of everything, Mairelon hadn't even said that she looked nice.

Her depression lifted when they entered the opera house. The ornate foyer was crowded with toffs. Most of the men wore dark coats and pantaloons; the younger women wore muslin gowns in soft colors; and the older ones wore silks, velvets, and a profusion of jewels that almost made Kim regret having given up thieving. Lady Wendall, Renée, and Mairelon seemed in no hurry to reach their box. They moved slowly through the crowd, greeting acquaintances, chatting with friends, and introducing Kim to more people than she could possibly remember.

Eventually, they reached the box, but this only set off another round of socializing as people in other boxes saw them and left their places to come and visit. Kim was not at all sure how they decided who stayed in a box and who came to visit, but there had to be some sort of system, or too many people would pass each other in the hall.

After what seemed hours, the traffic lessened and a few people began to take their seats in preparation for the overture. Many, however, continued talking and visiting despite the music. As the curtain rose, Kim noticed a slender young man watching them from the opposite box. She leaned over to mention this to Lady Wendall, but was frowned into silence. The show began.

On the whole, Kim decided, opera compared favorably with the puppet shows, hurdy-gurdy men, and balladeers of the marketplaces. The actors had better costumes, and everybody sang on key, and every so often a thoroughly implausible fight would erupt, with lots of leaping about and everyone still singing at the top of their lungs. On the other hand, she couldn't understand a word of it, and without the words, the actions didn't make much sense. She wasn't entirely convinced they were supposed to. It didn't seem to matter to anyone else; most of the audience was more interested in talking to each other or observing the toffs in the boxes than in the events on stage.

Halfway through the first act, Kim felt the unmistakable tingling sensation that heralded a spell in process. She stiffened, and looked around for the wizard, noting absently that Mairelon, Lady Wendall, and Renée D'Auber were doing the same. No one else seemed to notice; on stage, the opera continued forward without pause, and the audience was as rapt as they had ever been, which was not much. Mairelon spoke two rapid sentences in a low voice, and the tingling intensified. Then, abruptly, the feeling vanished.

Kim wanted desperately to question Mairelon, but again Lady Wendall gestured to forbid speech. Renée, Mairelon, and Lady Wendall continued watching the performance with outward calm, while Kim shifted restlessly in her seat for the rest of the act. As the curtain closed and the stage crew rushed to replace the candles in the giant candelabra that provided light to the stage, she turned to Mairelon and demanded, "What was that?"

"A scrying spell, I think," Mairelon said. "Someone wanted to know where we were."

"You *think?*" Renée said, lifting her eyebrows.

"The spell had an unusual construction. It was similar to the basic look-and-see spell everyone learns as an apprentice, but it wasn't identical by any means." He smiled. "It will be interesting to see who turns up during the interval."

An expression of mild relief crossed Lady Wendall's face. "You think that's all—oh, good evening, Lady Lidestone. Allow me to present my son's apprentice and ward, Miss Kim Merrill."

Kim rose and bobbed a curtsey as an elderly woman in a purple turban entered the box. "I am pleased to make your acquaintance, Lady Lidestone," she murmured.

Lady Lidestone raised a gold lorgnette and studied Kim. "Better than I had been led to believe," she pronounced after a moment. "So you really do intend to introduce her to Society, Elizabeth?"

"Of course," Lady Wendall said. "It will add a bit of spice to this year's Season."

Lady Lidestone gave a crack of laughter. "You always have been one for spice. I'll look forward to more entertainment than I've had in a long while." She gave a nod of approval that included Kim, and moved on.

She was replaced almost at once by a tongue-tied young woman and her Mama, who had ostensibly come to give their regards to Lady Wendall, but who seemed far more interested in being presented to Mairelon. They were followed by several amiable young men who wished to pay their respects to Renée, and the box began to seem more than a little full. Kim frowned, feeling hot and a little dizzy but not knowing quite what to do about it.

"You're looking a bit overheated," Mairelon's voice said in her ear. "I believe we should take a turn in the corridor."

Kim jumped, then nodded gratefully. With a few words, Mairelon extricated them from the polite conversation, and a moment later they were in the relative cool and quiet of the corridor.

"That's a relief," Kim said with a sigh as they walked toward the foyer.

Mairelon raised an eyebrow in inquiry.

"This is all . . . it's just . . . it's so *much*," she said.

"A bit overwhelming?" Mairelon nodded. "You'll become accustomed."

"Maybe," Kim said dubiously.

They walked in companionable silence to the foyer, nodding in passing to several people on their way to visit boxes.

The foyer was, once again, full of toffs and the scent of candle smoke. They stood in the doorway for a moment, watching as people surged and shifted, then moved sideways to stand against the wall and out of the traffic.

A few enterprising vendors had slipped into the opera house with baskets of fruit or comfits to sell to the toffs; one had even managed a tray of steaming drinks. Kim watched in professional admiration as he maneuvered through the crowd without spilling a drop. His customers were not always so fortunate; even as she watched, someone jostled a tall gentleman holding one of the drinks. The liquid sloshed over the rim of the mug and over his hands and sleeves. Cursing, the man set the mug on the vendor's tray and stripped off his gloves. As he scrubbed uselessly at his sleeve, light gleamed on a gold ring carved in the shape of a flower with a red stone in the center.

Kim clutched at Mairelon's arm. "Mairelon! That toff burglar's here. Or somebody with a ring like his, anyways. Over there!"

Without hesitation, Mairelon shook off her hand and plunged into the crowd. Kim tried to keep the burglar in sight, but the constant motion of the crowd made it impossible. *If I'd known it was him sooner, I could have gotten a look at his face. Oh, well, maybe Mairelon will catch him.* But she knew that under these conditions, it would be the sheerest luck if he did. *At least now I know he's got light hair. I wish I could have seen his face, though.* She backed up to avoid being stepped on by a portly gentleman in a very great hurry, and bumped into someone standing behind her.

"Excuse me," she began, turning, and stopped short. Looking down at her was an impressively handsome man with sandy-brown hair and warm brown eyes. He appeared to be in his early thirties, and his clothes proclaimed him very well-inlaid. Without thinking, Kim glanced down at his hands, and was unreasonably relieved to see that he was not wearing a ring. *He can't be the cove Mairelon's chasing, anyway—he couldn't have gotten here from over there, not this fast.*

"It was my fault entirely, Mademoiselle, and I beg your pardon," the man said, bowing. His voice was deep and faintly accented, but all Kim was certain of was that he was not French. He straightened and smiled. "We appear to have no one to make proper introductions. Permit me to be incorrect. I am Alexei Nicholaiovitch Durmontov."

"I'm Kim."

"I am most pleased." Durmontov bowed again. "You are alone; may I return you to your party, to amend my clumsiness?"

Kim glanced over her shoulder, but there was no sign of Mairelon. *Well, Lady Wendall and Renée D'Auber keep saying that wizards can do what they like. So I will.* "Yes," she said, then added belatedly, "Thank you."

Durmontov offered her his arm, and she directed him down the hall to the box. Lady Wendall looked mildly startled when they entered, and gave Kim a pointed look of inquiry.

"Mairelon saw somebody he wanted to talk to," Kim said. "Mr. Durmontov offered to bring me back."

"Ah." Lady Wendall's expression cleared. "Thank you, Mr. Durmontov. I'm sure my son also appreciates your kindness to his ward. I am Lady Wendall."

"It is more correctly Prince Durmontov," Durmontov said almost apologetically. "Prince is not the most correct term, but it comes as close as your English can."

A prince? Kim suppressed the urge to shake her head in wonder as Lady Wendall went through the rest of the introductions, extracting the prince's full name in the process. *A prince, bowing to me. Tom Correy would never believe it.*

"You are, then, Russian?" Renée said with considerable interest once the courtesies had been attended to.

"Since my birth, Mademoiselle," Durmontov replied. "I currently stay with Countess Lieven, though next week I remove to the George."

"I will look forward to seeing you at the countess's when I call upon her Friday," Renée said.

"And what brings you to England, Prince Durmontov?" Lady Wendall asked.

The prince's smile vanished. "Family business," he said shortly.

"Forgive me if the question was indiscreet," Lady Wendall said, unperturbed. "I find your country fascinating, but I fear I am not well acquainted with your customs."

"In your country, it is I who must comply with English customs," Durmontov replied.

"Ah, Kim, you made it back," Mairelon said from the entrance to the box. "I had no luck, I'm afraid; he got away in the crowd. Did you get a good look at his face?"

"No," Kim answered.

"Richard." Lady Wendall's voice held just the faintest note of reproach. "Allow me to present Prince Alexei Durmontov. Prince, my son, Richard Merrill."

"It is a pleasure," the prince said, but his eyes were skeptical and faintly wary.

Mairelon did not appear to notice. "Durmontov, Durmontov. Now where have I . . . ? Oh, yes. You don't happen to know a Miss Letitia Tarnower, do you?"

"I do not believe so," he replied, looking startled. "Why is it that you ask?"

"I expect you'll meet her fairly soon, then," Mairelon said. "That would explain it nicely."

"Explain what?" Lady Wendall said.

"Monsieur Merrill is very often most provoking, particularly when it is a matter of information," Renée informed the puzzled Russian prince. "Do not mind him in the least."

"I shall do my best to take your advice, Mademoiselle," Durmontov said. "It would be less difficult, however, if I had some small idea to what he refers."

"We met Miss Tarnower at that tea party last week," Kim said to Lady Wendall, feeling some explanation was called for. "She asked about Prince Durmontov."

"Yes, she put on a splendid show of hen-wittedness," Mairelon said. "Nobody is that silly by accident. I wonder what, exactly, she has in mind?"

"It is entirely unimportant," Renée said with somewhat more emphasis than was strictly necessary. "And I very much regret it, but it is nearly time for the second curtain."

"I regret it also, Mademoiselle, and I look forward to our future meeting," Durmontov said, and took his leave.

There was no time for more; the curtain rose almost as the prince left the box. It was not until they were in the carriage on the way home that the conversation resumed.

"*Did* anyone else interesting turn up in the interval?" Mairelon asked as they rattled over the cobblestones toward Renée's townhouse.

"A Russian prince is quite enough, I think," Renée said.

"But was he the one who cast the scrying spell?"

"How is it that I would know that?" Renée demanded. "It is not a thing one can tell by looking."

"The Marquis of Harsfeld, Lord Franton, arrived after you left," Lady Wendall said with some satisfaction. "He wished to be presented to Kim, and was quite disappointed to find that she was not there."

"Harsfeld? He must be nearly eighty," Mairelon said, frowning. "What does he want with Kim?"

"No, no, Richard, you're thinking of the fourth Marquis of Harsfeld," Lady Wendall said. "He died last year; it is the *fifth* marquis who was asking after Kim. He is quite a young gentleman—not much above twenty, I think. He was the grandson of the previous marquis."

"Oh. I expect that's all right, then," Mairelon said, but he continued to frown.

Lady Wendall looked at him, and turned the topic to the evening's performance. As this involved much comparison with previous performances, and speculation as to what certain different singers might have done in some of the roles, the discussion lasted until they reached the house in Grosvenor Square. Lady Wendall and Mairelon were arguing amicably as they entered, only to be interrupted by a loud thump from upstairs.

"What was that?" Mairelon said.

The unmistakable sound of china shattering, followed by an inarticulate shout, was the only reply.

"Maximillian!" Lady Wendall cried, and flew up the stairs.

TEN

Mairelon and Kim exchanged glances and followed Lady Wendall, though somewhat less rapidly. Halfway up the stairs, Kim unexpectedly felt the tingling pressure of magic. Her eyes widened; whatever was going on up there, it wasn't just the monkey. Mairelon must have felt it, too, for he started taking the stairs two at a time and elbowed his way rapidly through the little crowd of servants that had gathered in the upstairs hall, following his mother. He paused only once, to speak briefly to Hunch. Kim, hampered by her skirts, followed as fast as she could manage, only to bump into Mairelon from the rear when he stopped dead in the library doorway. The magical pressure was stronger here, and for a moment Kim thought that was what had brought Mairelon to a halt. Then he moved aside, and she got a clear view of the library.

Shards of white pottery littered the hearth, and one of the unlit candlesticks from the mantel had fallen among them. The heat from the fire was in the process of melting the candlewax, gluing everything firmly to the hearth rug. The table in the center of the library had tipped over, strewing books and papers across the floor. Harry, the footman, hovered uncertainly by the monkey cage. Inside the cage, Maximillian swung from bar to bar in high agitation, chattering loud reproaches. Kim's first thought was that their burglar had returned; then she saw Mrs. Lowe.

She stood in the far corner, her back to the bookshelves. Her expression was grimly determined, and her hands were wrapped around the fireplace poker, brandishing it as if it were a club. Behind her, one of the housemaids cowered in terror. In front of them, at about chest height, hovered a small book with a blue leather binding—Marie de Cambriol's *livre de mémoire*.

Lady Wendall had stopped two paces inside the library. "What on earth—"

The monkey shrieked loudly, and the blue book hurled itself forward. Mrs. Lowe whacked the book with her poker, and it dipped and retreated. An instant later, it streaked toward the bookcase beside her. It hit with considerable force, knocking several volumes to the floor. Apparently, this was not the first time the book had performed this maneuver; two of the shelves were already empty, and a third held only one book lying flat. The monkey shrieked again as the book backed up and made a dive at Mrs. Lowe. She hit it with the poker once more, square on.

"A nice flush hit!" Mairelon said. "Have you ever thought of playing cricket, Aunt?" Though his words were careless, Kim noticed that his hands were already moving in the gestures of a spell.

"Richard, your levity is singularly ill-timed," Mrs. Lowe said, keeping a wary eye on the floating book. "You are supposed to be a magician; do something about this ghost, if you please."

The housemaid wailed. The book wobbled, then angled upward and flung itself at the bookcases again. It hit the top shelf, which was still filled, and all of the books jumped. Fortunately, this time none of them fell.

"It isn't a ghost," Lady Wendall said calmly. "It's a spell." She picked a candle from the candlebox on the side table next to the door. "*Fiat lux,*" she said, and the candle burst into flame. Kim blinked; she hadn't realized that Mairelon's mother was a wizard. Lady Wendall held the candle out to Mairelon. "If you'll assist with the warding spell, dear. . . ."

"Not just yet, Mother," Mairelon replied. "I'd like to analyze this first."

"Stop it and *then* analyze it!" Mrs. Lowe gave Mairelon a withering look, then hastily returned her attention to the flying book. It was now making short runs against the bookcase, and its edges looked rather battered.

"But it's much simpler to analyze a spell in process," Mairelon said. "*O xenoi, tines este, pothen pleith' hugra keleutha.*"

The book paused in midflight, hovered for a moment, and then fell to the floor with a thud. The suffocating sense of magic eased. Mairelon looked startled, then began muttering rapidly under his breath. Lady Wendall, imperturbable once again, began pacing slowly around the room with the lighted candle, reciting the familiar warding spell as she went.

Mrs. Lowe hesitated, then lowered the poker and pulled the whimpering housemaid out of Lady Wendall's way. Kim waited a moment longer, to be certain that she would not accidentally disrupt the spells Mairelon and Lady Wendall were working, and then began picking up the books and papers littering the floor. She kept away from the blue volume that had apparently caused all the trouble. After a moment, the footman joined her.

"There," Lady Wendall said, placing the lighted candle in a holder next to the candlebox. "That should hold things for a little, I think."

"For a little?" Mrs. Lowe's voice wavered, then steadied into indignation. "Do you mean that we may expect a recurrence of this . . . this *event?*"

The housemaid apparently did not find Lady Wendall's comment very reassuring either; she shook off her paralysis at last and began having strong hysterics instead. Kim rolled her eyes, set down the books she was carrying, and looked around for a water jug or a vase of flowers. If the library had ever had any such things, they had not survived the activities of the flying book.

Lady Wendall moved swiftly to the housemaid's side and gave her a resounding slap. The maid gasped and coughed, then began sniveling quietly. When she was sure the girl was not going to begin screeching again, Lady Wendall turned to the footman and said, "Thank you for looking after Maximillian, Harry. Why don't you take Tess down to the kitchen and give her something to settle her nerves? And yourself as well, of course. You've both had a very trying evening, I'm sure."

"Thank you, Mum," the footman mumbled, and ushered the housemaid out.

"He'll be into the brandy for certain," Mrs. Lowe said sourly when the door had closed behind them.

"That is precisely what I intend," Lady Wendall said. "I think they deserve it, and if it makes the rest of the servants wonder whether this is all the result of some odd drunken revel, they will be less likely to give notice due to fear of ghosts."

"Ghosts? Not at all," Mairelon said, looking up from his observation of the now-quiescent book. "Good heavens, this house has had magicians and wizards in it for donkey's years. No ghost would dare come near it."

"Well, perhaps it would be a good idea if you explained that in the servants' hall tomorrow morning, Richard," Lady Wendall said. "Otherwise we may end up doing the cooking and floor-waxing for Kim's ball ourselves."

"Hmm? No, I'll get Hunch to do that. He'll be much more convincing.

"So long as it *is* convincing, dearest," Lady Wendall said. "Are you quite finished? Because if you are, we had better set up a ward around the house."

"I thought you were going to do that after the cracksman piked off," Kim said to Mairelon.

"Yes, well, it slipped my mind," Mairelon said. "It wouldn't have helped with this, anyway, not with as much power behind it as it had."

"You will not forget this time," Lady Wendall said firmly. "Only think of the difficulties another such disturbance would create! We are going to cast a full ward; we shall do so as soon as possible; and we shall maintain it at least until Kim's ball."

"A full ward?" Mrs. Lowe looked inquiringly at Lady Wendall.

"To keep this from happening again." Lady Wendall's wave encompassed the entire library. "All this excitement is very bad for Maximillian."

"I should think that that monkey would be the least of your worries!" Mrs. Lowe said. "If that was some sort of spell, I want to know who was responsible." She looked suspiciously from Mairelon to Lady Wendall to Kim.

"I'd like to know that myself," Mairelon said. Bending, he picked up the blue book that had caused all the commotion. Mrs. Lowe flinched. Apparently oblivious, Mairelon went on, "It was another puzzle-spell, stuck together out of pieces that didn't quite fit. A bit of summoning here, a bit of levitation there, a few other odds and ends, and a really awkward binding holding it together like a piece of string. It couldn't have lasted much longer, even if we hadn't arrived when we did."

"That book didn't look to me as if it were getting tired," Mrs. Lowe said. "And it had been bashing itself against the wall for a good half hour."

"*Half an hour?*" Mairelon blinked at his aunt. "Oh, come, you can't have been holding it off with the poker that long."

"I didn't say I had," Mrs. Lowe replied dryly. "It's only been about five minutes since that extremely foolish girl panicked and ended up in the corner. Your precious heroic footman was no use whatever, and something had to be done. I trust it will not be necessary again."

Lady Wendall tilted her head to one side and looked at Mrs. Lowe. "If you were not belaboring it with the poker for half an hour, what *were* you doing, Agatha?"

"Writing a letter to Lady Percy in my room," Mrs. Lowe replied. "The noise in the library disturbed me, so I rang for a footman—who took an amazingly long time to arrive—and sent him to put a stop to it. He proved unable to do so, but did not think to report back to me when he discovered the cause of the disturbance. When the noise did not subside after ten minutes, I came down to see for myself what was going on. By then, half the household had gathered, and while I was considering what was best to be done, the book made a more than usually erratic swoop and that silly girl panicked. I make it approximately half an hour from the time I first noticed the noise to your arrival."

Mairelon looked down at the book in his hand with a thoughtful expression. "This gets more interesting all the time."

"Why's that?" Kim demanded. She could see that neither

Lady Wendall nor Mrs. Lowe was going to ask, and she knew that if no one asked, Mairelon wouldn't think to explain.

"For one thing, it means I was mistaken about the scrying spell at the opera," Mairelon said. "The caster wasn't looking to see whether we were there; he was looking to make sure we *weren't* here."

"Very clever of him," Lady Wendall murmured encouragingly.

"Furthermore, the spell on that book was an incredible mishmash. Holding it together for even a few minutes would take a lot of power," Mairelon went on. "To hold it together for half an hour—well, there are only two or three wizards in England who could manage it. That I know of."

"Then one may presume this wizard is no one you know of," Lady Wendall said.

"More than that," Mairelon said. "I think he's someone I *couldn't* know of. I think he's either largely self-taught, or foreign. *Very* foreign."

Kim thought instantly of the handsome Russian prince at the opera, and she could see the same thing occur to Lady Wendall. "Why?" she said again.

"Because I've found very little trace of any traditional spell structures in any of the spells he's cast so far," Mairelon said, waving the blue book for emphasis. "That scrying spell this evening, for instance—no one who's had a proper magical education would bother reinventing something like that, not when every apprentice learns the standard scrying spell by the end of the second year. So our mystery wizard hasn't had the kind of magical education magicians get in England, which means he's either self-taught or foreign."

"If it's a he," Kim said. Something was niggling at the back of her brain, something important that she couldn't quite get hold of.

"That fellow who tried to burgle the library last week was a man," Mairelon pointed out.

"He was a toff," Kim objected. "You said this wizard had to be self-taught; toffs get training. At least, more training than this." She looked around at the library.

"An excellent point," Lady Wendall said. "Though very few gentlemen practice, any more than they read Catullus in the original once they have left school."

"They read Catullus if they read anything," Mairelon said. "He's too salacious to be so easily forgotten."

"Virgil, then," Lady Wendall said impatiently. "The point is that anyone who attended Oxford or Cambridge has learned at least a little magic."

"I should rather say they have been exposed to a little magic," Mrs. Lowe said austerely. "Whether they have learned any of it is another matter."

"Ladies are not so universally educated in magic as gentlemen are," Lady Wendall went on. "And such a display of vindictiveness as this—"

"What display of vindictiveness?" Mairelon said with a puzzled frown.

Lady Wendall gestured eloquently. Mairelon looked around as if seeing the chaos for the first time, and his puzzled expression vanished. "Oh, the mess. That's all just a side effect, really."

"A side effect?" Mrs. Lowe said indignantly. "Next I suppose you'll tell me that this object wasn't attacking me!"

"It wasn't," Mairelon said. "It was simply trying to get somewhere in as straight a line as possible. If this house were on the east side of the square instead of the west, the book would have smashed through a window in one or two tries and been gone."

"East?" Lady Wendall looked at the wall of bookcases. "Yes, I see. What a pity; practically all of London is east of us. If it had been heading south or north, we could have eliminated a great many more possibilities."

"If that book was just trying to get somewhere, why *didn't* it just smash a window and go?" Kim asked.

"That's one of the things that makes me think we're dealing with a self-taught wizard," Mairelon said. "The way that spell was cobbled together was so thoroughly inefficient that he didn't have room for an additional element, and so unstable that my analytical spell unbalanced it completely. What he left out were the comprehensive directional controls and the visual component. He could make a bit of change up and down and side to side, but he couldn't adjust the primary axis of movement at all, and he had no way of knowing which way he ought to send it. He's either very stupid, very careless, very ignorant, or very close; even if he'd gotten the book out of the house, it couldn't have gone far without running into something else."

"Do you mean to say the person responsible for this outrage may be standing in the street outside at this very moment?" Mrs. Lowe demanded.

"Possibly," Mairelon said. "I thought he might be, even before I came into the library, because of the power level. So I sent Hunch to look. He should be—"

Someone knocked at the library door. "That will be him now," Mairelon said. "Come in, Hunch."

The door opened and Mairelon's manservant entered, wearing an expression even more dour than usual. He nodded respectfully at Lady Wendall and said to Mairelon, "There weren't nobody around but a couple of toughs in back. They ran off when they saw me."

"Possibly a coincidence," Mairelon said. "Or possibly they were hired to catch Mme. de Cambriol's book when it flew out a window, and then bring it to our mysterious spellcaster. That would have gotten around the problem of flying the thing through the London streets."

"I ought to 'ave stopped them," Hunch said, chagrined.

"I told you to look for a spellcaster," Mairelon said. "I didn't realize, at the time, that there might be other possibilities."

"I still ought to 'ave stopped them," Hunch said stubbornly.

The thing that had been niggling at the back of Kim's brain suddenly came clear. "Ma Yanger!" she said before she thought to stop herself.

Everyone looked at her. "She's a witcher that lives up on Ratchiffe Row by the Charterhouse."

Mairelon's eyebrows rose. "And you think she's involved in this?"

"I might have guessed it would be something like that," Mrs. Lowe said, giving Kim a dark look.

Kim shook her head. "Not exactly. She used to do spells for people, though, and I think she put them together out of bits and pieces, like you said this one was. Tom Correy told me she's given up witching people, but she's got to do *something* to eat. Maybe she sold the idea to somebody, or sold them part of the spell they used."

"An interesting idea," Mairelon said. "We'll pursue it tomorrow. In the meantime, Mother, you and I should get to work on that warding spell. Kim, you'll watch; you're not quite ready for a long-term spellworking yet, but watching one will give you some idea what's ahead of you."

"I'll leave you, then," Mrs. Lowe said. "Kindly let me know

when it will be convenient to have the servants come and clean up."

"I will see to that," Lady Wendall said. Mrs. Lowe nodded and left.

As the door closed behind her, Mairelon let out a long breath. "Good. Now, Kim, I take it you wish to visit this witch friend of yours tomorrow?"

"It's a place to start," Kim replied with a wary look at Lady Wendall.

"When, exactly, were you thinking of going?" Lady Wendall asked. "There's a new bonnetmaker I wished to investigate, and we are engaged for dinner with the Blackburns."

"It'll have to be after dark," Kim said, resigning herself to the bonnetmaker. "I won't pass for a boy in daylight."

"I'll make your excuses to Lady Blackburn, then," Lady Wendall said.

"Mine as well, Mother," Mairelon said, and looked at Kim. "The same procedure as last time, I think? Hunch and I waiting in the carriage."

Kim was too surprised by the ease with which everything had been arranged to do more than nod.

Lady Wendall looked thoughtful, then smiled. "I shall tell Lady Blackburn that you have both been called away on some magical project. It will raise your stock with her considerably; she's terribly intrigued by wizards, though she's not in the least magically inclined herself. And it has the additional merit of being entirely true."

"That's settled then." Mairelon tucked the battered little book absently into his jacket pocket. "Now for the general warding spell. We'll need four candles, Kim, as closely matched in size and shape as you can manage. Hunch, will you fetch the largest lump of coal you can find from the kitchen? Mother, would you like to be the Respondent or shall I?"

Hunch nodded and left, Kim began hunting through the candlebox, and Lady Wendall moved to Mairelon's side to discuss their respective parts in the upcoming spell.

ELEVEN

For the second time in less than a fortnight, Kim slipped through the dark London streets in her boys' clothes. She was considerably more nervous, though she did not have as far to go—Ma Yanger's rooms were only a block and a half down Ratchiffe Row from Bath Street, where Mairelon and Hunch waited with the carriage. Because she was not answering a summons from Tom this time, it was earlier in the evening, and there were more people about. Several bricklayers clustered around an iron brazier on the corner, warming their fingers, while on the opposite side of the street a toothless old woman offered a cup of soup to anyone with a ha'penny to pay for it. A collier strode toward the bricklayers, possibly hoping to sell them another lump or two of coal before they packed themselves up. Huddled in a doorway, a young girl with haunted eyes took a swig of bottle courage from a flask. As Kim passed, the girl pulled the neck of her dress lower and started toward the bricklayers in a cloud of gin fumes, her hips swaying suggestively.

It was with a degree of relief that Kim arrived at the tenement at last. Like most such buildings, it was a rickety wooden structure—Ratchiffe Row was an alley well away from the center of London, and no one enforced the laws that, since the Great Fire, had required bricks to be the principal building material. The rates, however, were collected regularly, and as a result most of the windows had been blocked up to avoid the window tax, giving the exterior a hodgepodge look and making the interior gloomy and airless.

Kim climbed the dark stairs with care; it was early to find squatters sleeping on the steps and landings, but some liked to stake out a space before the competition got too intense. She stepped over one man who was already snoring loudly, but from the smell of him, it was liquor and not opportunity that had put him to sleep.

Ma Yanger had two rooms on the third floor, a palatial home by the standards of the place. No one had ever dared to complain that she was taking more than she should—not when the occupant of the rooms was commonly known to be a witch. So long as the landlord received his rent on time, the rooms were hers . . . and possibly longer. It was widely speculated that the only reason this building hadn't collapsed like so many others was because of Ma Yanger's spellworking.

Once, Kim had believed those speculations like everyone else. Now, with her magical training and her sensitivity to spells, she was fairly certain that the only thing holding the building up was good fortune. Even right outside Ma Yanger's door, there were no traces of magic.

Frowning, Kim rapped at the door. There was no answer; well, Tom Correy had said that Ma had holed up in her rooms and wasn't seeing any customers. But unless she'd cut off her friends as well, she'd have to answer the door to find out which it was. Kim's frown deepened, and she rapped again.

There was still no response. Kim glanced quickly up and down the hall to make certain that no one was in sight or earshot, then pulled a bit of wire from her pocket. She was out of practice, but the locks in a place like this wouldn't be much. She bent toward the lock, then hesitated. The locks wouldn't be much, but Ma Yanger was a magician of sorts, and she'd know that as well as everyone else. And Ma was too canny to rely on her reputation to keep the cracksmen away. If she'd witched the lock . . .

Kim straightened and returned the wire to her pocket. That spell Mairelon had taught her last week would tell her whether the lock was enchanted, but she hadn't thought to bring paper or ink with her. Well, Mairelon was always working spells without actually drawing the diagrams; maybe she could, too.

Slowly and carefully, she traced the diagram in the air, visualizing it as her hands moved. *"Epistamai, videre, l'herah, revelare,"* she said, and with the final word she felt the spell take hold.

The lock did not glow even faintly green. Puzzled but relieved, Kim retrieved her wire and bent to her work. Two minutes later, the lock clicked open, and she slipped inside.

Ma Yanger's front room was one of those that had had its window blocked up to save taxes; it was nearly pitch black and smelled suffocatingly of herbs. Nothing in it glowed green, either, though Kim could feel that the spell she had cast was still active. *How come a witch doesn't have anything magic in her rooms?* But Tom Correy had said that Ma hadn't done any witching for two months; maybe she had let her personal spells lapse, too, if she'd had any.

"Ma?" Kim called into the darkness. "Ma Yanger? It's Kim, from the Hungerford Market. I got to ask you something."

There was a shuffling noise in the next room, which subsided almost immediately. "Ma?" Kim called again.

No one answered. Kim thought about working the light spell she had shown Tom Correy, but Mairelon was always warning her about overextending herself, and she had a great deal of respect for his advice in matters magical. Her eyes were adjusting to the gloom, and there was no great hurry. She waited a moment longer, then began picking her way toward the far door, past a table strewn with anonymous packets and a set of shelves laden with jars. At the far door, she hesitated again. "Ma? Ma Yanger?"

On the other side of the door, something grunted. Kim's throat clogged, and she almost turned and ran. *It's just one of Ma Yanger's tricks to discourage visitors,* she told herself firmly. *And anyway I probably know more magic than she does, now.* Whether it was the sort of magic that would do her any good in a confrontation with Ma was something about which Kim refused to think. Taking a deep breath, she opened the door.

Ma Yanger was clearly visible in the faint green-glowing haze that surrounded her. She sat on the edge of a low, lumpy bed, one corner of which was propped up by an orange crate because the leg was broken. Gray hair hung in rat-tails around her face. Her eyes were empty and her mouth hung slack; a thin trickle of drool trailed from one corner.

"Ma?" Kim whispered.

"Uuunh," said the woman on the bed. The noise was clearly only a reflex; no trace of sanity or intelligence showed, even for a moment, on her face.

Kim started forward, then paused. Mairelon hadn't glowed green when she cast the magic-detecting spell before; only the button on his jacket that he'd enchanted to foil pickpockets had responded. Ma Yanger wasn't glowing green because she was a witch. She was glowing because someone had cast a spell on her. And there was no knowing what the effect would be if Kim touched her while the spell was active; the contact might cure her, or it might kill her, or it might afflict Kim with the same bizarre malady.

This is too much for me. I'm getting Mairelon. Kim backed out of the bedroom and hurried across the front room. By the time she reached the stairs, she was running. She vaulted the drunk and pelted up the street at top speed, ignoring the attention she attracted.

By the time she reached them, Mairelon and Hunch were out of the carriage and scanning the street behind her for pursuers. "Easy, Kim," Mairelon said as she leaned against the coach, panting. "No one's after you."

"I know," Kim said, forcing the words out between gasping breaths. "That . . . ain't it."

"What is it, then?"

Still panting, Kim told them. Mairelon's face grew grim as she described what she had found. "No wonder you were shaken," he said when she finished. "Do you want to stay here with Hunch while I go back?"

"No!" Kim and Hunch said together. They exchanged glances of perfect understanding, and then Kim went on, "You'll need someone to cast a ward, if you're going to do anything about that there spell on Ma."

Mairelon studied them for a moment. "Very well, then. The sooner, the better, I think. Though I'm afraid you will have to stay with the horses, Hunch."

"O' course I 'as to," Hunch said sourly. "And I'll 'ave them ready to move the minute you come running back."

"Very good," Mairelon said, oblivious to his servant's tone. "Let's go, Kim."

They started up the street in silence. Half a block later, Mairelon said in a musing tone, "You know, you were very fortunate with that spell of yours. There are a number of unpleasant things can happen to a wizard who dispenses with written diagrams too soon."

"Like what happened when I tried it in English?"

"Worse. If you get the diagram wrong—if the lines don't quite connect in the right places, or they overlap somewhere because you can't actually see what you are doing—then the energy of the spell will not be correctly shaped. At best, the wizard can be drained of all magical ability for weeks or months. At worst, one can end up in a condition similar to your friend Ma Yanger."

"But not dead?"

"I said *at worst*," Mairelon pointed out.

Kim digested this while they continued. "You haven't told me not to do it."

"I don't intend to tell you that," Mairelon said as they entered the tenement. "You've done it once; you obviously have the capacity to visualize a diagram clearly without having an actual, physical drawing. Just make certain that you always know the diagram well enough. Simple ones are easiest; the more advanced spells require too much precision, even for the very few wizards with absolutely perfect recall."

The reached the top of the stairs and turned down the hall. "Did you leave the door open?" Mairelon said, nodding at a wide-open entrance just ahead.

"That's Ma Yanger's place, but I don't think I left it open," Kim said. "I'm . . . not positive, though. I was kind of in a hurry."

Mairelon nodded. "We'll go carefully, then. *Fiat lux.*"

A ball of light appeared on Mairelon's palm. Resisting the impulse to point out that a light spell was not consistent with her ideas of "going carefully," Kim followed him into Ma's rooms. Mairelon took only a cursory look at the front room.

"Workshop and business parlor both, hmm?" he said, and headed for the far door.

Ma Yanger was gone. Nothing else had changed; the lumpy bed still bore the dent where she had been sitting during Kim's first visit.

"She *was* here," Kim said.

"Yes, well, given your description of her condition, she can't have gone far if she's just wandered off."

"*If* she's just wandered off?"

"Someone may have come and fetched her," Mairelon said. "Let's have a look around, shall we?"

They did not find Ma Yanger, and no one they spoke would admit to having seen her in weeks, with or without companions. A small boy on the lower floor admitted to leaving food at her door every day for several months, but said he never saw her. He would give a special knock, a shilling would slide out under the door, and he would depart, leaving the package of food behind. No one else had had even that much contact with her. After half an hour of fruitless searching, they returned to her rooms, where Mairelon made a quick but thorough investigation that made Kim blink in respect.

"You would of made a top-drawer cracksman, the way you sort through things," she said with considerable admiration.

"I got plenty of practice when I was in France," Mairelon replied absently. "And it's easy to be fast when there's nothing of interest to find." He frowned, then glanced toward the bedroom. "Wait here a minute."

"What are you planning?" Kim demanded.

"Something I should have done at once," Mairelon said. "Check for residuals." He made three sweeping gestures and spoke a long, involved sentence. Kim felt the spell, but nothing seemed to happen. She looked at Mairelon. He was turning slowly, studying everything in the room with narrowed eyes.

It must be something like that magic-detecting spell, that only shows things to the wizard who casts it, Kim thought.

Mairelon crossed to the bedroom and stood in the doorway, looking at it for a moment. "That's odd."

"What's odd? What did that spell do?"

"I told you, it's a check for residuals. Spells leave traces, and these rooms are full of them—but every last one of them is over two months old. No one has done any magic here in all that time."

"Tom said Ma Yanger had given up witching people," Kim said, uncertain of what point Mairelon was trying to make.

"Yes, but she can't have been incapacitated until very recently," Mairelon pointed out. "From your description, she doesn't sound as if she can clean or cook any longer; she'd have starved to death if she'd been like that for two months."

Kim thought of the empty eyes and the expression void of intelligence, and shuddered. "You're right about that. Maybe someone has been taking care of her."

"Possibly," Mairelon said. "But would whoever-it-is also take care of her herbs and spellworkings? There's no dust on these shelves; they've certainly been cleaned in the past day or so. And look at the table."

Kim looked. A candle stub sat in a puddle of melted wax; next to it, a wilted violet lay on top of a heap of crushed herbs. "It looks like the makings of a spell," she said cautiously.

"It is," Mairelon said. "It's a traditional spell for averting harm or bad luck. It's very old and not terribly reliable, which is why I haven't bothered to teach it to you—there are much better spells available nowadays."

Kim looked at the table again. "That flower isn't much wilted. Somebody set this up yesterday, or maybe the day before."

"Exactly. I'll wager that the somebody was your Ma Yanger. Somehow, she knew that something was going to happen to her, and she tried to avoid it."

"But you said nobody's done magic here in two months!"

"They haven't," Mairelon said, and his tone was grim. "She set this up, but she either didn't have time to use it, or couldn't for some other reason."

"Maybe that spell hit her and . . . and made her like that before she could cast this," Kim said.

"Possibly. But if it was a spell that incapacitated her, it can't have happened here, because there's no trace of it. And as far as we know, she hadn't left these rooms in two months."

Kim stared at Mairelon. "Then what happened?"

Mairelon looked at her. "That *is* the question, isn't it?"

TWELVE

M airelon and Kim stayed a few minutes longer, turning out Ma Yanger's bed and checking the iron kettle they found underneath it, but they came no nearer to answering Kim's question. When they returned to the coach at last, Hunch was wearing his most sour expression, from which Kim concluded that he had been worried. He refused to drive anywhere, or to allow Mairelon to do so, until Mairelon set up a protective spell around the coach. Mairelon eventually did so. Once they arrived home, he informed Hunch with insufferable smugness that the spell had not even been tested during the drive.

It was something of a shock to return to the trivialities of a social schedule the following morning. The London Season was under way at last, and invitations were pouring in. To Kim's surprise, many of them included her.

"At present, people are merely curious," Lady Wendall said. "That will change when they meet you, and I am quite certain that between us we can see to it that the change is a positive one. To that end, I should like you to accompany me on a few morning calls."

Kim sighed. "Morning calls are boring."

"That depends largely on just whom one is calling upon," Lady Wendall replied gently. 'Wear your jaconet morning dress with the pink ribbons, I think."

Kim rolled her eyes, but nodded. She let Wilson dress her and arrange her hair, then joined Lady Wendall in the salon. Shortly thereafter, they were on their way. The first two stops were houses Kim had visited during the horrible week with Mrs. Lowe, but to Kim's astonishment, Lady Wendall did no more than send in her card. As they pulled away from the second house, Kim ventured to ask why.

"One cannot cut someone dead simply because they are dull, but one need not endure their conversation in order to maintain the social niceties," Lady Wendall replied.

Their next stop was quite close, and this time Lady Wendall climbed down from the coach to rap on the door. A moment later, they were ushered up to the drawing room, where they found their hostess, Lady Clement, already engaged with several earlier visitors. Kim was dismayed to see that one of them was Miss Annabel Matthews, who had been at Mrs. Hardcastle's disastrous tea.

Lady Wendall presented Kim, and Lady Clement introduced her guests. Miss Matthews was accompanied by her mother; the tall, brown-haired girl beside her was Miss Marianne Farrell. Miss Farrell's aunt completed the company of ladies. Across from them was a handsome, blond man in his mid-twenties, who was introduced as Lord Gideon Starnes. As he rose and bowed, Kim's eyes flashed automatically to his hands. They were ringless.

A little uncertainly, Kim made her curtsey. To her relief, Miss Matthews welcomed her warmly, though her mother frowned disapprovingly. Lord Starnes, Kim noticed, did not seem pleased either; his eyebrows rose slightly and his lips curved in an ironic smile as she took her seat.

"I am so glad to see you again," Miss Matthews said in a low tone. "And if you would be so good as to pretend to be absorbed in conversation with me for a few moments, I would be deeply grateful."

"Why?" Kim asked.

"I do not wish to speak with Lord Starnes," Miss Matthews said. "And he *will* not take a hint."

"Is he—" Kim could not think of a polite way to finish her question.

"There! He has struck up a conversation with Mrs. Farrell, and we are safe."

"Why don't you like him?" Kim asked.

"It is not that I don't like him, exactly," Miss Matthews responded. "But it is very wearing to be solicited constantly as a go-between, particularly when it would be decidedly improper of me to agree."

Kim blinked in surprise. In her experience, the need for a third party to carry messages or arrange other things occurred only when something illegal was involved. But Miss Matthews was an unlikely choice as either a fence or a bawd. "Who does he want you to—to go between?" she asked cautiously.

Before Miss Matthews could answer, her mother looked over and said, "Annabel, dear, come and tell Lady Clement about that Brussels lace we found at the market last Thursday. You are much better at describing such things than I am."

Miss Matthews looked a little surprised by this request, but all she said was, "Of course, Mother," and the two changed places.

"And then I wish to hear all about this ghost of yours," Lady Clement said to Lady Wendall. "I understand it smashed an entire set of Crown Derby china and sent three of the housemaids completely out of their minds?"

Startled and a little worried, Kim looked at Lady Wendall, but Lady Wendall only smiled. "Nothing so dramatic as that. An extremely ugly Sèvres vase was broken, and one of the housemaids had hysterics."

"But the ghost?" Miss Farrell said breathlessly.

"A magical experiment that got out of hand," Lady Wendall said.

"I suspected as much," Lady Clement said with satisfaction. Miss Farrell appeared to have suffered a severe disappointment.

"It was really very careless of Richard," Lady Wendall went on, "and I have informed him that in the future he is to use the laboratories at the Royal College."

"An excellent idea," Lady Clement said. "You really cannot have anything like that happening during your ball. It has been an age since your last party, and I am quite looking forward to this one. Though I trust you do not plan to serve frogs' legs this time. Unusual refreshments are all very well, but there *are* limits."

"My son has already made the same request," Lady Wendall replied. "And since it is to be his ward's come-out, I felt it only proper to accede to his wishes."

"So there *is* going to be a ball!" Miss Farrell said. "I thought it must be true when you came in with—That is, how splendid!"

Mrs. Matthews looked slightly startled. "You are indeed presenting your son's . . . ward, Lady Wendall? I had heard some talk of a ball, but I made sure it was idle speculation, circumstances being what they are."

Lady Wendall's smile had very little warmth in it. "Circumstances? I have not the slightest notion what you mean."

"Well . . . that is . . . I was no doubt misinformed."

"Miss Tarnower was probably just mistaken," Miss Farrell said soothingly.

Lord Starnes stiffened, and his expression turned dark as thunderclouds. "I hope you are not criticizing Miss Tarnower," he said.

"Anyone can make a mistake," Miss Farrell said hastily.

"Perhaps she was confused because my sister-at-law, Mrs. Lowe, acted as Kim's chaperone for a few days until I arrived in London," Lady Wendall said. "But it would be quite improper for anyone other than myself to present my son's apprentice and ward to Society."

"Apprentice?" Miss Matthews said, with a puzzled glance at Kim.

"Kim is to be a wizard."

"Oh, I *see.*" Mrs. Matthews looked relieved. "That explains everything."

"I thought it might," Lady Wendall murmured sweetly.

"Yes, yes, but now you must tell us about this ball," Lady Clement said, and the talk turned to the festivities. Kim found it very dull. So, apparently, did Lord Starnes, for after a very few minutes he rose to take his leave. He bowed punctiliously to each of the ladies, but when he came to Miss Matthews, he gave her a look that, even to Kim's inexperienced eye, was fraught with significance. Miss Matthews reddened and shook her head slightly. Lord Starnes's face darkened once again; with a curt nod to Kim, he left.

"Such a handsome young man," Lady Clement said as the door closed behind him. "What a pity he had not a feather to fly with."

"If someone truly cared for him, his lack of fortune would not weigh with her," Miss Farrell proclaimed, tossing her head.

"Yes, between the title and that face of his, he may do very well in spite of his financial situation," Mrs. Matthews said. "Though I understand he has a penchant for gaming which may add to his difficulties." She looked at her daughter and added pointedly, "It is unlikely, however, that he would express serious interest in any young woman whose means are but modest. He cannot afford it."

"Oh, Mrs. Matthews, you cannot mean that the way it sounds," Miss Farrell said earnestly. "Why, you make Lord Starnes out to be the veriest fortune hunter!"

Although Kim was quite sure that this was exactly what Mrs. Matthews had intended, the woman disclaimed any such intention, and the talk turned to various social events once more. Lady Greythorne's upcoming musicale was the focus of much interest; rumor had it that over a hundred and fifty cards of invitation had been sent out, and that nearly everyone had accepted.

Several well-known singers had been asked to perform, in addition to an Austrian harpsichordist, and there were to be refreshments afterward, and a card room for those who were not musically inclined.

Kim found the conversation alarming. The invitation to Lady Greythorne's musicale had been delivered two days before, and Lady Wendall had accepted it that morning. Kim was rather vague as to what a musicale was, and had been picturing something rather like the opera. From the ladies' discussion, it was clear that there would be considerably more activity than that. It was also clear from Miss Farrell's remarks that rumors about Kim and her exact status were already circulating. The thought of facing over a hundred members of the *ton* was intimidating enough for a former street thief without adding worries about what they might have heard.

Kim voiced her concerns to Lady Wendall as soon as they were alone in the carriage again after leaving Lady Clement's.

"All the more reason for us to make a push to establish you properly," Lady Wendall said. "In fact, that is one of the reasons I particularly wished you to join me today. You may be sure that after this morning Lady Clement will inform all her acquaintance that you are a very prettily behaved young woman, and her word carries considerable weight. If we can stop in to see Lady Harris, and perhaps Lady Jersey as well, we will have done a good day's work. I do hope Sally Jersey is at home. She is the dearest creature, and the greatest gossip in London."

Kim prepared herself for another boring morning, but the rest of it went much better than its beginning. Lady Harris was a lively woman with a wide range of interests; she had clearly heard of Kim's background and equally clearly found it fascinating. Lady Jersey was even livelier; she talked nearly nonstop for the entire visit and at the end of it pronounced Kim's conversation to be thoroughly unexceptionable.

They arrived home to find Mairelon scowling over Marie de Cambriol's battered book. "Mother, do these ingredients sound familiar to you? 'A quart of red wine, three handfuls roses, and the pills out of two pomegranates.' The pomegranates are heavily underlined; they must be important, though I can't see why. I thought at first it might be a variation on the de Quincy fire spell, but I can't see why anyone would need that much wine for it."

"It's a receipt for a cough remedy, dear," Lady Wendall said. "It was quite popular when I was young, on both sides of the Channel."

"Cough remedies." Mairelon closed the book with a snap.

"You mean it's just a book of recipes?" Kim said.

"Not *just* recipes. There are portions of spells, incantations, at least two shopping lists, and several lists of directions which are utterly useless because they don't mention where one is supposed to begin." Mairelon shook his head. "I cannot think why anyone would go to such lengths to get hold of this book. I've been through it twice, and everything in it is either commonplace or incomprehensible or both."

"A *livre de mémoire* isn't supposed to make sense to anyone except the owner," Lady Wendall said. "She only copied into it the bits of things she couldn't remember. That's probably why the pomegranates are underlined."

"Maybe whoever-it-is doesn't know that there's nothing useful in it," Kim said.

"Yes, but that's no help at all," Mairelon said crossly.

Lady Wendall laughed. "I doubt that our wizard is trying to be helpful. Kim is probably right, and you will only strain your eyes staring at that book. Come and have tea."

Mairelon came, but he was not so easily discouraged. For the next several days, while Kim and Lady Wendall paid social calls and attended teas, he painstakingly catalogued the contents of the book, identifying as many spell-bits as he could. Kim's magic lessons suffered somewhat from this obsession. She missed them sorely, and not only because she was back to studying dry and difficult books instead of discussing theory with Mairelon. She missed the daily quiet hour in the library with him, away from the toffs who crowded the saloons and parlors of upper-crust London.

For despite Lady Wendall's best efforts, and all her assurances that things would improve, Kim was not really enjoying the preliminaries of a London social Season. She would have much preferred tackling burglars in the hallway or chasing down mysterious wizards, but there were no more attempts made to steal the odd little book and no spells tested the strength of the protective ward that Mairelon and Lady Wendall had put in place around the house. Kim was left with shopping, morning calls, and the other activities that occupied ladies of Quality. Lady Wendall's acquaintances were much more interesting than Mrs. Lowe's, but Kim was simply not comfortable among them. Consequently, Kim was not much pleased when Lady Wendall announced that the two of them were going for a drive in the park.

"It will do you good to get a little air, and I can begin to introduce you to the *ton*," Lady Wendall said. "In the future, you may ride, if you wish—that is, *do* you ride?"

"No," Kim said with somewhat more force than she intended.

"Then you won't need a riding habit," Lady Wendall said with unimpaired calm. "What a good thing I hadn't ordered you one yet. Now, go and put on your cream muslin, and we will go to the park. And take care not to disarrange your hair!"

Kim did as she was bidden. It was amazing, she reflected as she donned the walking dress, how much less annoying Lady Wendall's acerbic comments and peremptory commands were than Mrs. Lowe's had been. But then, Lady Wendall at least *listened* to Kim's objections, and if she overruled her, she usually gave a reason. And Lady Wendall didn't seem at all inclined to make bloodless propriety the center of her life; quite the contrary. She knew exactly how near the line of acceptable behavior to tread, and how far over it she went in privacy was an entirely different matter. *But she's a toff born, and I'm not.* Frowning, Kim shoved the thought away, picked up her reticule, and left the room.

Hyde Park was not as crowded as it would be in another week or two, but it was certainly busy. Traffic crawled along as carriages paused to let their passengers converse with ladies and gentlemen on horseback or with the occupants of other carriages. No one seemed to mind; the object of coming to the park, after all, was to see and be seen.

Lady Wendall's landau was one of those most responsible for holding up traffic. She seemed, Kim thought, to be on speaking terms with every one of the gentlefolk in the park, from Lady Jersey on down. After being presented to upwards of a dozen persons in fifteen minutes, Kim stopped trying to remember the names and simply smiled and nodded in acknowledgment of each new introduction.

The brief conversations that followed the introductions all consisted of talk of people Kim did not know and places she had not been. Lady Wendall seemed to be enjoying herself enormously, but Kim was beginning to wonder how much longer the ordeal would last when she saw Renée D'Auber in a carriage ahead of them.

"There's Mlle. D'Auber," she said as Lady Wendall finished her conversation with the latest set of acquaintances and leaned forward to instruct the coachman.

"Where?" Lady Wendall asked. "I don't see her."

Kim pointed.

"Ah yes; how interesting. She's with the Countess Lieven. In the future, do not point in public. Or at least, try not to do it often. Jackson! Pull around by the Countess Lieven's carriage. I wish to speak to her before we return home."

"Is the Countess Lieven a fr—a magician?" Kim asked as the coachman maneuvered the landau through the snarl of traffic.

"Not at all; I never met anyone with less of a sense for magic," Lady Wendall replied. "But she is one of the Patronesses of Almack's, which makes her a power in Society. Now, what was that you almost called her? Fr—something," she added helpfully when Kim gave her a puzzled look.

Kim's face grew hot. "Frogmaker. It's cant."

"I rather thought it might be," Lady Wendall said, nodding. "You must tell me more some evening when we are at home and private."

Kim had no idea how to respond to such a request, but fortunately, she did not have to. The landau drew up beside Countess Lieven's barouche, and yet another round of introductions began. Kim suffered an interesting mixture of feelings when she discovered that the third person in the barouche, who had not been visible when she spotted Renée, was Prince Alexei Durmontov.

"I am enchanted to greet you again, Miss Merrill," he said.

"Thank you," Kim replied, considerably taken aback.

"I see you are determined to make your ball the highlight of the Season," the Countess Lieven said to Lady Wendall. "Five hundred cards sent out, from what I hear."

Lady Wendall smiled. "It is the first party I have given in a considerable time, and since it is in honor of my son's ward, I wish it to be especially memorable."

"It is of all things the most likely," Renée D'Auber said.

"No doubt," the countess said dryly. "Lady Wendall has always had a reputation for . . . originality, even before the curried snails in aspic. I trust such inventive dishes will not be prominent at *this* party?"

"I try not to repeat myself," Lady Wendall said with a

charming smile. "May we hope to see you and your guest?"

"I believe you may count upon Lord Lieven and myself," the countess said. "Prince Durmontov will do as he sees fit, though I believe he would enjoy it. Magicians always seem to enjoy talking to one another."

"Ah! You are a magician, Lady Wendall?" said the prince.

"A mere dabbler," Lady Wendall answered. "My son is the true practitioner in the family, though I understand that Kim is coming along nicely."

"Then I look forward to speaking with him of your English enchantments," the prince said. "I, too . . . what did you say? 'Dabble.' I dabble in magic."

"But you are too modest," Renée said. "Have you not just told me that your family is of the finest wizards in Russia?"

"Some of my family are, indeed," Durmontov replied. "But I am not yet among them. One reason I journey here is to enlarge my skills."

Kim's stomach clenched. *He can't be the burglar,* she told herself. *He doesn't wear a ring, and he was behind me at the opera when Mairelon went after that other cove.* But the wizard and the burglar weren't necessarily the same person, and if the wizard had to be either self-trained or foreign . . .

"Then you must come to Kim's ball," Lady Wendall said without hesitation. "Some of the greatest wizards from the Royal College of Magic will be there, and I shall be sure to ask my son to introduce you."

"I am in your debt, Madame," the prince replied.

After exchanging a few more pleasantries, Lady Wendall extracted herself and Kim with effortless politeness and gave the coachman orders to return to Grosvenor Square. She was silent and thoughtful through much of the drive home, putting Kim forcibly in mind of Mairelon in one of his brown studies. Had it been Mairelon sitting beside her, she might have attempted a comment or two, in hopes of finding out what he was thinking, but she did not know Lady Wendall well enough to risk interrupting her thoughts, and so she, too, was silent.

THIRTEEN

The rest of the week went by without incident. No spells tested the house-ward that Mairelon and Lady Wendall had set up, nor were there more burglars. Shoreham sent no news regarding the French wizards, and none of Mairelon's spells elicited any trace of Ma Yanger. Hunch made several forays into the lower-class portions of London, but the only information he could obtain was that Ma Yanger was missing. The general presumption was that she had left for parts unknown.

Kim dutifully accompanied Lady Wendall on rounds of calls and attended several small dinner parties, about which she had very mixed feelings. Lady Wendall's friends had, thus far, been very kind, but Kim could not help feeling rather like the central attraction in a bear-garden. She could only be thankful that Lady Wendall had decreed a quiet schedule until after the come-out ball, which she was already looking forward to with considerable apprehension, and she was a bit dismayed that Lady Greythorne's musicale was considered quiet enough to meet Lady Wendall's exacting standards. Her attempts to explain her real worries fell on deaf ears, so she fell back on something the toffs in the household would understand.

"What if that wizard tries something while we're gone?" she asked at dinner the day before the event.

Mrs. Lowe looked alarmed, but Lady Wendall only smiled. "The warding spell can handle anything he is likely to cast, and a great deal that he isn't," she told Kim. "Richard and I renewed it just this morning."

"I meant like that scrying spell at the opera," Kim said. "Not something here."

"I thought of that," Mairelon said with a touch of smugness. "I hope he does; I've been working on something that will give him a surprise. And with any luck, it will let us know the identity of our mystery wizard."

"I would prefer to receive assurances that there will be no disturbance at all," Mrs. Lowe said. "Here *or* there."

"What, exactly, are you planning, Richard?" Lady Wendall said. "Lady Greythorne is an understanding hostess, but for a wizard to cast spells in the home of a nonwizard without being requested . . . well, no matter what the provocation, it is not *done*."

"I won't be casting anything," Mairelon assured her. "I'm using the same technique as our burglar—infusing an object with a spell to be invoked later. The only one who will notice will be the other spellcaster."

"I sincerely hope you are right," his mother said. "Your reputation cannot stand another scandal. And don't tell me that your name has been cleared. Another muddle, and no one will believe it." She paused, considering. "Unless, of course, it's a more *usual* sort of scandal. I would rather you didn't lose your fortune at cards, but if you could contrive to fall in love with someone's wife, that might answer."

"Really, Elizabeth!" Mrs. Lowe said in scandalized tones. "It would be much more to the point to advise him to behave with propriety."

"There is no point to giving him that sort of advice," Lady Wendall said. "Richard would never follow it. But an *affaire* is another matter, and might answer very well to reestablish him in Society, as long as he doesn't take things too far."

"I assume you would consider dueling over the hypothetical lady to be 'too far,'" Mairelon said, amused.

"Much too far," Lady Wendall replied seriously. "That is precisely the sort of extreme you need to avoid."

"I think I can promise you that."

"It is not a joking matter, Richard! You could find yourself a social outcast permanently, not to mention ruining Kim's prospects and damaging the rest of the family." Lady Wendall paused, then laid a hand on Mairelon's arm. "I am only asking you to take care, my dear. You can't deny that sometimes you forget to do so, especially when you are absorbed in one of your projects."

"I most certainly can deny it," Mairelon said. "Of course, if I did, I'd be lying. Very well, Mother, I'll keep your recommendations in mind."

But Kim noticed that Mairelon had not agreed to actually abide by any of them. She was almost relieved. The thought of Mairelon setting up a flirtation was . . . awkward. Uncomfortable. Unpleasant. She picked up her fork, and applied herself to food that had gone suddenly tasteless.

Lady Greythorne's townhouse was a palatial residence filled with footmen, silver, marble tables, and delicate, uncomfortable chairs. A cracksman could have made his fortune in ten minutes in the Green Saloon—except that, Kim judged, this was one of those houses where the guests did not depart until three or four in the morning, at which point the kitchen staff and housemaids would already be stirring in preparation for the following day. The rooms were even more crowded than Kim had anticipated, and much to her dismay, Letitia Tarnower was the first person to greet them as they entered the drawing room after paying their respects to their hostess.

"Mr. Merrill!" the Beauty said to Mairelon. "I am so very pleased to see you again. And you also, Mrs. Lowe."

Mrs. Lowe nodded stiffly, then immediately excused herself to go and speak with someone who had just entered on the far side of the room. Miss Tarnower looked up at Mairelon expectantly.

"Miss Tarnower," Mairelon said gravely, and then, with an exquisite correctness that made Kim instantly suspicious of his motives, presented her to his mother.

"I am so very pleased to meet you, Lady Wendall," Miss Tarnower said, curtseying. She gave Kim a small nod; evidently she was not going to ignore Kim completely until she was sure of her status.

Lady Wendall murmured something politely noncommittal.

"I am so happy to be here tonight," Miss Tarnower went on in a confidential tone. "I was quite honored to receive a card, for you know that Lady Greythorne is so very *choosy* in her guests."

"I was certainly used to think so," Lady Wendall said blandly.

Annoyance flashed in Miss Tarnower's eyes; she gave Mairelon the briefest of calculating glances and then said sweetly, "Oh, but everyone knows that Lady Greythorne's parties are very nearly as exclusive as Almack's! Surely you are funning me!"

"Not exactly," Mairelon said. "It will do for an interpretation, however,"

Miss Tarnower smiled and widened her eyes at him. "I am excessively bad at interpretations," she said. "Particularly of music, though I do love it so. And I particularly wish to understand the pieces tonight. Perhaps you would be good enough to explain them to me, Mr. Merrill?"

"Do forgive us, Miss Tarnower," Lady Wendall broke in firmly, "but we really must pay our respects to Lady Castlereagh. It won't do, you know, to interrupt her once the music has begun."

"Then I hope I will have a chance to talk with you later, Mr. Merrill," Miss Tarnower said, yielding gracefully. As she moved off, several young men closed in around her. Prominent among them was Lord Gideon Starnes, and Kim wondered briefly whether he had ever persuaded anyone to carry his message to Letitia for him.

"That was rather unnecessary, Mother," Mairelon said as they made their way through the crowd toward Lady Castlereagh. "Now it will take twice as long to find out what it was she really wanted."

Lady Wendall gave him a pitying look. "What she wants is obvious, dear."

"Mmm? Possibly, but nobody is that obvious by accident. Or that hen-witted."

"I didn't say it was accidental." Lady Wendall pursed her lips. "I think it is a good thing that Andrew is in Suffolk this Season. I must write and tell Lord Wendall to be sure and keep him there on some pretext, should they finish their business with the canals a bit early."

Kim felt suddenly queasy. Despite Mrs. Lowe's preoccupation with matchmaking, it hadn't occurred to her that Mairelon was an extremely eligible bachelor. *He's a wizard, he's well-born, he's got forty thousand in the Funds, and he's under thirty.* She stole a glance at him. *And he's not bad-looking, either.* That wouldn't weigh with the Mamas of the innocent hopefuls who flocked to London during the Season in hopes of catching a husband, but it would certainly weigh with the hopefuls themselves. *He's a younger son, and he hasn't got a title,* she reassured herself, but that wasn't much help. Forty thousand pounds was more than enough to offset such trifling disadvantages.

At least he wasn't taken in by that Tarnower chit. Somehow, the thought was not entirely reassuring.

They paid their respects to Lady Castlereagh and wandered through the rooms, conversing with the other guests and admiring the furnishings and the figures painted on the pediments above the doors. Several rooms were designed with recessed alcoves in the corners, most of which were lined with narrow tables on which the hostess had chosen to display a variety of enormous, ornate silver urns, marble statuettes, and other valuable items. Kim was particularly taken with a pair of candlesticks that looked to be solid gold—they were small enough to be easily portable, and they'd fetch at least fifty pounds apiece at Gentleman's Jerry's.

As they proceeded, Kim made a point of observing the gentlemen's hands. Though she saw a great many rings of varying value, none was the ruby-centered flower she was looking for. Twice, she saw Renée D'Auber passing into another room. Prince Durmontov was also present; when Kim spotted him, he was listening with apparent attention to Letitia Tarnower while Lord Starnes stood by in barely concealed irritation. Kim found herself hoping that the Beauty was hanging out for a title after all.

"Kim," Lady Wendall said, calling her back from her reverie. "Allow me to present Lord Franton, Marquis of Harsfeld, who particularly desires to meet you."

Kim turned. A slim young man with dark hair bowed immediately; as he straightened, she recognized him as the gentleman she had seen observing her at the opera, before the scrying spell and Prince Durmontov's appearance had driven everything else from her mind. "I am pleased to meet you, Lord Franton," she said.

Lord Franton smiled. He had a very nice smile, and his expression was openly admiring. He looked to be no more than twenty-two or twenty-three, but he had an air of self-confidence that made him seem older. "Not nearly so pleased as I am to meet you at last, Miss Merrill," he said to Kim. "I have been trying to arrange an introduction for a week, but you have been remarkably elusive."

"I have?"

"So it seems to me. Now that I have managed it at last, will you allow me to procure you a seat for the music? I believe they are about to begin."

Feeling a little dazed, Kim looked at Lady Wendall, who nodded encouragingly. Like a puppet, Kim's head bobbed as well, and a moment later she found herself being escorted to the music room by the marquis. His arm was firm under her gloved hand. Her breath had gone odd, and she was abruptly conscious of the depth of her gown's neckline. *Nobody ever really looked at me like I was a girl before,* she thought suddenly. *No man, anyway.* She stole a glance upward and encountered another warm smile that almost made her stumble. She felt tingly all over, rather as if someone were doing magic nearby, only different. *I could get to like this.*

"I hear that you are studying wizardry, Miss Merrill," Lord

Franton said. "I have very little skill myself, but I admire those who do. How did you come to it?"

"Mairelon—that is, my guardian decided to teach me," Kim said. "It's a long story."

"I would be happy to call on you next week to hear it at more leisure," Lord Franton said.

"Sure," Kim replied. "I mean, that will be fine, Lord Franton."

They found seats in the fourth row of hard, straight-backed chairs and sat down to wait for the harpsichordist to begin playing. "Are you enjoying your first Season, Miss Merrill?" Lord Franton asked.

"I'm still getting accustomed to it," Kim answered cautiously. She risked another glance upward, and found him watching her face with a keen admiration that renewed her tingling. Hastily, she averted her eyes.

"You find it still so new, even after a year? I understood that you have been Merrill's ward at least that long."

"Yes, but we were in Kent for most of it, and Mairelon— I mean, my guardian isn't much for house parties."

"Why do you call him Mairelon?"

"It's the name he was using when we met." She hesitated, but the circumstances were no secret, and neither Mrs. Lowe nor Lady Wendall had forbidden her to discuss them. "He was working Hungerford Market as a stage magician, and I broke into his wagon. And got caught." She grimaced in remembered disgust. "The toff who hired me forgot to mention that Mairelon was a real frogmaker, and not just a puff-guts making sparkles for the culls."

Lord Franton looked at her, plainly intrigued. "And that was when he made you his ward?"

"No, that came later. I told you, it's a long story."

"I am even more eager to hear it than I was before," Lord

Franton said. "And I must remember to compliment Mr. Merrill on his perception. You clearly were meant to grace the drawing rooms and country houses of the *ton.*"

No, I wasn't, Kim thought as the first harpsichordist appeared at last and the conversation ceased in a round of polite applause. Though the marquis plainly meant what he said, and though she could not help being flattered by it, she could not pretend, even to herself, that she felt truly comfortable among so many toffs.

Lord Franton, however, was a different matter. *Comfortable* was not, perhaps, quite the right word for the way he made her feel; nonetheless, she found that by the first break she had promised to go driving in the park with him later the following week, and to grant him two dances at her come-out ball. She was profoundly relieved when he offered to bring her some punch and took himself off for a few moments. Finding a quiet spot beside a large marble bust, she waited, scanning the milling toffs for familiar faces.

A corpulent gentleman entered the room, saying something about the music to a tall woman in a feathered turban. As he went by, waving his arms with considerable animation, Kim stiffened. *He's wearing that burglar's ring! But he can't have been the cove in the library; I'd have noticed for sure if he'd been that fat.*

"Your punch, Miss Merrill," Lord Franton said.

Kim turned. "Find Mairelon right away," she said. "Mr. Merrill, that is. Tell him to come here; it's important."

"I beg your pardon?" Lord Franton said, blinking.

"Never mind," Kim said. "There he is. Excuse me, I got to talk with him right away."

Abandoning the puzzled marquis and his cup of punch, she threaded her way through the crowd to Mairelon's side. "Mairelon, the cove with the ring is here," she said. "Only it's not the right cove."

Mairelon turned, frowning slightly. He blinked at Kim, and then his expression cleared. "Who is it, then?"

"The jack weight talking to the mort with the green feathers in her hat," Kim said. "I'll go bail he wasn't the cracksman, but he's got the ring. Or one near enough like it to be its twin."

"Ah, Lord Moule. Let's find out how he came by it, shall we?"

Mairelon offered her his arm, and they crossed the room together. Though Mairelon nodded to several of the people they passed, he did not pause to converse, and Kim could tell that his attention was focused sharply on the fat man with the ring. Despite her own curiosity, Kim could not help comparing Mairelon's attitude to Lord Franton's, and she found herself wishing that Mairelon were not *quite* so single-minded.

They reached the discussion which, judging from the degree of Lord Moule's animation, was reaching its climax. As Lord Moule paused to draw breath, Mairelon said, "Excellent point, Moule. I was just saying something similar to my ward, wasn't I, Kim? Do allow me to present you."

The ensuing round of introductions completely derailed the conversation and allowed the lady in the green feathered turban to escape. As soon as she had, Mairelon said, "Interesting ring you're wearing, Moule."

"This?" Lord Moule studied the gold ring that was squashed onto his littlest finger. "Yes, I thought so. Won it at play last week."

"Naturally," Mairelon said. "From whom?"

"Some young chub or other," Lord Moule replied. "You know how it is—White's, three in the morning, claret been flowing for hours, things get a little fuzzy. But it's a nice piece, and I'm glad to have it."

"I should think so. It's not everyone who's that lucky at

play. Though I understand there's rather a good game going in the card room."

"Is there?" Lord Moule brightened. "Excuse me, Merrill. Your servant, Miss Merrill." And he departed in a hurry that was barely seemly.

"And that disposes of the one fact we thought we had," Mairelon said, looking after him. "I wonder whether it was cleverness or mere bad luck that led our burglar to stake it?"

"Don't they keep records or something at those clubs?" Kim said.

"The betting-books? Those are for long-term wagers, not for what's won or lost at table of an evening." Mairelon sighed. "It's a pity. Ah, there's Renée and that Russian in the back corner. Let's see what they're up to."

They made their way around the room to the alcove where the other two stood. Prince Durmontov did not look best pleased to have Mairelon and Kim join his nearly private conversation with Mlle. D'Auber, but he greeted them politely nonetheless. Renée gave Mairelon an amused look and said to Kim, "How is it that you are enjoying yourself?"

"It's a little confusing," Kim said.

"It will become less so," Renée told her.

"My mother tells me you're a wizard, Prince," Mairelon said to Durmontov.

"Of no great measure, I fear," Durmontov said. "I hope while I am here to study your English methods."

"You seem more intrigued by French ones," Mairelon murmured in a provocatively innocent tone.

"I have some familiarity with French magic already," replied Durmontov. "One of my aunts—"

A prickle of magic ran across Kim's skin, and she stiffened. So did the other three wizards. Mairelon's eyes lit. "Now, then!" he said, and reached into his pocket. Kim heard a sharp crack, like a twig breaking. An instant later, power ripped across her in a sudden wave.

I thought he said you couldn't tell when someone invoked a spell instead of casting it, she thought fuzzily, clutching at Mairelon's arm, and then the sensation was gone completely.

"M. Merrill!" Renée said, her voice full of concern.

Kim looked up. Mairelon's eyes had gone blank, and his face was gray-white. He swayed on his feet, and she clutched at his arm again, this time to support him. "Mairelon!" she said, her voice wobbling in sudden terror. "Mairelon?"

FOURTEEN

Mairelon blinked and a little color returned to his face. "That was . . . unexpected," he said in a shaken voice.

A little reassured, Kim shook the arm she held. "What happened?"

"I, too, am full of the curiosity," Renée said. "And so will be a great many other persons, and very soon, I think."

"It appears not," Prince Durmontov said. "Your English seem entirely uninterested."

Kim glanced over her shoulder. Lord Starnes stood against the far wall, arms crossed, glowering at the ring of gentlemen hovering around Letitia Tarnower; Lord Franton was deep in conversation with an elderly gentleman; knots of ladies talked placidly with each other or with gentlemen, or moved with studied grace from one room to another. No one gave any indication of knowing that something out of the ordinary had occurred.

"Good," Mairelon said. "Though that, at least, isn't a surprise."

"No?" Renée studied Mairelon for a moment. Her concerned expression lessened, to be replaced by one of annoyance. "My friend, if you are not at once more clear, I shall become what it is that Mademoiselle Kim says wizards are, and turn you into a frog. Why is it not surprising that no one has noticed this spell?"

"No one noticed the spell at the opera, either," Mairelon said. "This was the same thing, I think. I got that much before he . . . broke off."

Renée nodded. "That is a good beginning. Continue, if you please."

Prince Durmontov frowned. "Spell at the opera? To what do you refer?"

"There, you see?" Mairelon said to Renée. "No one but us noticed it. I was rather hoping that wizard would try again, whoever he is; I had an analyze-and-trace spell all ready for him." He shook his head. "I didn't expect him to chop everything off in the middle the minute the trace got to him, and I caught a bit of back blow, I'm afraid. Now, if you'll excuse us, Kim and I have to be getting home immediately."

"What?" Renée said, alarmed once more. "Why?"

"Because the last time whoever-he-is tried this, he attempted to run off with something from my brother's library." Mairelon's cheerful tone sounded forced to Kim, but neither Renée nor the prince seemed to notice. "I didn't catch him here; maybe I can catch him there. Come along, Kim."

"What about Lady Wendall and Mrs. Lowe?" Kim said as they started toward the door, leaving Renée to attempt to explain Mairelon's cryptic utterances to the prince as best she could.

"I'll send the coach back for them as soon as we get home," Mairelon said. There was an undercurrent to his voice that made Kim want to break into a run. *Whatever happened back there, he hasn't told it all yet. And it isn't good.*

In the coach, Mairelon gave the orders to the coachman and then leaned back against the squabs and closed his eyes. Even in the dark interior, Kim could see his face settle into lines of unnatural exhaustion. She waited, not daring to think for fear of what thinking might lead to, watching the rise and fall of Mairelon's chest as if he were a child on a sickbed.

The carriage lurched into motion. After a few minutes, Mairelon spoke, without opening his eyes and in a voice so low that Kim had to lean forward to hear it over the sound of the carriage wheels. "You'll have to check the house-ward as soon as we get home. You shouldn't have a problem; you've watched Mother and me do it enough times, and I'll be there to talk you through it."

"What?" Surprise and shock made her tone sharper than she intended. "Why? If you're there—"

Mairelon's eyes opened, and the bleak despair in them cut Kim off in midsentence. But his voice was steady as he answered, "I won't be doing it because I can't." He hesitated, then shook his head as if to clear it and took a deep breath. "At the moment, I haven't got enough magic to light a candle."

"*What?*"

"Whatever my tracing spell hit, it didn't get cut off and blown up back at me." Mairelon closed his eyes again. "It got sucked into something, and everything else . . . went with it. So you'll have to check the house-ward."

"Oh." Kim wanted to say more, but Mairelon's pose forbade the sympathy and comfort she didn't know how to express anyway. It hurt to look at him, but she couldn't stop. "How long do you think it will last?" she asked carefully after a moment.

There was another long pause. "I don't know," Mairelon said finally. "If I'm very lucky, I'll be back to normal in the morning. If not, perhaps a week or so. Perhaps longer."

Perhaps never hung unspoken in the air between them, and supper congealed in Kim's stomach like three-day-old porridge. *What will he do, if he can't work magic anymore, ever?* she thought, and then, *And what happens to me?* She frowned suddenly, wondering what she had meant by that. It wasn't as if Mairelon were dead, and even then Lady Wendall wouldn't throw Kim back out on the streets. To do her justice, neither would Mrs. Lowe. *What am I worried about?*

Abruptly, she realized the answer, and her eyes widened in shock. *All the wizards in St. Giles—Tom said they were working for Mannering, or they weren't working. Ma Yanger hadn't done any spells for two months, and then she . . . she . . .* The memory of Ma Yanger's vacant expression and the grunting sound that had been all the speech she could manage made bile rise in Kim's throat. *Not Mairelon!*

She looked across at him, suddenly frantic with worry. His eyes were still closed; he hadn't noticed her reaction. She hesitated, but only briefly—they must be nearly to Grosvenor Square, and she didn't have much time left. "*Epistamai, videre, l'herah, revelare,*" she said, too softly for him to hear over the sound of the coach wheels, and sketched the pattern in the air.

A softly glowing green haze sprang up around Mairelon, twin to the one she had seen surrounding Ma Yanger in the tenement the week before. Despite herself, Kim gasped. Mairelon's eyes opened. "What is it?" he said.

Kim swallowed. If she needed further proof, she had it now; he hadn't felt the spellcasting. "I just did that spell you taught me, the one that shows what things are enchanted. And you're glowing green."

Mairelon's eyes narrowed, and his face lost some of its hopeless look in sudden interest. "Brightly? Evenly?"

"Not very bright, just sort of a mist. It's about three inches deep all over, near as I can tell." She leaned forward to measure more nearly, and Mairelon jerked away.

"No!" he said, and then, more gently, "Until we have a better idea just what happened and how, you'd better not try anything like that again. You don't want it to happen to you."

Kim sat back. The advice was good, but . . . "If you won't let nobody throw the wind at you, how are we going to figure out what sneaking bully fitch done this, let alone set it to rights?"

Mairelon frowned, looking yet more like himself. "I hadn't really thought it out. Shoreham may have run into something like this before, or one of his men may have. I'll see him in the morning. And Kerring—if it's a known spell, it'll be in the Royal College's library somewhere, and if it's there, he'll find it."

And if it's an unknown spell? But she couldn't bring herself to say it, not when the thought of being able to do something about the spell had banished the haunted look from Mairelon's face.

The carriage pulled up, and for once Mairelon waited for the footman to open the door. The house was quiet as they entered. Mairelon nodded toward the darkened dining room and said, "We'd best check the ward before we do anything else. The check is a small variation of the warding spell you already know, like this. . . ."

Kim followed his directions, but found nothing; the warding spell remained untouched. When she reported this to Mairelon, he frowned. "Either we've arrived in good time for whatever he's planning, or he isn't planning to do it here," he muttered.

"Or he's done it already," Kim said.

"Eh?" Mairelon looked up, startled.

"It was a trap," she said patiently. Mairelon's face set, and she went on quickly, "Maybe that's all he meant to do."

"Ah. If he thinks that I'm the only full-fledged wizard in the household, he'll expect the ward to dissipate in a day or two, because ward spells require maintenance and I . . . can't do that any longer. All he would have to do is be patient, and he'd have a free hand." Mairelon dropped into a chair and began drumming his fingers on the dining-room table. "But as soon as he realizes that the ward isn't weakening, he'll know that someone else is maintaining it. Then he'll come after you and Mother."

"And maybe we can trap him."

Mairelon's expression went bleak. "That's what I thought I was going to do, and look what happened. No, that's not a good idea at all, unless . . ." He paused, and a hint of the familiar gleam appeared in his eyes. ". . . unless we convince him that his first trap didn't work at all."

Kim blinked, then caught on. "You mean, make him think you still have all your magic?"

"Exactly." Mairelon rose to pace up and down alongside the table. "When the ward doesn't collapse, he'll wonder; all we'll need is a public demonstration to convince him. And we have the perfect opportunity in a week's time."

"What's that?"

"Your come-out ball," Mairelon said with a shadow of his old grin. "You and I will do the illusion display, just as we've planned. Only you'll do a bit more of it, and Mother will handle the rest. If we arrange it correctly, no one will realize that it's not me actually working the spell."

And it would be arranged correctly, Kim was sure. If there was one thing Mairelon understood, it was showmanship.

When she had first met him, he had been performing stage magic—sleight-of-hand illusions, coin tricks, and other such things—in the Hungerford Market, and turning more than a few shillings at it without employing any real magic at all. But . . . "If this frogmaker thinks you still got your magic, won't he come after you again?"

"Thinks I still *have* my magic," Mairelon said. "Yes, that's the whole idea. He can't do anything more to me, after all."

Kim thought of Ma Yanger, and shivered. But Mairelon would think of that himself, soon enough, and if he didn't she could point it out later. And as long as he was busy with Shoreham and Kerring and figuring out how to pretend he still had his magic, he wouldn't go haring off on some long chance that only a bubble-brained, pigheaded flat would even think of.

Carriage wheels sounded outside, and a moment later Lady Wendall burst into the room, followed more sedately by Mrs. Lowe. "Richard!" said Lady Wendall. "What happened? Why did you and Kim leave so early?"

"Our mysterious wizard had another try, and Kim and I thought we should come home and check the ward," Mairelon said. "But it's held up fine."

Lady Wendall gave Mairelon a sharp look, but held her peace.

"I trust that next time you will bring your mother, instead of dragging Kim away from a promising situation," Mrs. Lowe said. "She will be fortunate indeed if the Marquis of Harsfeld does not take exception to the manner in which he was deserted this evening."

"Bosh, Agatha!" Lady Wendall said. "If Kim had gone to the musicale as one of Lord Franton's party, he might justly have been offended, but she came with us. And it will be just as well if he is not too particular in his attentions. It is much too early in the Season for Kim to allow her name to be linked with that of any one gentleman."

"I should think so!" said Mairelon, sounding rather startled.

"If the pair of you intend to encourage Kim to pass up a brilliant match, simply because it does not suit your sense of timing, then I shall say nothing more," Mrs. Lowe announced.

"Really, Aunt Agatha, that's coming on a bit too strong," Mairelon said. "Kim only met Lord Franton this evening."

"The marquis was clearly very taken with her," Mrs. Lowe countered. "I can only hope that Kim will have sense enough to pursue the matter before he comes to his senses."

Everyone looked at Kim; remembering Lord Franton's polite-but-very-interested attention, Kim flushed. Mairelon frowned. Lady Wendall cocked an eyebrow and said, "Well, my dear?"

"He asked for two dances at our ball next week," Kim admitted. "And he said he'd come to call, and asked me to drive in the park."

"There, you see?" Mrs. Lowe said triumphantly to no one in particular.

Lady Wendall smiled. "It is an excellent thing, to be sure. However, Kim still has the remainder of the Season ahead of her. And may I remind you, Agatha, that the purpose of this come-out is to see Kim launched and well-established in Society, not necessarily to find her a husband."

"She could not possibly be more well-established than she would be if she were to marry a marquis," Mrs. Lowe countered.

"She might marry a duke, as Elizabeth Gunning did," Lady Wendall murmured provocatively.

"That was over sixty years ago." Mrs. Lowe pointed out.

Lady Wendall considered. "Only the first time. Her second marriage, which you will recall was likewise to a duke, was not quite sixty years ago."

"If you intend to make a joke of this, Elizabeth, I shall leave you," Mrs. Lowe said. "I hope you will think about what I have said." With massive dignity, she swept out of the room.

"There!" Lady Wendall said. "I began to think she would never leave. Now, Richard, tell me—what scrape have you fallen into this time? I made sure it was something when Renée told me you had run off, and when I saw your face, I was certain of it."

"It's a good deal worse than a scrape, Mother," Mairelon said. "You had better sit down."

Kim glanced at his face, and then away. It had been hard enough for him to admit to her what had happened, even in the darkness of the closed carriage. She didn't think he would want her to watch him tell the story over again to his mother. Silently, she slipped out of the room.

The hall was empty, and Kim hesitated. She wanted to talk to Hunch, but the thought of being the one to break the news of Mairelon's incapacity to him was more than she could face on top of the rest of the evening. Tomorrow—tomorrow she would talk to Hunch, and then go see Mannering. If he was behind what had happened to Mairelon . . . She climbed the stairs to her bedroom, and found Wilson waiting patiently to assist her in undressing.

Kim allowed the abigail to work in silence for a few minutes, her own thoughts and emotions still churning. Finally she said, "Wake me early tomorrow. I got some errands to do before people start calling."

"Very good, miss," the abigail said. "Will you be wanting me to come with you?"

Kim considered a moment, then shrugged. "I don't know

yet. It's part wizard things and part . . . personal. What do you think?"

"I'll be ready, then," Wilson said. "I can sit in the coach for the wizardly bits. Turn around, miss, if you please, so's I can undo the back."

The abigail finished her work and left. Kim climbed into bed and blew out the candle, then lay staring into the dark for a long, long time.

FIFTEEN

Kim slept very badly, and she was wide awake and had already made a trip to the library downstairs when Wilson returned the following morning. Wilson made no comment, but went about her work with quiet efficiency. "What will you wear today, miss?" she asked at last.

"I don't know," Kim said. "What have I got that'll impress somebody?" Some of her plans had firmed during the long dark hours before dawn, but clothes were not among them. All she knew was that there was no point in wearing her boy's disguise today. Jack Stower worked for Mannering now; Jack knew she was a girl, so Mannering must, and she couldn't pass for a boy by daylight anyway. What she *would* wear was not something she had considered.

"I suggest the slate-colored walking dress with the Spanish puffs, miss," the abigail said.

Kim nodded and let the abigail help her into it without paying much attention. When she finished dressing, she put the bit of wire she used for lockpicking in the matching reticule and slid her carefully chosen book into her pocket. Then she said, "Now I got to talk to Hunch. Do you know where he is?"

"Below stairs," Wilson replied. "And in a right temper this morning. I'll fetch him at once, miss."

"No, that'll take too long. Just come down with me," Kim said.

"Very good, miss."

They found Hunch out in back of the kitchen, cleaning carriage tack and chewing on his mustache. As soon as she saw his face, Kim knew that Mairelon had told him what had happened. He glowered at her, but Kim ignored it.

"Hunch, I need to get down to the City," she said without preamble.

"What for?" Hunch demanded suspiciously.

"To see a sharper that might have something to do with what happened last night," Kim said.

"You'll want a 'ackney, then," Hunch said, rising. "Master Richard won't 'ave no trouble figuring out that you've gone and done something if you take the carriage." His eyes met hers in perfect understanding.

"I want a pistol, too, if you have one," Kim said.

Hunch stopped. "I better come with you, then."

"No. Mairelon'll want you when he goes to see Lord Shoreham. And I don't know if we'll be back by then."

" 'E'd want me to come with you. And 'e'll raise merry 'ell when 'e finds out, if I 'aven't. I'm coming, or else you ain't going."

None of Kim's arguments moved Hunch in the slightest. Finally, she gave in, feeling secretly relieved. Visiting a cent-per-cent wasn't quite so bad as wandering some of her former haunts in girl's clothes would have been, but it was enough to make her nervous nonetheless.

Hunch procured a hackney coach, and Kim gave the driver the direction. No one spoke for some time as the coach rattled over the cobbles. Then Hunch looked at Kim and said, "You think this'll 'elp?"

"I don't know," Kim said. "Maybe. I got to try, anyway."

Hunch nodded and relapsed into silence. The coach pulled up in front of a row of small, slightly shabby buildings. Kim climbed out carefully and told the driver to wait, then marched toward the near door without waiting to see whether Hunch or Wilson followed. She had to ring the bell vigorously two or three times before there was any response, but finally a watery-eyed clerk opened the door a crack and said, "We're closed."

Kim shoved her foot into the opening before the clerk could shut the door. "Not to me, you ain't."

The clerk's eyes widened as he took in Kim's fashionable and expensive dress, and he gobbled incoherently for a moment. Kim took advantage of his surprise to push the door out of his lax hands and walk through it into the dim, dusty hallway beyond. "Where's Mannering?" she demanded.

"He ain't here," the clerk said. "I told you, we're closed."

"I didn't ask if you were closed," Kim said. "I asked where Mannering is."

"Mr. Mannering ain't here," the clerk repeated sullenly.

Kim looked at his face and decided he was telling the truth. *Now what?* She frowned at the clerk and said irritably, "You told me that before, cully, and I heard you then. Where's his office?"

"It don't matter; there's no use you waiting. He ain't here, and he ain't coming back today."

Forgetting her girl's clothes, Kim reached up and grabbed hold of the clerk's muffler. One good yank pulled his astonished face down level with hers, and she snarled into it, "Listen, you mutton-headed nodcock. For the last time, where's Mannering's office? Or I'll tie your tongue in a bow-knot behind your ears and find the place for myself."

"Th-that one," the clerk said, pointing. "But you can't go in there, it's locked and I ain't got the key, and Mr. Mannering—"

"Ain't here, you said that, too," Kim said, releasing him. She dusted her gloves and stepped back, to find Hunch and Wilson standing in the doorway. "See this cove don't shab off just yet, will you, Hunch?" she said. "I might want to talk to him again after I've had a look at Mannering's office."

Hunch nodded. Kim walked down to the doorway the clerk had pointed out and studied the lock. It was new and shiny against the aged wood of the door; pretty much what you'd expect to find at a moneylender's place of business. But this moneylender had been collecting wizards. Frowning, Kim cast the spell that allowed her to see enchantments. To her relief, the lock did not glow. She fished her lockpicking wire from the bottom of her reticule and set to work.

Opening the lock took some time; Mannering had paid for the best, and gotten it. Kim felt considerable pride when it clicked open at last. The feeling turned to strong dismay when the door opened and she got a look at the room beyond.

Everything indicated that someone had been here before her: the heavy lockbox lying open and empty on the desktop, the dustless squares here and there on the shelves where objects had lain, the half-open drawers, the wrinkled cravat lying forgotten underneath the chair. Kim bit back a curse and started forward. Maybe the other cracksman had left something she'd find useful.

As she sifted through what was left in Mannering's office, she quickly became convinced that this was no robbery. No thief would have bothered to take pages from the ledgers, or missed the pound note stuck under the lockbox. Mannering had taken the things he considered important and piked off, and he'd done it in a tearing hurry, too. Kim frowned. This didn't make sense . . . unless he thought that Mairelon's tracing spell had worked, and had expected to find the Runners on his doorstep this morning instead of Kim.

Methodically, Kim began pulling out the desk drawers and examining their contents. Most contained paper or old ledgers. The center drawer had a small lock, which had been thrown—but in his hurry, Mannering had not shut the drawer completely, and the lock had not engaged. Pleased to be spared the work of picking it, Kim opened the drawer.

The drawer was half full of notes and partially completed spell diagrams. Kim looked at one or two of them and frowned. They all looked the same, or rather, nearly the same—on this page, the top line twisted up; on the next, it twisted down; on the one after that, it was straight as an old Roman road. *Variations on a spell design*, Kim thought. *But Mannering wasn't ever a frogmaker, and George and Jemmy and Wags don't know this kind of magic. Who's he got helping him?* Some of the notes bore a line or two of almost illegible writing, with frequent crossings-out and insertions. Kim puzzled at one of the inscriptions for a while, then shook her head. Reading was hard enough when she could tell what the letters were supposed to be; Mannering's scrawl was hopeless. Maybe it was instructions for the spell. She gathered up the papers and stuffed them in her reticule. Mairelon or Lord Kerring or Lord Shoreham might be able to make something more of them.

When she finished, she rejoined Hunch, Wilson, and the clerk, who was by turns sullen and terrified. "I'm done, Hunch," she said. "We'd better go."

"You—I—What am I going to tell Mr. Mannering?" the clerk babbled. "You can't do this!"

"Tell him I heard he wanted to see me," Kim said. "Tell him I got something he wants." She pulled a small blue book from her pocket, just far enough for the clerk to get a look, and then shoved it back out of sight. It had taken her half an hour to find one that was a reasonable match for Marie de Cambriol's *livre de mémoire*, and she wasn't going to give anyone a close enough look to see that it wasn't the real thing. "Tell him that if he pulls any more tricks like last night, he won't see this, or me, or anything else he wants. I ain't got much patience with jingle brains or shag-bags."

The clerk nodded dumbly. They left him staring goggle-eyed after them, and returned to the hackney. "Where to now, miss?" the jarvey said.

Kim hesitated, then shook her head. "Back to Grosvenor Square," she said.

"Find anything?" Hunch said as the coach started off.

"Not what I thought," Kim said. "The cull has piked off, right enough. I think he was scared of something."

"Good."

Kim glanced at him, startled by the savagery in his tone. She wasn't really surprised, though; it was the way she felt whenever she thought about what had been done to Mairelon. "He left some notes. Maybe they'll help."

Hunch nodded and lapsed back into his usual silence. Kim stared glumly out the carriage window, watching the tradesmen on the street without really seeing them. Mairelon was not going to be pleased to find out what she had done, but she'd have to tell him; *she* certainly wasn't going to be able to make sense of all those bits and pieces and scrawls.

The other members of the household were at breakfast when Kim and Wilson slipped through the back door. Kim sent Wilson off with her bonnet and pelisse, while she went up to join the family. When she entered the room, she could tell from everyone's faces that this modest attempt at conceal-ment had been pointless; they were already aware that she had left the house, and Mairelon and Lady Wendall, at least, had been worried.

"Kim!" Mrs. Lowe said. "Where *have* you been at such an hour?"

"I had an errand to run," Kim said, heading for the side-board. "Don't jaw me down now; I ain't had breakfast yet."

"Mind your language!"

"Sorry," Kim said absently as she filled her plate. "I . . . haven't . . . adjusted back yet."

"Adjusted back?" Lady Wendall raised her eyebrows.

"Don't tell me that after all my warnings, you went to see some of those low friends of yours!" Mrs. Lowe said.

"No." Kim took a seat and began tucking in to the sausage. "Not a friend."

Mairelon's eyes narrowed. Oblivious, Mrs. Lowe shook her head at Kim. "Where *did* you go, then? After all the worry you've caused—"

"I'm sorry you were worried," Kim said, glancing at Lady Wendall apologetically. She couldn't quite bring herself to look at Mairelon yet. "I thought I'd be back before anybody noticed I was gone."

"That is no excuse," Mrs. Lowe said. "It is highly improper for a young lady to wander about London unescorted."

"I took my abigail," Kim said. She sneaked a glance at Mairelon. "And Hunch."

"Did you?" Mairelon's expression was closed; she hadn't ever seen him quite like this before. Not knowing how to respond, Kim said nothing.

"Very sensible of you," Lady Wendall put in approvingly.

"I must entirely disagree," Mrs. Lowe said. "Running 'errands' at this hour of the morning is plainly an excuse. I insist that Kim explain—"

"Aunt." Mairelon's voice was quite level and not very loud, but Mrs. Lowe broke off in midsentence and looked at him. In the same level tone, he continued, "My apprentice and ward will explain *to me* immediately after breakfast. I trust that is clear?"

"As you wish," Mrs. Lowe replied stiffly.

Kim finished her meal quickly in the uncomfortable silence that followed. "I'm done," she said.

Mairelon rose. "Then you can explain yourself to me in the library." He waited only long enough to see Kim nod before he left the room.

She caught up with him on the stairs and followed him into the library. As soon as the door closed behind them, he said, "Well?"

"I went to Mannering's office."

"*What?* Are you mad? Didn't you think at all? If Mannering is behind this—"

"I thought for most of the night," Kim said, and looked at Mairelon apologetically. "I saw right off that Mannering was in this somewhere, but I didn't think you had yet."

"Then why didn't you mention it?"

Kim hesitated. "Because I was worried you'd go off and do

something goose-witted," she owned at last. "You've done it before."

Mairelon stared at her in silence for a moment. "Not after I said I wouldn't," he said at last.

"When—" Kim stopped. He'd promised her, when she'd come back from seeing Tom Correy two weeks before, that he wouldn't go investigating Mannering without talking to her first. She hadn't remembered . . . but she hadn't remembered because, she realized, she hadn't really believed that he would hold to his promise now that the situation had changed so radically. "I forgot," she said lamely, and then, looking down at her hands, she added, "Nobody ever—I never knew anybody before that . . . that would do that. Not with something this big, not when it was only somethin' they said to me."

"I see." Mairelon's voice had lost its coldness; he sounded torn between amusement and some other emotion she couldn't identify. After a moment, he went on lightly, "So to keep me from doing something goose-witted, you did it yourself. Why? And why in heaven's name didn't you at least tell me what you were planning?"

The bantering tone didn't fool Kim; she could hear the hurt underneath the lightness. She turned away and said to the monkey cage, "I had to do *something*. You looked . . . you were . . . I just had to do something, that's all. And I didn't say because I was afraid you'd stop me. I can see now I should of trusted you, but— Well, I never had nobody I *could* trust like that before. I'm not used to it."

There was a long silence. Kim wiped at her eyes with the backs of her hands. After a long time, Mairelon said, "Anybody you could trust. Not 'nobody.'" His voice sounded hoarse.

"Anybody," Kim repeated. "Anyway, I'm sorry."

"I'm afraid I have to apologize as well," Mairelon said. She turned to find him looking at her with an expression she could not interpret. "I didn't mention Mannering for the same reason you didn't—because I didn't want you haring off after him. I forgot that *you* hadn't promised anyone not to."

"Well, I won't do it again," Kim said.

"Good." Mairelon hesitated. "I suppose you've thought of the possible connection to your friend Ma Yanger, as well?"

Kim licked her lips. "First thing last night, practically."

"Well." Mairelon looked down, and for a brief moment his expression was grim. Then he shook his head and said, "Well, then, how *was* your little visit with Mannering?"

"He wasn't there," Kim said. "Looks like he took all his valuables and piked off in the middle of the night."

Mairelon stared at her, then sat down very slowly in one of the reading chairs. "Gone, is he? Now that *is* interesting. I wonder why?"

"I been—I *have* been thinking about that," Kim said. "What if he doesn't know that *you're* the one he caught in that spell? If he thinks it was me—"

"—then he'd have expected a very angry wizard in his office bright and early in the morning, and he didn't think he could handle it," Mairelon said. He gave Kim a rueful grin. "He appears to have been quite right, too, though perhaps not in exactly the way he'd been thinking."

"He left some notes in his desk," Kim said, and began pulling them out of her reticule. "They look like bits of spell diagrams and such, but I can't read half of them."

"You're right," Mairelon said, glancing at the drawings. "Someone was experimenting." He squinted at one of the scribbled notes and frowned. "This looks as if it could be part of a spell chant, but—"

"But?"

"It's in English."

Kim stared at him. "But if the spell is in English, it won't work right for an English wizard," she said at last.

"Exactly." Mairelon tapped the note. "Now, if you don't mind, tell me just what happened during your visit to Mannering's offices this morning, and then we'll go through these a little more carefully."

SIXTEEN

It took Kim some time to give Mairelon the precise account he wanted. He did not interrupt, but listened with a bemused expression, sorting Mannering's notes into two neat piles as Kim talked. When she finished, he shook his head.

"None of this adds up properly," he said. "You say Mannering isn't a wizard, and is certainly English, but he has a drawer full of magical diagrams and spell bits that no English wizard could use. We have a Russian wizard nice and handy, but he can't possibly have cast those spells last night—not with you, me, and Renée standing right next to him. One of us would have noticed. We have a mystery wizard who is willing to waste power in prodigious amounts in order to get hold of a useless *livre de mémoire*, and a singularly inept burglar who seems to be, in his better moments, a gentleman of sorts. And we have a batch of untrained criminal wizards who, for no reason anyone knows, have suddenly forsaken their independent ways and gone to work for Mannering—except for one, who first gave up or lost her magic and then vanished completely under suspicious circumstances. It doesn't *fit*."

And none of it looks like it's helping to get your magic back. "I could have a talk with Jemmy or Wags," Kim offered, but Mairelon was shaking his head before she even finished speaking.

"No. I'll ask Shoreham to have his people look into it. It's not, strictly speaking, part of the business of the Ministry, but he owes me a favor or two, and I think he'll do it." He eyed Mannering's notes thoughtfully. "I'll take these with me when I visit Shoreham later, if you don't mind. He may have a few more ideas."

"If I don't mind?" Kim said, astonished.

Mairelon gave her a crooked smile. "You're the one who went and got them."

Kim could only nod her assent.

"Meanwhile, I think it would be advisable to make a copy." Mairelon handed her the stack of diagrams. "You do these; I'll see what I can make of the others."

They set to work, side by side at the table. Mindful of the need for accuracy, Kim worked with painstaking care, duplicating even the lines that looked to be accidents or scribbles before she turned the paper face down to go on to the next one. On the third page, she turned the note over and stopped. "Mairelon. This one has writing on the back."

Mairelon looked over. "So it does. Let's see—" He stopped abruptly, frowning at the writing.

"What is it?" Kim said, peering down at it. The writing was, like that of the other notes, nearly illegible, and there were circles and arrows and check marks on top of it that made it even harder to puzzle out.

"It's a list of names," Mairelon said. "French names."

"Not those wizards Mlle. D'Auber was telling us about?" Kim guessed.

"Right the first time," Mairelon said. "But there are only six of them. M. László Karolyi, Mlle. Jeannette Lepain—that one is circled—the Comtesse Eustacie de Beauvoix, the Comte Louis du Franchard—he's circled them, too, and there's a check mark next to the comte's name—Mme. Marie de Cambriol—circled, but no check mark—and the Duchesse Camille Delagardie."

Kim ran quickly through her memory of their conversation with Renée D'Auber. "It's missing Henri d'Armand."

"Yes."

"But what does it *mean?*" Kim said in frustration.

"I don't know." Mairelon looked down at the page, and a muscle by the corner of his mouth spasmed briefly. "But it's the first real evidence we have that Mannering is connected with our bits-and-pieces wizard—the one who was after the de Cambriol book."

And the one that set that trap. Kim scowled at the papers. "Well, it doesn't help much."

"It's something." Still studying the pages intently, Mairelon said, "Let's finish this, and then we'll see what Shoreham has to say."

"We?"

"Yes, of course." Mairelon did not look at her. "He'll want to hear about your visit to Mannering's office, and it will be better if you're there to tell him in person. And there may be . . . other things."

Kim's startled comments died on her lips as she realized belatedly just what "other things" Mairelon was referring to. Spells. If the Earl of Shoreham had anything to recommend, or needed a second wizard to help with any test he wanted to run, someone besides Mairelon would have to be there to do it. And Mairelon would want it to be someone who already knew of his . . . difficulties, which meant either Lady Wendall or Kim.

Feeling more than a little nervous, Kim nodded and returned to her copying. Edward, Earl of Shoreham, wasn't just another toff; he was one of the top men at the government's Ministry of Wizardry, head of a semiclandestine department that was responsible for a great deal of intelligence gathering by both magical and nonmagical methods. He was the one who had persuaded Mairelon to do all of his spying on the French during the last few years of the war. Kim had only met him twice before: once, when he had turned up during the recovery of the Saltash Set, and once a few weeks later, after she and Mairelon had returned to London. Shoreham was, unquestionably, a right knowing one, and though he did not seem to dislike her, he made her uneasy nonetheless.

But when they finished making their copies and arrived at the Ministry of Wizardry with Mannering's original notes, they found that Shoreham was not there. "Gone down to Brighton to meet one of our chaps coming in on the packet," the secretary, an earnest young man, said. "He should be back tomorrow."

"Tell him we'll be by at ten o'clock," Mairelon said.

"He's meeting with the minister then," the secretary replied, checking a book lying open on the desk.

"Eleven, then," Mairelon snapped, and left in more of a temper than Kim could ever recall seeing him in before.

Their visit to the Royal College was slightly less frustrating—Lord Kerring was there, and though he was deeply immersed in some magical project that Kim did not quite understand, he set it aside at once when he heard that Mairelon was in need of help. After hearing their story, he studied the spell affecting Mairelon from several angles, but then shook his head.

"There's nothing I can do about this today. I need an analysis, and from what you say, the standard spell is . . . inadvisable." Lord Kerring scratched his bushy beard. "I'll have to design something that works less invasively than the usual methods."

"How long will it take?" Mairelon said.

"Hard to say," Kerring replied. "I know you're in a hurry, and I don't blame you, but . . . some things, you just can't rush. I'll send you word as soon as I have something feasible, but don't expect it before next week. And it might be longer. It depends on how tricky the interlocks turn out to be."

Mairelon nodded; from the quality of his silence on the ride home, Kim concluded that he had been hoping for a quick solution. When they arrived back at Grosvenor Square, Mrs. Lowe informed them that they had had several visitors in their absence.

"The Marquis of Harsfeld was among them," she said with a significant look at Kim.

"Lord Franton?" Kim said. "He did tell me he was going to call, but I didn't think he meant right away."

"When he discovered that you were from home, he did not stay," Mrs. Lowe said. "I trust that he will have better fortune on his *next* visit."

Mairelon frowned. "Who else did we miss?" he said abruptly.

"Your French friend, Miss D'Auber," Mrs. Lowe replied. "She said that she wished to see how you did. I cannot think where she could have gotten the impression that you were unwell."

"She may have mistaken something I said last night," Mairelon said.

Mrs. Lowe nodded, satisfied. "I told her it must be some misunderstanding."

"Did she say anything else?" Kim asked, hoping to turn the subject before Mrs. Lowe accidentally precipitated a crisis.

"She mentioned that she overheard the Marquis of Harsfeld tell Lady Greythorne that you were even more charming in person than from afar," Mrs. Lowe said. "I am pleased that you managed to make such a good impression last night, though it would have been far better had you been here to receive him when he called today. Oh, and there has apparently been something of a rash of thefts and burglaries lately."

"Really?" Mairelon was suddenly all attention. "Did Renée say who, or when?"

"Someone stole a painting from Mr. Winton's library last week, and Lord Bancroft and his wife lost an urn that had been in the family for several generations, though it was only silver plate. That was Monday. And last night, someone broke in at the George."

"Someone tried to rob a *hotel*?" Kim said incredulously.

"It does seem a bit unusual," Mairelon said.

"It's a mug's game," Kim told him. "People who're putting up at hotels don't cart their silver along with them, and if they've got jewels, they're out wearing them at night. And there's the hotel staff, as well as everybody's servants, so there's at least three times as many people to avoid. Milling a gentry ken is a lot safer, and they're not exactly easy marks."

"Kim," Mrs. Lowe said reprovingly, "you really *must* be more careful about your language. Those . . . cant terms are simply not suitable in polite company."

"I wonder what the cracksman took," Mairelon said.

"Miss D'Auber didn't say," Mrs. Lowe replied stiffly, frowning at him.

"Pity. Kim, I'll want to see you in the library after lunch;

we've a good deal of work to do if we're to have that illusion ready for your ball." And with an absent nod, Mairelon escaped up the stairs, leaving Kim with his aunt.

Kim had expected the rest of the day to be quiet, but she was quickly disabused of that notion. Mairelon had not been joking when he said they had a lot of work to do to prepare for the illusion spell, and most of the work was Kim's. Fortunately, Lady Wendell could take over some of Mairelon's part, but there were limits to what she could accomplish from the sidelines without letting it become obvious to everyone that it was she, and not her son, who was assisting Kim with her come-out illusion. The additional parts fell to Kim, and she burned candles late into the evening trying to memorize them all.

Promptly at eleven the next morning, she and Mairelon were at the Ministry of Wizardry once again. The Earl of Shoreham did not keep them waiting long. "I suppose you're here about those French wizards again," he said to Mairelon as they found seats in his office.

"Not directly," Mairelon said. "There have been developments."

"With you, there are always developments," Lord Shoreham said, amused.

"Someone seems to have developed themselves right into my magic, and me out of it," Mairelon said with an unsuccessful attempt at lightness.

"What? Richard, you don't seriously mean—" Lord Shoreham looked at Mairelon, and his amusement vanished, replaced by concern. "You'd better start at the beginning. What has this got to do with your French wizards?"

"If I knew that, I'd be considerably farther along than I am now," Mairelon said testily. "The beginning, so far as I know, was an inept burglar who tried to steal a book from my brother's library. Kim heard him in process, and interrupted before he got what he was after. The book was a *livre de mémoire* written by a French wizard named Marie de Cambriol and rather grandiosely titled *Le Livre de Sept Sorciers*, and so far as I've been able to tell, there's no reason at all why anyone would want to get hold of it.

"Last week someone had another go at it while Kim and Mother and I were at the opera. He used a scrying spell to make certain we were away from home, and then put together a sort of summoning-cum-levitation to bring the book to him. He failed mainly because he didn't have sense enough to find out which side of the house the library was on before he cast his spell; according to my aunt, the book spent half an hour trying to batter through a wall when it could have nipped through one of the windows and been gone."

"Amateur work, then?" Shoreham said.

"Possibly. There was a lot of power behind the spell, but it was very badly balanced; it fell apart almost immediately when I tried to analyze it. I'd guess self-taught, or foreign, or both."

"Ah." Shoreham leaned back in his chair. "Go on."

"The spell reminded Kim of an old . . . acquaintance of hers that lives up by the Charterhouse, a Ma Yanger."

Shoreham nodded. "One of the rookery witches. She's one of the canny ones—we have reason to think she turns an occasional spell for some of the professional thieves, but she's been careful enough that we haven't caught her at it. Most of her trade is minor household-level magic—removing corns, easing aches, the odd love spell. Some of it is the genuine article, but a good deal of it is mere sham."

"From what Kim and I found, she hasn't cast any spells for

at least two months, and she's not likely to be doing anything at all for a lot longer than that." Mairelon nodded at Kim. "Tell him."

Startled, Kim hesitated for a moment, and Shoreham gave her an encouraging look. She swallowed and, trying not to feel as if she were betraying her old friends, she explained what Tom had told her about wizards working for Mannering, and then described what she had found at Ma Yanger's.

"Hmph," said Shoreham when she finished. "I'll have to get on to MacArdle; he's supposed to be keeping up on the minor wizards, especially the ones around St. Giles and Smithfield. If he overlooked something like this, we shall have words. Continue."

"Two nights ago, at Lady Greythorne's musicale, our mystery wizard tried his scrying spell again," Mairelon said, and stopped.

"And knowing you, you were ready for him," Shoreham said.

"Not ready enough," Mairelon said. "I had a trace-and-analyze spell infused in a splinter of kindling, all ready to go, and when I felt the scrying spell, I invoked it. But—well, the scrying spell didn't just fracture and fall apart this time; it sucked down my enchantment like quagmire sucking down a horse. And not just the enchantment, either."

"I see." Lord Shoreham looked seriously concerned. "I can't say I've heard of anything like this before, but I'll put some people on it immediately. In the meantime—"

"Kerring's working at the enchantment end of things," Mairelon said. "I spoke to him yesterday."

"Are you sure that's enough?"

"I don't exactly like the thought of everyone knowing that I can't so much as light a fire without flint and tinder,"

Mairelon said testily. "The fewer people who have the details, the better."

"As you wish." But Shoreham continued to frown, and after a moment he looked at Kim. "It's not really the thing to be asking another wizard's apprentice this, but have you learned Gerard's Refuge yet?"

"No, she hasn't," Mairelon said before Kim could answer. He did not look at all pleased, but Kim could not tell whether he was annoyed with Shoreham, or with her, or with himself.

"What is it?" Kim asked, looking at Mairelon uncertainly.

Mairelon remained silent. Shoreham glanced at him, then said, "It's a minor protective spell, rather like the standard ward but less complex and easier to cast. It doesn't last as long, and it isn't intended to absorb or block magic, the way a ward does."

"Then how can it protect anything?" Kim asked.

"It deflects spells," Shoreham said. "Sort of shoves them to one side where they can go off without doing any harm." He glanced at Mairelon again, then looked back at her. "I think it would be a good idea for you to learn it as soon as possible."

"Teach it to her now," Mairelon said. "I should have thought of that myself." He sat scowling at the front of Shoreham's desk while the earl explained the spell and ran her through casting it several times. It was, as he had promised, quite simple—a single gesture and a word—and it did not take long for her to master it.

When they finished, Shoreham turned to Mairelon. "Now, about those French wizards. I've done some checking since you were last here. *Les Griffonais* were of considerable interest to the Ministry in the early years of the French war, even though they had all left France well before the trouble began, so there was more information lying around than I'd expected."

He pulled a sheaf of papers toward him and read from the

top of the first page, "M. László Karolyi, Hungarian—close friend of the current Vicomte de Bragelonne. He helped the vicomte escape France during the Terror, in fact. Karolyi was apparently much in sympathy with the aims of the *sans-culottes,* but thoroughly disgusted by the eventual direction their revolution took. He returned to Hungary and has spent most of his time there for the last thirty years, though he has visited England upon occasion—or rather, he has visited those of his French friends who sought sanctuary from the Terror here."

"Lately?"

"No, not since Waterloo," Lord Shoreham said. He turned to the next page. "Mme. Marie de Cambriol—traveled in Italy and Greece after leaving France, then came to England with her husband in 1799. Died of a putrid fever some months later.

"M. Henri d'Armand—also, apparently, inclined to travel after leaving France, but not so successfully. He was on his way to Milan to attend the opening of an opera when his ship sank."

"What?" Mairelon sat up. "D'Armand is dead?"

"And has been for nearly thirty years," Shoreham said. "The accident happened only a month or two after he left France. Is that significant?"

"His name was missing from Mannering's list," Mairelon said. "That may be why."

"The de Cambriol woman is also deceased," Shoreham pointed out, turning over another page. "If I may continue? The Duchesse Camille Delagardie—settled in England with her husband. She has a reputation as both a recluse and an eccentric, though from what I can gather, it's founded mainly on a dislike of making the rounds in Society. She has a small but devoted circle of friends, many of them wizards. Before you ask, yes, she's still alive; I believe she and her husband are somewhere in the North at the moment. They have a little place in Hampstead, when they're in Town."

"Hampstead!" Mairelon said. "Good lord. That's not in Town."

"It apparently does very well for them," Shoreham said. "The Comte Louis du Franchard and the Comtesse Eustacie de Beauvoix—also settled in England, but returned to France last month, possibly to repossess the estates that were confiscated from them during the revolution. Unlike the duchesse and her husband, they socialized rather freely during their twenty-some years here."

"And finally, Mademoiselle Jeannette Lepain—also lived in England for a few years, but in 1801 she married a Russian wizard-prince, one Ivan Durmontov, and moved—"

"Ivan *Durmontov?*" Mairelon interrupted. "Now that *is* interesting."

"So I gather," Lord Shoreham said dryly. "You wouldn't, by chance, care to enlighten me as to why?"

"There's a Prince Alexei Durmontov in London for the Season," Mairelon said, and smiled. "I think perhaps I should have a talk with him. It appears we may have some interests in common."

"Richard—" Lord Shoreham began, and then sighed. "I'd much rather we found out a bit more about him before you go stirring things up. I suppose there's no use telling you to wait?"

"None whatever."

"Very well, then, but for heaven's sake, be careful. If he *does* have anything to do with this . . . this situation—"

"Then I intend to find out what it is as soon as possible," Mairelon said, and his tone was deadly serious. "Anything else, Edward? No? Then we'll be going. Let me know if you find out anything."

"Be sure I will," Lord Shoreham said gravely.

SEVENTEEN

As soon as they returned to Grosvenor Square, Mairelon sent Hunch off with a note requesting Prince Durmontov to call at his earliest convenience. Hunch returned an hour later, while Kim and Mairelon were still in the library rehashing Shoreham's comments. He reported that he had left the note, but Prince Durmontov had not been at his lodgings to receive it.

"What?" Mairelon said.

" 'E ain't there," Hunch repeated. "The 'otel staff said 'e was upset by the robbery and 'e went off to stay with some friends in the country."

"Upset by the—Good Lord, that's right! He did say he was moving to the George." Mairelon studied Hunch. "He wasn't by chance one of the people who was burgled?"

Hunch nodded. "The 'housemaid says 'is rooms were turned up a rare treat, but 'ooever it was didn't take nothin' valuable."

"That doesn't make sense," Kim said.

"Neither does anything else we've learned," Mairelon said. "Did they take anything at all, Hunch?"

"Some family 'eirloom, she said." Hunch shrugged. "That's why 'e was so cut up about it."

"An heirloom," Mairelon said. "A book, perhaps? That would certainly be convenient—a little *too* convenient, I think. When is the prince returning to London?"

"Nobody knows," Hunch said.

If not for the expression on Mairelon's face, Kim would have been almost thankful to have the visit to the prince put off for a few days. Between Mairelon, Lady Wendall, and Mrs. Lowe, she was run nearly ragged learning her illusions, helping to check and maintain the protective wards on the house, being fitted for her come-out dress, memorizing what seemed like thousands of instructions for her conduct at the ball, and practicing acceptable social behavior during morning calls, teas, and other social outings.

The attentive Lord Franton added to the number of things that had to be fit into each day. He called several times, and held Kim to her promise to drive with him in Hyde Park two days after the musicale. But though his visits were certainly enjoyable while they lasted, Kim could not help resenting them because of how much more hectic things always were afterward.

Except when Mairelon drilled her in the spells for the illusion, she saw less and less of her guardian as the ball neared. He spent most of his days at the Royal College or at the Ministry of Wizardry, closeted with Kerring or Shoreham. Whatever they discussed, it was plain that they had made no progress regarding the spell that affected Mairelon's magic. Each evening when he returned, he was quieter than he had been the previous day. Lady Wendall developed a small vertical worry line between her eyebrows that deepened whenever she looked in her son's direction. Only Mrs. Lowe seemed unaware that anything was wrong.

The day of the ball, Kim did not see Mairelon at all. She and Lady Wendall were busy most of the morning with preparations for the illusion, drawing diagrams on the ballroom floor with rosewater made in a mirrored bowl, and she spent the afternoon being dressed. After having her hair fussed over, her gown examined and reexamined for creases, and everything from her stockings to her hair ribbon studied and commented on, Kim was nearly ready to scream. Fortunately, the arrival of a charming posy tied up with peach-colored ribbons distracted her well-meaning helpers in the nick of time.

"The very thing!" Lady Wendell said. "Look at the card, Kim, and see who it is from."

"Lord Franton sent it," Kim said after studying it for a moment. She set the card aside, trying not to feel disappointed and wondering why she did.

A second box arrived a few moments later, though it was far too small to hold flowers. "Now, what is this?" Lady Wendall said, frowning slightly.

Kim lifted the lid. Inside, on a small pillow covered in white velvet, lay a gold sunburst the size of her thumbnail, hung on a delicate chain. It looked a little like the first spell she had ever cast, a small explosion of light recreated in metal, and she was not really surprised to find the card with the single word "Mairelon" scrawled across it.

"Ah," said Lady Wendall, peering over Kim's shoulder. "I'd been wondering—I'm very glad he remembered."

So am I, Kim thought, feeling suddenly much more cheerful.

When all the fussing and fixing-up was done at last, they

went down to await their guests. This, too, was a longer and more complicated process than Kim had expected. She and Lady Wendall and Mairelon stood at the head of the stairs receiving the company for over an hour and a half, and the flow of arrivals was so steady that there was no time to pass even a few remarks among themselves. Renée D'Auber came early, and Lord Kerring and his lady wife soon after, but most of the other guests were not well-known to Kim. It was a relief to spy the occasional truly familiar face; even Letitia Tarnower, who had somehow managed to be included in the party from Kirkover House, was almost a welcome sight. For the rest, Kim's part was no more than to smile and curtsey as Lady Wendell presented her to those guests whom she had not previously met. This gave her far too much time to think about the upcoming illusion. By the time the stream of incoming guests began to thin, she had worked herself into a fair case of jitters.

The Marquis of Harsfeld was among the last to arrive. He smiled politely as he greeted Lady Wendell, but his eyes strayed to Kim's hands, and his smile warmed noticeably when he saw his flowers attached to her wrist. "I had not dared to hope you would accept my tribute," he said softly when he reached Kim.

"I'm— It was— Thank you," Kim said, and passed him on to Mairelon.

"I notice that Durmontov hasn't shown up yet," Mairelon commented when the marquis had passed out of hearing.

"Renée D'Auber tells me that he does not return to Town until some time next week," Lady Wendell said, and Mairelon frowned. Lady Wendall turned to Kim. "Ten minutes more, and we shall go in. We really cannot delay the dancing any longer than that."

Kim swallowed. Ten minutes, and she would have to perform a spell before several hundred members of the *ton*, with most of whom she had barely a nodding acquaintance. If it were just for Mairelon and Lady Wendall and Renée D'Auber, and maybe Lord Kerring and Lord Shoreham, it wouldn't be so nervewracking.

"The last few minutes before the show are always the worst," Mairelon said, as if he knew exactly what she was thinking. "You'll do very well." Kim smiled at him gratefully, then belatedly connected his remark with the performances he had once given in the Hungerford Market. Maybe he *did* know exactly what she had been thinking. The thought that even Mairelon had been nervous before his shows made her feel a little better. Still, it seemed as if far less than ten minutes had gone by when Lady Wendall signaled to Mairelon to take Kim in to the ballroom.

As they entered, the hum of conversation sank to a mere murmur and heads turned to look at them. Kim shivered slightly; she was more used to avoiding attention than accepting it. Almost involuntarily, her free hand rose, seeking reassurance, and touched the gold sunburst that Mairelon had given her.

Mairelon led her to the center of the floor. She hardly heard his introduction; she was suddenly, frantically certain that she did not remember a single word of the illusion spell. *Brevis lux, nox . . . nox . . . What comes after* nox? And then Mairelon drew his arm away and stepped back, and she stood isolated under the eyes of more toffs than she had ever thought to see, let alone draw the attention of.

She took a deep breath, and her self-consciousness receded. Fixing her eyes on a candle sconce on the far wall, she raised her arms and—in a clear, steady voice—began the invocation.

At the end of the first five lines, Mairelon's voice joined

hers as if he were supporting and assisting in the spell. This was the trickiest part, for it was Lady Wendall who was really performing the magic. As the primary spellcaster, Kim had to merge the two enchantments into one—a difficult task indeed when she not only could not hear Lady Wendall's voice, but also had Mairelon's to distract her.

Somehow, she managed it all—keeping the timing right, reciting her own part, and building the images in her own mind as she spoke. She knew, as she said the final phrase, that it was going to work, and with a triumphant sense of satisfaction she brought her hands down and together in the gesture that set the spell in motion.

All of the candles went out. The guests gasped, then hushed again as a glowing cloud of white smoke erupted from the bare floor in front of Kim, where she had knelt all morning with the rosewater. From the center of the smoke, a voice called, "Come one, come all! Prepare to be amazed and astonished by the one, the only—Mairelon the Magician!"

With the last words, the smoke dissipated. Where it had been rose the image of a wooden stage, and in the middle of the stage stood Mairelon as Kim had first seen him, in a black opera cape and top hat, wearing a small, neat mustache. He raised a silver-headed walking stick, and a grubby, dark-haired boy in a ragged jacket jumped out of the darkness onto the stage beside him. The two images held the pose for a long moment while a murmur of surprise rose from the watchers, and then the real Mairelon and Kim stepped forward and took their places beside the images of their former selves. The candles flickered into flame once more, and the illusion faded, leaving only the true Mairelon and Kim in their formal finery.

A scattering of applause broke out. Light-headed with relief and triumph, Kim grinned at Mairelon. Mairelon smiled back at her, bowed, and stepped forward to take her hand as the musicians began the opening dance.

Other couples fell in behind them after the first few bars. Kim let the music lead her feet without paying much conscious attention; after the successful spellcasting, a mere misstep held no terrors for her. Indeed, she felt as if she *could not* put a foot wrong this night.

At the end of the first dance, Mairelon relinquished her to a throng of intrigued gallants and retired to the sidelines. Kim had more than half expected that the illusion, with its reminder of her too-humble origins, would put a damper on her social prospects; instead, it seemed to have significantly increased the number of gentlemen taking an interest in her. Mindful of Lady Wendall's—and Mrs. Lowe's—strictures, she was careful not to agree to more than two dances with any of them, but there were so many that she was on her feet for most of the evening. Several times, she caught sight of Mairelon watching her as she danced, but he did not return to claim a second dance for himself.

Lord Franton presented himself promptly for his first dance, and though he did not press her for another immediately afterward, he seemed always to be nearby when she finished a turn with some other partner. He would make light conversation for a moment or two, and then yield his place to the next gentleman. After a while, Kim began wondering when he would claim his second dance, and whether his attentions would be as assiduous once he had had it.

The dance the marquis chose at last revealed that he was no mean strategist—it was the supper dance, and since Kim had not previously engaged with anyone to take her down to supper, Lord Franton naturally claimed that privilege when the dance ended.

"Now, that is the outside of enough!" said one of the other

gentlemen, arriving just too late to put forward his own claim. "It's taking unfair advantage, that's what it is. You'd be justly served, Harry, if my friends were to call upon you in the morning."

"You've no one but yourself to blame," the marquis said, grinning unrepentantly. "If you hadn't been so determined to cut me out for the galliard earlier, you might have secured this last dance yourself."

"If you weren't given to underhanded tactics, I wouldn't have needed to," the other retorted.

Lord Franton only laughed and swept Kim off on his arm.

As they made their way in to dinner, Lord Franton said, "I don't believe I've told you how impressed I was by your introductory illusion."

"I was worried that no one would like it," Kim confessed. Although "not liking it" wasn't quite what she meant. But she couldn't bring herself to tell Lord Franton, Marquis of Harsfeld, that she hadn't been sure about the wisdom of flaunting her past as a street thief in front of a bunch of toffs, no matter what Mairelon and Lady Wendall had said. Judging by people's reactions so far, however, they had been right in advising her not to fret.

"It was . . . unusual," the marquis said in a thoughtful tone. "I assume the details were accurate?"

"We spent a lot of time getting it right," Kim said. "I think climbing roses would have been easier."

The marquis laughed. "So someone told you that that's what the young ladies normally do. This was much more original and memorable, believe me." His face grew serious. "It's a bit like the Cinderella fairy tale for you, isn't it? Except that you've had a magician for a godfather instead of a fairy godmother."

"And my clothes won't turn to rags at midnight," Kim said

lightly. "And I don't have to try to dance in glass slippers." *And Cinderella didn't have to be talked into it; she* wanted *to go to the ball.*

"I can't imagine how your magical godfather happened to overlook so many important details," the marquis said, shaking his head in mock sadness. "It seems a shocking oversight."

"He's . . . had a lot on his mind," Kim said.

"At least he has not stinted in the matter of handsome princes," Lord Franton said. "There seem to be any number of candidates eager to apply for the position." He nodded in the direction of the still-faintly-glowering young man who had hoped to take Kim in to supper.

"Well, it's a good thing there are," Kim said, falling in with his bantering tone. "The Prince of Wales is above my touch, and the only other prince I know of is Prince Durmontov. He was invited, but he's away until next week."

"Ah?" Lord Franton gave her a sharp look. "Perhaps that is as well for the rest of us." He did not pursue the matter further, but instead turned the conversation to Mairelon's exploits during the French war. He seemed quite disappointed when Kim professed ignorance of any details.

"You'll have to ask Mairelon about that," Kim told him. "Or Hunch; he was there for a lot of it."

"Hunch?" Lord Franton looked puzzled.

"He's . . ." Kim hesitated, unable to think of a suitable description. "He works for Mairelon."

Lord Franton nodded. "I wanted to join the army, when I was younger," he said a little wistfully. "I even thought about running away and enlisting."

"You did? Why? I mean, why didn't you?"

"Responsibilities. By the time I would have been old enough, I was the heir to the title and there was no getting out of it." He grimaced. "The army is much too risky a place for a future marquis."

"Oh." Kim found it difficult to understand why anyone would want to hare off to some foreign country in order to eat short rations and get shot at, but it wouldn't do to say so. Still, it was one thing to join up because you didn't want to see the French marching up High Holborn, and quite another to go off just because you wanted an "adventure." Toffs could be incomprehensible.

Lord Franton seemed to sense her mood, and did not pursue the subject. Instead, he amused her with unexpected comments and stories about the dignified ladies and gentlemen conversing with such elegance around the tables. It made Kim feel much more at ease to learn that the formidable Lord Benton was still known as "Piggy" because he had fallen off his horse into a sty during his second hunt, that the Carringtons kept eight pug dogs at their house in Town and a great many more at their country seat, and that the correct Lady Catherine Abelside had tried to elope with her dancing master two weeks into her first Season.

After dinner, the dancing resumed. The last of the guests did not depart until nearly three in the morning. With evident satisfaction, Lady Wendall pronounced the party a triumph, and sent Kim off to bed, warning her once again to be sure to stay late in bed the following day.

"Casting that illusion was more draining than you will have realized, and with the rest of the evening's excitement, you will be far more tired than you expect," Lady Wendall said.

"I will make your excuses to any callers," Mrs. Lowe put in.

Kim nodded, though receiving callers had never been prominent among her reasons for getting up in the morning, and went up the stairs, her head still whirling with the dizzying idea that she, Kim, was an unqualified social success.

EIGHTEEN

Despite Lady Wendall's warning, Kim was amazed to find that it was long after noon the following day by the time she awoke. When she came downstairs, she was further astonished—and a bit dismayed—by the size of the stack of cards and invitations that had accumulated while she slept. Her dismay proved well-founded. When Lady Wendall reviewed them, dealing out the invitations with all the concentration of a cardsharp dealing to a bunch of flats, the pile of engagements to be accepted was enormous.

The remainder of the week passed in a dizzying round of social activity. Kim drove in the park with no less than four gentlemen, including Lord Franton; attended a Venetian breakfast, two balls, three dinner parties, and a card party; and paid and received more calls than she could keep track of. Lord Franton called twice and turned up at dinners, balls, and assemblies with such regularity that Kim suspected he had somehow got hold of her schedule.

She hardly saw Mairelon at all, for though he accompanied Kim and Lady Wendall to a few of the events, he generally excused himself the moment they entered the doors and went off to the card rooms. After the second ball, Kim realized that he only joined them at events where Shoreham or Kerring was likely to be present, and he could speak with them privately. It seemed excessive to her, when Mairelon already spent most of his days in one or another of their offices, but the deepening lines in Mairelon's face prohibited comment.

As far as Kim could tell, there had still been no progress in defeating the spell that had removed Mairelon's magic. She did not like to ask; refraining from making irritating comments was practically the only thing she could do to help. Two days after her come-out ball, she tentatively brought up, for the second time, the subject of talking to Jemmy and Wags, and was informed that they had dropped out of sight as completely as had Mannering, at least as far as Shoreham's informants were concerned. Privately, Kim was convinced that her chances of locating them were much better than Shoreham's, but with all her social commitments, she did not have an unsupervised moment in which to try, even if she had been willing to break her promise to Mairelon not to do so.

She began to look forward with considerable anticipation to Prince Durmontov's return to the city. At least talking with the prince would give Mairelon something new to do, rather than just sitting around fretting himself to flinders.

Kim was not the only one who had noticed Mairelon's erratic social performance. At Lady Souftmore's rout-party, a week after Kim's come-out, she was accosted by Letitia Tarnower, who paid her several compliments as fulsome as they were insincere and then said, "I cannot help but wonder that your guardian does not accompany you. Shall we see him later in the evening?"

"No," Kim said. "He's working on something."

Letitia raised her eyebrows. "He is very devoted to his work, then?"

"Yes," Kim said. "Excuse me; I think Lady Wendall wants me for something."

She made her escape, but spent the next hour wondering whether she ought not to have made a push to find out more from Miss Tarnower. She felt as if she ought to tell Mairelon about the conversation, but there was so little to tell that when she imagined herself repeating it to him, she felt foolish.

Her preoccupation continued, and after answering Mr. Cromie twice at random and throwing Lord Rencombe into a pother by the unguarded remark that his mother strongly resembled one of the apple women in Covent Garden, Kim decided that she had better get out of the crush and think for a moment.

The throng of guests made escape difficult and privacy all but impossible. Kim checked several of the small rooms along the hall, only to find them filled with card players. She returned to the ballroom, hoping that a corner of the balcony might be empty and quiet.

The glass balcony doors had been blocked off by a China silk screen placed several feet in front of them to prevent drafts. Kim rounded the edge just in time to see Letitia Tarnower step out onto the balcony. Another encounter with Letitia was the last thing Kim wanted; fortunately, Letitia hadn't seen her. As she moved away from the screen and back into the ballroom, she saw Lord Gideon Starnes coming toward it from the opposite side, scanning the crowd anxiously over his shoulder as if to see whether anyone was following him. He hesitated briefly, then slipped behind the screen. An instant later, Kim saw the tops of the balcony doors open and close, the movement only just visible above the silk screen.

Uneasy curiosity warred briefly with Lady Wendall's instructions on proper behavior. Curiosity won. Kim eased herself behind the screen and pushed the near door open a cautious inch, then backed into the shadows behind the brocade curtains, where she was not likely to be seen from outside, and set herself to listen.

"—can't mean that!" Lord Starnes was saying in low, passionate tones.

"Really, Gideon, don't be absurd," said a light female voice that Kim had no trouble identifying as Letitia Tarnower's. "I most certainly can and do mean it."

"After all your promises, you could not be so heartless!"

"Promises? Stuff! I was seven years old, and you no more than ten. It was children's play, no more."

"I felt it more," Lord Starnes said heavily. "I thought you did, as well."

"No, Gideon, you *haven't* thought," Letitia said. "I do feel something for you, but what of it? You haven't a feather to fly with, and I *won't* spend the rest of my life scrimping and fending off bailiffs the way Mama has."

"If it's only the money—"

"If *you* had spent your life penny-pinching and wearing made-over dresses, you wouldn't say that it was *only* the money," Letitia replied sharply, and for once Kim found herself in sympathy with the other girl. "This is my once chance at something better, and I don't intend to waste it, Gideon."

"But I'll *have* money soon," Lord Starnes protested. "More than enough. If you will only wait . . ."

Letitia gave a tinkling laugh. "What is it this time, a sure thing in the races at Newmarket? Or will you stake your stickpin on the turn of a card, and mend your fortunes with the winnings? And when that doesn't come through, you'll ask me to wait for a cockfight that's certain to pay you a hundred to one, or for the dice to favor you. No. If you have your fortune in hand before I get Humphreys or Merrill up to scratch, you may speak to me about it then, but I won't gamble my future on your luck."

Kim's budding sympathy evaporated. It shouldn't have been a shock to hear Letitia state her intentions toward Mairelon so baldly, not after the way the girl had been behaving, but a shock it was, nonetheless.

"Lord Humphreys," Lord Starnes said with disgust. "He's ten years older than your father!"

"So much the better," Letitia replied. "I won't have to put up with him for long."

"And Merrill. Of all people, why Richard Merrill?"

Kim tensed; she had been wondering that herself. Mairelon didn't seem the kind of person that would attract someone as relentlessly social as Letitia Tarnower.

"He's wealthy, he's well-connected, and he's the sort that will be so preoccupied with his little magical projects that he won't notice or care what his wife does," Letitia answered promptly. "I'd thought of that Russian Prince Durmontov for a while, but he's a bit too wide awake to suit me, and he's the sort everyone watches. Merrill isn't so prominent that the old cats will scrutinize every step his wife takes. That ward of his will have a harder time than she thinks once she's married to Lord Franton."

"Is that settled?" Lord Starnes said, momentarily distracted. "Because I haven't seen him here tonight, and I've got a bet in the book at White's . . ."

"No, it's not settled and he isn't here, but anyone can see which way the wind is blowing," Letitia said. "And everyone can also see you making a cake of yourself every time I'm at a party. I wish you wouldn't."

"But Letitia, I love you!" Lord Starnes said desperately.

"Yes, you've said so often enough," Letitia said. "About once a month for the past three years, ever since I turned fifteen. And you're quite personable, and very amusing when you aren't pouring your heart out at my feet, and I do like you. But one can't live on love and wit, my dear. Find yourself an heiress, and let me be."

"You are entirely heartless."

"No, merely practical. And if you cannot behave yourself in company, I do not wish to see you again. Do I make myself clear, Lord Starnes?"

"Abundantly."

"Then I give you good evening." There was a rustle of skirts and Kim shrank back into the curtains as the balcony door opened. To her relief, Letitia Tarnower swept out into the ballroom without glancing around. Kim gave her a moment to get clear, then slipped around the far edge of the silk screen. She'd heard all there was to hear, and Lord Starnes would be leaving the balcony, too, in another minute.

Kim's mind was in considerable turmoil. Mairelon had been quite right; Letitia Tarnower was not the widgeon she pretended to be. Indeed, if she had settled on anyone other than Mairelon as a prospective husband, Kim would have been more than a little sympathetic to her position. *If it was anyone but Mairelon .. . .* And *was* everyone expecting the marquis to make an offer of marriage for Kim?

The rest of the evening seemed to drag on forever. Kim was even more distracted and preoccupied than before, until she noticed Lady Souftmore and Mrs. Lowe exchanging significant looks. After that, she exerted herself to pay attention, but though the gentlemen redoubled their efforts to be charming, she was considerably relieved when the time came to leave at last.

When they arrived back at Grosvenor Square, Kim lingered in the hall for a moment to charge the footman not to let Mairelon out of the house next morning until he had spoken with her. She still wasn't sure what she was going to tell him, or what good it might do if she did. *At least maybe it'll distract him some.*

As she reached the top of the first flight of stairs, she saw a gleam of light coming from the half-open library door. Curious, she stepped forward and peered around the door.

The fire had died to embers; the light she had seen came from a single candle, burned down to barely an inch above the socket, which stood near the far end of the library table. Next to the candle stood a cut-glass brandy decanter, over half empty. Slumped in the chair at the end of the table, cradling a glass in both hands, was Mairelon. His dark hair looked as if he had run his hands through it several times, and there were shadows like bruises under his eyes. *He looks as if he hasn't slept in a week,* Kim thought, and unconsciously took another step forward.

The movement attracted Mairelon's attention, and he looked up. He frowned for a moment, as if collecting his thoughts from somewhere very far away, and then said, "Ah, Kim! Come in and toast your good fortune." His voice had an unfamiliar, almost mocking edge to it.

"My good fortune?" Kim stepped into the room and studied Mairelon for a moment. "You're foxed," she said in mild surprise. She'd never seen Mairelon even a bit on the go before, not for real, though she'd seen him play the part once or twice.

"I'm not foxed yet," Mairelon said. "The decanter isn't

empty. There's another glass somewhere; sit down and join me."

Uncertainly, Kim pulled up another chair and sat down on his right. Mairelon blinked owlishly at her. "Don't look so glum," he said, the mocking edge strong in his voice. "You should be celebrating. Though I'll grant you, the prospect of congratulating Aunt Agatha on her perspicacity might take some of the satisfaction out of it."

"You *are* foxed," Kim said. "What are you on about?"

Mairelon raised his eyebrows. "Dear me, don't you know?"

"No, I don't." Kim clenched both hands in her lap to hold in her temper.

Mairelon's eyes narrowed and he studied her for a moment; then he sat back, his mouth twisted in a self-mocking smile. "Ah. Obviously I was mistaken."

"*Mairelon,*" Kim said, exasperated. "You're just as annoying foxed as you are sober. Mistaken about what? What are you talking about?"

"Lord Franton, Marquis of Harsfeld, visited me earlier today," Mairelon said. "He asked my permission to pay his addresses to you."

"He—You mean that Tarnower chit was *right*? He's going to make me an *offer*?"

"I believe that is what I just said." Mairelon sank down in his chair, studying his brandy glass. "He seemed to have no doubt about your answer."

"He wouldn't," Kim said in disgust. "Of all the sapskulled things to do! I don't want to marry a toff, and certainly not a marquis!"

Abruptly, Mairelon's eyes focused on her with alarming intensity. "You don't?"

"Well, I don't have anything against marquises in general," Kim said, considering. "But I don't want to marry Lord Franton."

"Why not?" Mairelon said, still with the same intense focus. "He's rich, he's titled, he's nearer your age than . . . He's near your age. And Aunt Agatha was quite right—you couldn't be better established than to marry a marquis."

Kim shook her head, searching for words. "If all I wanted was money . . . Lord Franton's nice enough, but . . ."

"You're not still worried about being socially acceptable, are you?" The edge was back in Mairelon's voice. "Not after the triumphs of the past week!"

"Triumphs!" Kim snorted. "I'm a novelty, like a performing bear, that's all."

Mairelon's eyes dropped to his glass. In a completely colorless tone, he said, "Lord Franton doesn't seem to think so."

"Lord Franton ain't got no sense," Kim said flatly.

"I didn't think him so utterly senseless as that," Mairelon said, and an odd smile flickered over his lips.

"Well, you ain't got no sense sometimes, neither," Kim retorted. "Thinking I'd get leg-shackled to a marquis just because— If I'd of been that interested in money, I wouldn't of worked so hard to stay out of the stews all those years."

Mairelon blinked, plainly startled. "It's not the same thing at all."

"It ain't?" Kim shook her head and shivered slightly. The brothels of Southwark had been among her worst nightmares since she had first learned of their existence when she was five or six. "Marrying a marquis because he's rich and titled would be more comfortable and more permanent than working Vauxhall or Drury Lane, but I can't see that there's much other difference."

"Ah. I had never considered it in that light." Mairelon raised his glass and drank, then set it too-carefully on the table.

"Jenny Correy didn't marry Tom because he was well off,

because he wasn't, then," Kim went on, half to herself. "And a lot of folks said she was throwing herself away on him, when she could have had Barnabas Totten, who's got his own pub, or Henry Miller down at the shipyard. But Jenny and Tom are a lot happier than the ones who picked the best catch. They . . . like each other, and they get on well. Most of the time. More than anybody else I know, anyway."

"I am justly chastened," Mairelon said, sounding more like himself. "Is there, perhaps, some other gentleman among your suitors whose addresses you *would* welcome? The marquis gave me to understand that he knew he was being a bit hasty, but he was desirous of, er, beating the competition to the gate."

"You mean he thinks I'm going to get *more* offers?" Kim said, appalled.

"He doesn't seem to be the only one who thinks so," Mairelon said. "Aunt Agatha mentioned it to me yesterday afternoon. *Is* there anyone, or would you prefer that I turn the lot of them away?"

Kim shook her head. "There isn't anyone."

Except you.

The revelation was so blindingly sudden that the words almost slipped out, and she had to bite her tongue and look away. *And you thought Lord Franton hadn't got any sense,* she castigated herself. But sense had nothing to do with it. She swallowed hard, and tears stung her eyelids. If a beauty like Letitia Tarnower couldn't interest Mairelon, and a brilliant wizard like Renée D'Auber hadn't attracted him in all the years they'd known one another, what chance did she, Kim, have?

"Kim. . . ." There was a long pause, and then Mairelon said in an altered tone, "You know, I believe you are right; I *have* had a little too much of this brandy."

With a lightness she did not feel, Kim replied, "If you

hadn't, you wouldn't have been so nattered about Lord Franton. Silly clunch."

"Is that remark meant for me, or for Franton?" Mairelon said. "Never mind. If anyone else wishes to propose to you, I shall send him away, but I'm afraid you'll have to deal with the marquis yourself."

"I don't—" A prickle swept across her shoulder blades, and she stiffened and broke off in midsentence. After a moment, she realized that she had cocked her head as if she were listening for something, which was ridiculous—you couldn't hear magic. "Something just touched the houseward," she told Mairelon. "It's still up, but—" Another twinge interrupted her. "There it goes again."

"A probing spell?" Mairelon said urgently. "Or a steady pressure?"

"Not steady," Kim answered. "Not really like a probe, either, at least, not like the ones your mother showed me. More like—" she groped for the image, "—like somebody throwing a rock through a window and running away."

"Probably nothing that needs immediate attention, then," Mairelon said. "I hope it didn't wake Mother."

Kim nodded. In the silence that followed, they heard a loud creak from the lower stairway. Immediately, Mairelon leaned forward and pinched out the candle. In the dim glow from the dying embers of the fire, he rose and made his way carefully to the library door, where he flattened himself against the wall. After a moment's thought, Kim also stood. Taking care not to make any noise, she slipped toward the bookshelves behind the door. There was nothing she could do about the pallor of her lilac gown, but at least she would be out of the line of sight of anyone entering the room.

There was another creak, louder and nearer, and then the library door swung wide and a dark figure entered. Mairelon waited until the man had passed him, then kicked the door shut and jumped. The two shapes went down with a thump. Kim snatched up a vase, then hesitated, unable to tell which figure to brain with it.

"I have him," Mairelon's voice said a moment later. "If you'd be good enough to manage the lights, Kim? I'm a bit occupied at the moment.

"*Fiat lux,*" Kim said hastily, and a rather wavery ball of light appeared above the two combatants. She frowned and concentrated more carefully, and the light steadied.

"Well, well," Mairelon said. "Lord Gideon Starnes. To what do we owe the pleasure of this unusual call, my lord?"

NINETEEN

Lord Starnes stared at Mairelon for a moment, and then all of the tension left his body and he sagged toward the floor. "It *would* be you," he said bitterly, and his words slurred very slightly as he spoke. "I suppose now you'll tell her, and I'll have no chance at all."

"I should be more concerned about my telling the Runners, if I were you," Mairelon said.

"I haven't done anything," Lord Starnes said with as much dignity as he could manage while lying on his back with Mairelon half-kneeling on top of him.

"Breaking into a house is something," Kim pointed out. "Even if you aren't very good at it."

"And especially when it's the second time," Mairelon said.

Lord Starnes jerked. "How did you— It wasn't me!"

"Looby," Kim said. "If we hadn't guessed before, we'd know now." Holding the light spell steady, she crossed to the table and relit the candle, then fetched two more from the candlebox and lit them as well. It looked as if this was going to take awhile, and she wasn't sure how long she could keep the spell going, especially if Lord Starnes was going to start saying things interesting enough to distract her.

"Very good, Kim," Mairelon said when she finished with the candles and let the light spell fade. "Now, Lord Starnes, I should dislike having to summon the Watch or lay information against you in Bow Street—but I shouldn't dislike it enough to keep me from doing it. You had better explain."

"And hurry up, before the rest of the house gets here," Kim advised.

"Oh, that won't be a problem," Mairelon said. "I made it quite clear that I didn't want to be disturbed this evening."

Kim frowned, but she couldn't ask him anything in front of Lord Starnes, even if Starnes was, as he appeared to be, considerably more foxed than Mairelon.

"Letitia will never have me now," Lord Starnes said miserably at that moment, drawing Mairelon's attention back to him.

"Letitia?" Mairelon frowned. "Not the Tarnower chit? What has she got to do with you breaking into Andrew's library?"

"She told him to sheer off, tonight at Lady Souftmore's rout," Kim said. "She's hanging out for a rich husband, and he wouldn't be one."

Mairelon gave her an inquiring look.

"They were talking out on the balcony and I . . . happened to overhear," Kim said. "I was going to tell you, but we got to discussing other things."

"I can't imagine why you thought I would be interested in Letitia Tarnower's *amours*," Mairelon said. "No doubt you had your reasons."

"That wasn't all they were talking about. I'll tell you later."

"Do you mean that?" Lord Starnes said, raising his head. His voice was suddenly hopeful.

"Of course she means it," Mairelon said.

"No, did you mean what you said about Letitia—Miss Tarnower, that is?"

Mairelon frowned. "Do you know, I was under the impression that *I* was the one who was going to be asking questions and *you* were the one who was going to answer them. I can't think how I made such a mistake. Possibly it has something to do with the brandy."

"What brandy?" Lord Starnes said, bewildered. "I wasn't drinking brandy; I was drinking gin."

No wonder he hadn't noticed the smell on Mairelon's breath. Kim sighed and plopped into the nearest chair. If the two of them kept it up, this would take even longer than she had thought.

"Is that why you broke into my brother's house?" Mairelon said politely. "Because you've been drinking gin?"

"Of course not," Lord Starnes said. "Can't expect to find Blue Ruin in a place like this."

"Why not?" Mairelon said. "The cellars at Osterly House are half full of it, and the Racknetts practically bathe in the stuff. Not to mention—"

"Why *did* you come, then?" Kim interrupted before Mairelon ended up enumerating every gentry ken in town at which one could perfectly well expect to find gin in great quantities.

"I came for the book," Lord Starnes said.

"That, we know," Mairelon said. "The question is, why? It isn't good for anything."

"It is the key to a fortune!" Lord Starnes said dramatically, then broke out in a coughing fit. "Could you move your knee?" he asked Mairelon plaintively when he recovered.

"If I move my knee, I won't be able to balance," Mairelon said. "Get up, and we'll sit down at the table and talk in comfort."

"Oh, very well," Lord Starnes said.

They rearranged themselves according to this program, while Kim shifted impatiently in her chair. Then Mairelon looked at Lord Starnes and said, "Now, about this fortune?"

"It was the wizards," Lord Starnes explained. "The Frenchies. There were seven of 'em, and they knew the Terror was coming, so they put all their valuables in a secret vault and locked it with a spell. They each put part of the spell in a book, because they didn't trust each other, y'see, and then they left France. And the vault is still there, with a fortune in it seven times over, because they never went back. But it takes all seven books to get in."

"Fascinating," Mairelon murmured. "And how do you come to know all this?"

"M'grandfather knew one of 'em," Lord Starnes confessed. Having begun, he seemed almost eager to tell his story. "Fellow he met at a concert in Vienna, named d'Armand. They hit it off wonderfully, and d'Armand told him the whole story and gave my grandfather his book for fear of losing it."

"That sounds extremely unlikely," Mairelon said. "Especially since d'Armand was killed very soon after he left France. Have some brandy."

Lord Starnes shrugged as he took the glass Mairelon proffered. "My grandfather had d'Armand's book, and he said that d'Armand must have had a what-you-call-it, a vision that he was going to die, because a week later he drowned. And since grandfather didn't know any of the other Frenchies, and had no idea how to get in touch with them, he didn't do anything."

"That sounds even more unlikely," Mairelon said.

"You never met my grandfather." Lord Starnes sighed. "Lucky man."

"Me, or your grandfather? Never mind. What made you

decide to collect the rest of the books? I assume that is what you have in mind—collect all seven of the books and claim the fortune."

"Letitia Tarnower," Kim said. "That's what did it. I told you, she's hanging out for a rich husband."

"I will hear no word against Miss Tarnower," Lord Starnes said belligerently.

"No one has spoken any," Mairelon reassured him. "About these books—"

Lord Starnes heaved a sigh. "I would never have thought of it myself. But Mannering assured me that no one would know, and it would be the making of both of us."

Kim's eyes widened, and she and Mairelon exchanged glances. "Mannering?" Kim said in a careful tone.

"Yes, he's a cent-per-cent, a moneylender, that I've done business with," Lord Starnes said. Kim nodded, and helpfully refilled his glass. Lord Starnes took an absentminded pull and went on, "I gave him d'Armand's book last year as collateral, along with some other things. I thought he'd take it because he has a great interest in wizardry, though I didn't realize at the time that he was one himself."

"He isn't," Kim said before she could stop herself.

"I've seen him work spells myself," Lord Starnes contradicted her.

"When was that?" Mairelon said.

"About a month ago, right after he offered to take me into partnership over this French vault," Lord Starnes answered. His shoulders sagged. "I didn't realize he wanted a lot of poking and prying and sneaking into people's houses. I thought we'd just quietly buy up the other books somehow, and then I'd go to France and . . . and . . . collect everything."

"I see." Mairelon rubbed his chin thoughtfully. "And when

did you discover that the business was more complex than you had anticipated?"

"When Mannering sent me to get the first two books," Lord Starnes said. "I thought—but he gave me a couple of twigs that he'd set spells in and told me to break into the house. It was some awful place north of the city—"

"Not Hampstead?" Mairelon said.

"No, but near there, I think," Starnes replied. "It took me forever to find it, and then when I got inside it was a regular rabbit's warren. Books everywhere, stacks of them, in the drawing room and the dining room and even the *bedrooms!* I could only find one of the ones Mannering wanted. I think they only *had* one—they were the two wizards who were supposed to be married, you know, and what would they want with one each? Especially when they had all those others. But Mannering was very upset about it."

"Ah, that would be the Comte du Franchard and the Comtesse de Beauvoix," Mairelon said, refilling Starnes's glass once more.

Lord Starnes didn't notice. "Yes, that's right, the comte and comtesse. And then we had to track down the book you have, and I didn't manage to get hold of it, either." Lord Starnes sighed. "Mannering was livid. Said that if I couldn't get him the book, I'd have to make payments on the loan he'd given me! I had to go down to White's and it's a dashed good thing the cards were in my favor that night. Most of it."

"Is that when you lost your ring to Lord Moule?" Mairelon said. "The gold one with the ruby center?"

"Now, how did you know about that?" Lord Starnes said, astonished.

"Magic," Kim told him.

"Oh, of course." Lord Starnes tried to look intelligent. Failing, he took another drink of brandy instead.

"It's obvious how you were planning to, er, acquire the books that were here in England," Mairelon said thoughtfully. "But how were you planning to get hold of the Russian book? And the Hungarian one? Or didn't you know about them?"

"Oh, I knew the books weren't all in England," Lord Starnes said. "That's one of the reasons I never bothered to try for the seven of them myself. But Mannering said he'd arrange for the other two to be brought to London, and Durmontov showed up right on schedule. Whatever it was, it doesn't seem to have worked with the Hungarian, though."

"So Prince Alexei Durmontov is also involved in this interesting scheme of yours?" Mairelon kept his voice carefully neutral.

Lord Starnes looked startled. "No, of course not. If we'd gotten him involved, we'd have to split the money with him. No, no, Mannering tricked him somehow."

"That explains it," Kim said, topping off Lord Starnes's glass again.

"It didn't occur to you, I suppose, that the surviving wizards might want their belongings themselves?" Mairelon said in a deceptively mild tone.

"They've gotten along without them for thirty years," Starnes said sullenly. "If they wanted the treasure back, they should have made some push to get at it. And anyway, they can't get in without d'Armand's book."

Kim shook her head incredulously. "So you and Mannering decided to lighten *six wizards*? Of all the cloth-headed notions! Nobody with any sense tries to crack a frogmaker's ken, let alone six of 'em. It's too chancy."

"I'm a bit of a wizard myself," Lord Starnes said with dignity. "I got past your wards tonight, after all."

"It didn't do you much good, did it?" Kim retorted. "And anyway, you didn't get past them. You set off all the warning spells."

"I was afraid it was three circles, and not two," Lord Starnes muttered, suddenly deflated. "But if I'd gotten the spell right—"

Kim snorted. "It still wouldn't have done you no good. Amateurs! Magic won't help if you can't even put your feet down careful."

Mairelon's mouth twitched in amusement. "Yes, well, no doubt he didn't anticipate running across an expert on the crack lay," he said to Kim.

"Part of the job is looking ahead," Kim said crossly. "He should of known I was here."

"Should have known," Mairelon corrected. He leaned forward, and Kim saw an almost undetectable tension in his shoulders. "I don't suppose you know where Mannering is at the moment?" he asked Lord Starnes in a casual tone.

Lord Starnes shook his head. "He's gotten very . . . strange these last few weeks," he said in a confidential tone. "Flies out at people for no reason, that sort of thing. And then a week and a half ago, he closed his office. I was afraid he'd got hold of the other books without me and gone off to France, but it turned out it was no such thing."

"And how do you know that, if you haven't seen Mannering in a week and a half?" Mairelon said.

"Oh, I've *seen* him. Twice. I just don't know where he is."

Mairelon and Kim looked at him in wordless expectation.

"He sent me a note," Lord Starnes explained. "And then I went down to meet him at some warehouse off the docks. It was a dreadful place, worse than Hampstead. Took my valet half a day to get the smell of fish out of my coat."

"You said you'd seen him twice," Mairelon said, emptying the last of the brandy into Lord Starnes's glass. "Was it the same warehouse both times?"

"No. The second one was even worse." Starnes shuddered in remembrance. "Mannering didn't look well, either. I think his brain is turning. He talked of sending a couple of footpads after that Russian fellow. What's the point in that, when we've already got his copy of the book?"

"Footpads?" Mairelon said thoughtfully. "What a good thing for the prince that he's out of town."

"I've thought a couple of times that I'd be better off out of it," Lord Starnes said. "But there's Letitia. . . ."

"Yes, well, I doubt that Miss Tarnower will look favorably on your suit if you end up in gaol."

Lord Starnes' eyes widened. "I hadn't thought of that. But you know, you're right." He emptied his glass and gazed mournfully into the bottom.

Kim rolled her eyes. Mairelon gave her a stern look and said to Starnes, "You go home and think it over. If you have any more messages from this Mannering fellow, let me know and I'll deal with him. But if you do any more breaking into houses or stealing books—or even merely *trying* to steal them—I'll be down in Bow Street the next morning. Is that clear?"

Lord Starnes was initially disposed to argue, but between them, Kim and Mairelon got him out of the house at last, with the clear understanding that he was not to attempt any more amateur burglaries.

"Do you think he'll remember in the morning?" Kim said as they watched Lord Starnes wobble off down the street.

"He'll have the devil of a head after mixing gin and

brandy, but he's not so well to live that he'll forget what happened." Mairelon rubbed his forehead. "Neither am I, though I almost wish I were. The more we find out, the less sense any of it makes. If this keeps up, I'll be ready for Bedlam by the end of the week."

Kim swallowed hard as the memory of Ma Yanger rose unbidden in her mind. "Don't joke about it."

"What? No." Mairelon sighed. "I'm too tired to think straight now; it'll have to wait until morning. Don't run off with one of your swains tomorrow until we've had a chance to talk."

"I won't," Kim told his back as it retreated up the stairs.

TWENTY

K im did not get to sleep for a long time; she had too much to think about. She was no more satisfied with Lord Starnes's explanation than Mairelon had been—it left too many things unexplained. How could Mannering have so suddenly become a wizard? Who was the foreign wizard who had left those spells in English on Mannering's desk? And if Mannering was working with a foreigner, which of them had ensorcelled Ma Yanger and Mairelon? And why had they bothered? There seemed to be no connection between the spells and the supposed fortune that Lord Starnes was so eager to obtain, though it was certainly plausible that Mannering would be more than a little interested in the money.

On top of Lord Starnes and Mannering, Kim was concerned about Mairelon. He was taking the loss of his magic even harder than she'd realized, if he'd started drinking nights in the library. But the most disturbing thing of all, to which she kept returning like a tongue probing a sore tooth, was the realization that she had fallen in love with her guardian.

When had it happened? She wasn't quite sure. At their first meeting, she had feared his magic, but that had not lasted more than fifteen or twenty minutes. The often-exasperated fondness that had replaced the fear wasn't love. Nor was the gratitude she felt because he had taken her out of the precarious street life that was all she had known until then, nor the also-often-exasperated respect that she had learned for him as a teacher, nor the equally exasperated friendship that surfaced when they were poking around some problem together. Exasperation, in fact, seemed to be a keynote of her feelings toward Mairelon. Was that how you fell in love with someone, then—by getting exasperated with him?

It had certainly worked with Mairelon, though to the best of her recollection he had never shown any feeling for her except a mild and absentminded affection. Maybe she should try to make him exasperated with her. Kim sighed. Attractive as the idea was, she doubted that it would help any, even if she could manage to do it. Mairelon was harder to annoy than anyone she'd ever known; it was one of the things that made him so exasperating. She smiled fondly, then caught herself. Rolling over, she punched her pillow hard in frustration.

Stupid, stupid, stupid. Even if she could, by some miracle, get Mairelon to reciprocate her sentiments, what good would it be? For all his turns as a marketplace performer, Mairelon was a gentleman born, and she didn't know how to be a toff's wife. She didn't know how to be *anyone's* wife. She barely knew how to be a girl.

I used to be good at ignoring what I wanted, when I knew it was impossible. What happened? But she knew what had happened: she'd spent a year in Mairelon's company, learning wizardry and having dreams come true that she hadn't even known she'd had. And anyway, you couldn't ignore anyone as exasperating as Mairelon.

She buried her head in the pillow. *I am going to sleep. There is no point in thinking about this. I am going to sleep. Now.*

Eventually, she did. But she did not sleep well, and when she went down to breakfast the following morning, Mrs. Lowe commented that she appeared to have been overdoing her social life.

"Yes, you do look a bit hagged," Lady Wendall said. "Perhaps we should not go to Lady Sefton's tonight, after all."

Before Kim could answer, the door opened and Mairelon entered. He looked tired and drawn, and he winced a little at the light from the windows, but his expression was nonetheless more cheerful than she had seen it in several days. "Ah, good, you're up, Kim," he said. "Are you free of engagements this morning? I'd like you to join me on an errand or two."

"Richard," Mrs. Lowe said reprovingly, "we were just commenting that Kim has been doing too much. It would be much better for her to stay home and rest."

"I don't mind," Kim said quickly. If she had to miss something, she'd rather it was a fashionable do at Lady Sefton's than a few hours of Mairelon's company.

"You're sure?" An uncertain, anxious look crossed Mairelon's face.

It was gone in a moment, so quickly that even Lady Wendall did not notice, but Kim frowned. *This has to have something to do with his magic.* "Of course I'm sure," she said.

"That's all right, then," Mairelon said in a tone of mild relief that was altogether at odds with that brief expression of uncertainty. He picked up a plate and then hesitated, eyeing the eggs and sausage with evident doubt.

Mrs. Lowe frowned. "But, Richard—"

"I think it is a very good idea indeed," Lady Wendall interrupted. She had been looking sharply from Mairelon to Kim, but now she gave Mrs. Lowe her full attention. "We have been remiss in allowing Kim to fall behind in her magic lessons; and magic is, after all, a significant part of the good impression she has made. Of course she must go with Richard." She glanced at Mairelon and added sweetly, "And I am sure you will tell me *all* about it when you return."

"Oh, I doubt that there'll be much to tell," Mairelon said. "Errands are generally uneventful, you know."

"Not yours, dear," Lady Wendall replied.

Feeling considerably more cheerful herself, Kim applied herself to her breakfast. Mairelon did not eat much, so they finished at about the same time. "Don't forget your sunshade this time, Kim," Mrs. Lowe advised as they rose to leave.

Kim made a face, but made sure she had it with her as they left the house. Not listening to another one of Mrs. Lowe's thundering scolds was worth the minor inconvenience of carrying a parasol, especially since she could always leave it in the carriage.

"Where are we going?" she asked Mairelon as he handed her into the coach.

"The George," Mairelon said as he settled into the seat opposite. "If Prince Alexei Durmontov is back, they'll be the first to know where he's putting up; he'll have to let them know where to send his mail. And if the prince hasn't returned, someone may have an idea where he's gone. I don't like the sound of those footpads Starnes was talking about last night."

Kim frowned. Then, reluctantly but unable to resist asking, she said, "Why do you want me along for that?"

The coach began to move. Mairelon hesitated, then, with an evident reluctance more than equal to Kim's, said, "I promised Shoreham I wouldn't go anywhere without someone along who can handle protective spells."

"What?" Kim stared. "You mean, that's why you haven't gone anywhere unless Shoreham or Kerring was around?"

"Shoreham's worried about another attack," Mairelon said. "I think he's wrong; the only time the house-wards have even been tested was last night, and that turned out to be the congenial Lord Starnes. But that's Shoreham for you."

"And you're counting *me* as a wizard?" Kim said, completely thunderstruck. She wasn't nearly good enough for something like this; she could barely handle a standard warding spell!

"You've been doing the house-wards for a week and a half," Mairelon said in a low voice. "And Shoreham taught you Gerard's Refuge himself. Besides, I'm not anticipating any trouble."

"That's the problem," Kim grumbled. "You never do."

A reluctant smile tugged at the corners of Mairelon's mouth. "Never? Surely I haven't been *that* consistent."

Kim laughed in spite of herself. "I bet Hunch would agree with me."

"That's taking unfair advantage," Mairelon said.

"What's unfair about it?" Kim demanded.

The coach drew up outside the George, relieving Mairelon of the need to answer. Inside, the concierge informed them that Prince Durmontov had returned to town late the previous evening. It was a very great pity that they had not arrived a few minutes earlier; he had just that morning been to the George to pick up his letters. No, he had not left very long ago. Where? Probably on some errand. The prince did not discuss his schedule with the staff. Yes, he had had several messages waiting; Mr. Merrill's was undoubtedly among them. Well, he really wasn't supposed to talk about the guests' affairs, but since Mr. Merrill was so generous, and the prince was no longer really a guest . . . There had been a note from a lady—no direction, naturally, but quite clearly feminine in origin—and a number of invitations and cards, as well as two or three other personal notes, and a singularly odd missive delivered by a scruffy fellow with a sour disposition, not at all the sort that the George was accustomed to receiving. That one? Yes, now that Mr. Merrill mentioned it, it was after reading that note that the prince had left, and in a bit of a hurry. And he had asked for directions to Gray's Inn, though that was clearly not his destination; no gentleman would—

"Mannering owns a bowsing ken by Gray's Inn," Kim interrupted. "And around there, anyone who saw a couple of wild rogues taking a gentry cove would be careful not to take notice."

"We'll try that, then," Mairelon said. "Come on; if we hurry, we may catch up with him before they do." He tossed the concierge another guinea as they departed. As the carriage rattled over the cobblestones, Mairelon said, "Have you practiced Gerard's Refuge since Shoreham taught you?"

"A couple of times," Kim said warily. "Do you think we'll need it?"

"It's possible," Mairelon said. There was a new tension in his shoulders, and he leaned forward slightly in his seat as if urging the coach onward. "Mannering would be a fool to decoy a wizard without being prepared to deal with magic. And so far as we know, he's not a fool."

And we know how he deals with wizards. Kim shivered. No wonder Mairelon was in a hurry; the thought of another wizard falling prey to the same antimagic spell affecting him would make him wild.

"I don't suppose you'd be willing to stay in the carriage?" Mairelon went on, giving her a sideways look.

"No," Kim said firmly. "If anybody stays, it should be you. I'm just an apprentice; you're a wizard, and if they think you can do magic, they'll go for you first. And after the way we did the illusion at that ball, they have to think you can still do magic."

"That's true," Mairelon said, sounding more cheerful. "I'd forgotten."

Kim blinked. "Then you'll stay here?"

"What? No, of course not. With any luck—"

The carriage stopped abruptly, and they heard Hunch swearing from the coachman's perch. Mairelon opened the door and sprang out without waiting for the steps to be let down. "Cast the Refuge," he said over his shoulder, and ran forward.

Cursing her skirts, Kim struggled out of the carriage and looked around. Hunch was still occupied with the reins, though a groom had jumped down from the back of the coach and was running to take the horses' heads. Mairelon was halfway down a narrow, refuse-choked alley leading directly away from the carriage door. At the far end, two solidly built men with their faces wrapped in mufflers were dragging a third man toward a waiting cart. True to Kim's prediction, the few people in the vicinity were paying no attention whatever to the attack in progress; they seemed far more interested in the presence of a gentleman's coach-and-four in such an unlikely location.

Kim started forward, clutching her sunshade like a club. Then she heard the sharp-edged words of a spell coming from the far end of the alley, and hastily cast the refuge spell that Shoreham had taught her. An instant later, an enormous gout of flame exploded around the combatants, roaring from wall to wall as high as the second row of bricked-up windows, and she felt a magical pressure against her shield. Over the roaring of the flames came a loud, high-pitched whine that hurt the ears even as far back as Kim was standing.

The cart horse shied and bolted, taking the cart with it and leaving the attackers nowhere to take their victim. The attackers themselves lost interest in their erstwhile prey and ran hell-for-leather down the alley toward Kim. One of them slammed full tilt into Mairelon, and both men went down. The other villain continued toward Kim, oblivious to his companion's misfortune.

With great presence of mind, Kim stepped to one side and, as the runner passed her, thrust her sunshade between his feet. He fell headlong, and the force of his movement snapped the shaft of the sunshade in two. Before he could scramble to his feet once more, Kim sat down hard on his upper back, driving the breath out of his body. For the next moment or two, all the bully-boy could do was gasp for air, and by the time he at last managed to refill his lungs, Hunch had come up with them.

"You can get up now," Hunch told her. "I'll 'andle 'im if 'e tries anything."

Kim bounced once, just to make sure the fellow wasn't up to anything, and stood up.

"Get him into the carriage," Mairelon's voice said. Kim looked over her shoulder to find him standing behind her, half-supporting Prince Durmontov. The prince looked rather dazed, but seemed largely unharmed; Mairelon's coat sleeve was torn, his cravat had come half-undone, and he was liberally streaked with mud, but he, too, did not appear to be injured. "The other man got away, and I think there was a driver in that cart; there's no sense hanging around here until their reinforcements arrive."

The flames and the whining noise had stopped some time during Kim's encounter with the man she had captured. Glancing around, she was unsurprised to find the street deserted. Nobody wanted trouble with wizards.

Hunch nodded at Mairelon and hauled their prisoner to his feet. The man's muffler had come undone, and Kim blinked at him in surprise. "Jack Stower!"

"Well, well," Mairelon said. "This *is* going to be interesting. Into the carriage, Kim, Hunch."

Hunch pushed Jack forward without comment, but when they reached the coach, he frowned. "You ain't a-going to take this 'ere cove in there with you, are you?" he said.

"How else are we going to ask him anything?" Mairelon said. "He won't make any more trouble—not with three wizards keeping an eye on him."

Glowering, but unable to object publicly to this outrageous statement without giving Mairelon's incapacity away, Hunch did as he was told. A little nervously, Kim took the seat in the far corner from Jack; Mairelon helped the prince in opposite her, and slid in beside her himself. As the coach started off, he said, "Now, Mr. Stower, kindly explain your part in this little contretemps."

"I ain't sayin' nothing," Jack said sullenly.

"Very well," said Mairelon affably. "We'll just let Shoreham get it out of you. We're on our way to the Ministry now; I just thought it would save a little time if you talked to us first."

Prince Durmontov raised his head. "Ministry?" he said hazily. "What Ministry?"

"The Ministry of Wizardy," Mairelon said. "It's not far, and we'll take you back to the George after. Or wherever you prefer. You look rather done up."

"That spell is draining." The prince smiled a little wanly. "It is an old one, used in Russia to keep wolves off a sleigh. One use is all that is generally needed, so recovery does not need to be quick. If those men had soon returned, I would have been in . . . difficulty. I am in your debt."

"Spells," Jack said bitterly. "He said you didn't have no spells. Chicken-hearted gooseberry."

Kim felt Mairelon go tense beside her. "Mannering told you that?"

"How'd you know it was him?"

"Never you mind. What else did he tell you?"

Jack was disinclined to answer, but by the time they reached the Ministry, Mairelon had pried most of what he knew out of him. It was not much. Mannering had ordered Prince Durmontov brought to the cellar of a pub in Smithfield and left there; he had assured his men that Durmontov would not be capable of using spells against them; they were to pick up their payment from the clerk in Mannering's office the following day. Jack had no idea where Mannering was hiding, only that something had sent him scurrying for cover.

With that unsatisfactory information, they were forced to be content. They turned Jack over to Lord Shoreham, who accepted with equanimity Mairelon's muddy arrival and even muddier prisoner. Returning to the carriage, they found Prince Durmontov looking much more himself.

"Where now?" Mairelon said. "Back to the George?"

"No, if I may impose a little upon you," Prince Durmontov said. "I am concerned for family friends who may be also of interest to the man behind those—those—"

"Footpads," Kim offered.

"Yes," the prince said. "So I would like to go at once to Hampstead, to warn my friends."

TWENTY-ONE

K im and Mairelon stared at the prince for a long moment. "Hampstead?" Mairelon said at last.

"Yes, to Duc and Duchesse Delagardie," Prince Durmontov replied. "They are only just returned from Edinburgh, and—"

"By all means," Mairelon replied. "And we have a great deal to discuss on the way. How fortunate that it is such a long drive."

The prince blinked, but gave Hunch the direction. Hunch scowled disapprovingly at Mairelon, but climbed back onto the box without comment, and in a few moments they were under way once more.

"How is it that you know the duc and duchesse?" Mairelon asked.

"One of my aunts knew them many years ago in France," Durmontov replied. "It is, in fact, partially on their account that I came to England."

"That would be the former Mademoiselle Jeannette Lepain? One of the seven French wizards once known as *Les Grif-fonais?*"

"Yes," said the prince, frowning. "How is it you know this?"

"I have had occasion to find out," Mairelon said. "Perhaps it will enlighten you somewhat if I tell you that some years ago, my father purchased a copy of *Le Livre de Sept Sorciers: un livre de mémoire* by one Madame Marie de Cambriol, and that someone has twice tried to make off with it in the past month."

"Three times," Kim corrected.

"I don't think you can count Lord Starnes's little excursion last night," Mairelon said. "His heart really didn't seem to be in it."

"What is this?" the prince said, his frown deepening.

"Wait until we reach the duc and duchesse," Mairelon said. "There's no sense in going over everything twice. Besides, you were about to tell us what your aunt's former associates have to do with your being in England."

Prince Durmontov studied Mairelon for a long moment, then capitulated. "Very well. A little time ago, my aunt received a message of a . . . magical nature. It involved an obscure threat to the Duchesse Delagardie and advised my aunt to bring her *livre de mémoire* to England. Though this message was not entirely clear, it disturbed her greatly. She is, however, deeply involved in an extended study of magic on the Indian subcontinent, and did not wish to break it off at a critical point to make so long a journey, most particularly because she could not be positive that it was necessary."

"Ah. So she sent you instead."

The prince inclined his head. "As you see."

"And since your arrival . . . ?"

"I have been very much confused," Prince Durmontov admitted. "First there seemed to be no threat—the Duchesse Delagardie was not even in London. Then, at Lady Greythorne's musicale, came that scrying spell which sent you hurrying off, and when I returned to my lodgings, someone had gone through my protections and stolen my aunt's book. I felt then that it was urgent to speak with the Duchesse Delagardie, but she had not yet returned. So I went to look for her."

"And found her, I take it," Mairelon murmured.

"She had been visiting a friend in Edinburgh named Lady MacKay, and had broken her return journey in York. She, too, was much puzzled when I told her of my aunt's message, and very troubled that someone had succeeded in removing my protections and stealing her *livre de mémoire*. The spells I had used were, you understand, some of those that the Duchesse Delagardie and my aunt and their friends had invented for their own use, and it would take more than a common wizard to avoid them."

"There is at least one extremely uncommon wizard in this somewhere," Mairelon said grimly. "Go on."

"I have little more to tell," the prince said. "We returned last night from Edinburgh. When I returned to the George this morning to arrange these last few matters, I found a note waiting for me, bidding me to a certain public house to learn more of the matter which brought me to England." He shrugged. "There was also your message. Had I answered it first—But one cannot live in might-have-been."

"No." Mairelon's voice had an undercurrent of irony, and Kim knew he was thinking of his ill-fated attempt to trace the scrying spell at Lady Greythorne's musicale.

There was a brief lull in the conversation; then the prince looked at Mairelon and said, "How is it that you performed such a timely arrival?"

"We hurried," Mairelon said.

Kim choked back a snort of laughter.

"And how did you know that it was necessary to hurry?" the prince asked politely, looking from one to the other.

"We had it from an inept gentleman-burglar late last night," Mairelon said. "He mentioned, somewhat in passing, that you were likely to be set upon. When we reached the George to leave you a warning, and discovered that you had already been and gone . . . well, hurrying seemed like a good idea."

"But why should anyone attack me?" the prince said, frowning.

"If we knew that, we'd be considerably further along than we are," Mairelon replied.

"Maybe Mannering wanted to find out where this Duchesse Delagardie is," Kim suggested.

"Mannering?" said the prince. "Who is—" He broke off as the familiar tingle of magic swept over them. "Ah!" he said, and raised his hands in an arcane gesture.

Kim lunged across the coach and grabbed his wrists, forcing his arms down before the gesture could be completed and ruining whatever concentration the spell required. "No!" she said forcefully.

The prince and Mairelon both stared at her as the tingling receded, the prince with restrained anger, Mairelon with a mixture of alarm and speculation. "Another scrying spell?" Mairelon said tentatively after a moment.

"I don't know," Kim said, sitting back. "Something, anyway. And it's gone now, like the other ones."

"There is some reason why you did not wish this spell traced?" Prince Durmontov said coldly.

Kim looked at Mairelon, who sighed. "We would very much like that spell traced," Mairelon told him. "Unfortunately, tracing it seems to have . . . unpleasant consequences."

"Indeed?" Durmontov looked skeptical but interested. "Yes, I recall that at Lady Greythorne's musicale you took a backlash from the spell. But—"

"It was more than a backlash," Mairelon said harshly. "It was a trap. A particularly nasty one."

The prince raised an eyebrow inquiringly, but Mairelon did not continue. After a considerable pause, Kim said, "He needs to know. If we hadn't been here, and he'd done that trace . . ."

"Yes, yes, all right," Mairelon said testily. He looked at Durmontov. "When my tracing spell connected to the scrying spell at Lady Greythorne's, it got sucked straight into it. Along with everything else."

Durmontov blinked. "Everything else . . . ?"

"I haven't been able to sense a spell-in-process, much less work one of my own, for nearly two weeks," Mairelon said, clipping the words off sharply. His face was stony, defying comment or sympathy.

Prince Durmontov's eyes widened and he sat back heavily against the squabs. "I . . . see." He turned to Kim. "I would appear to be doubly in your debt." He hesitated, looking at Mairelon. "I can see that you do not wish this to be talked of. Nor would I, in your place. But when we reach the duchesse, she must be warned."

"Of course," Mairelon said without enthusiasm.

The conversation died. Kim thought of half a dozen questions she would have liked to ask, but in the face of Mairelon's heavy silence and the prince's contemplative one, she didn't quite dare. She found herself torn between sympathy for Mairelon and annoyance at his behavior. She knew, none better, how difficult it was to reveal a weakness or a vulnerability, even to a friend—but she also knew that if Mairelon hadn't blown the gab, he would have blamed himself for whatever grief the prince came to later on. He knew it himself, but he was sulking like a sweet-stealer with a pain in his tooth.

They reached Hampstead at last, and descended from the coach in front of a small white stone house set well back from the street. A flagstone walk led to the doorway, past short clumps of new-green plants and some kind of thorn-covered vine that was just leafing out. Inside, a housemaid showed them to a small drawing room that looked as if it had been hastily and rather incompletely tidied, and left to fetch her mistress. On closer examination, the air of disorder proved deceptive. The books and papers on the corner tables were arranged neatly between bookends; the silver candleholders gleamed, and the chairs and woodwork shone with beeswax. It was the number and variety of books and furniture that gave the impression of confusion.

A few minutes later, a short, plump, bespectacled woman entered the room. She wore her ginger hair unfashionably long and loose beneath her proper lace cap, and her blue velvet gown, while clearly expensive and in the best of taste, was not in the latest mode. "Good morning, Alexei," she said. "You have brought friends to meet me? But you have had some accident!"

"No accident," said Prince Durmontov. "I was set upon, but thanks to these two, I am not harmed. Allow me to present Miss Kim Merrill and her guardian, Mr. Richard Merrill. This is the Duchesse Camille Delagardie."

"You have no notion how happy I am to make your acquaintance at last," Mairelon said with feeling.

The duchesse's eyes twinkled behind her spectacles. "No? Then you must at once seat yourselves and explain, and I shall have Liza bring in tea. For it is obvious that there is some long explanation to come, and I find that long explanations always go well with tea. It is an English custom of which I thoroughly approve."

They followed this program at once. The account took some time, for, somewhat to Kim's surprise, Mairelon did not play off any of his tricks for avoiding explanation on the duchesse. Instead, he gave her a more detailed version of the story he had told Lord Shoreham, compressed but complete in all the essentials. The duchesse lost her twinkle almost immediately, and listened in thoughtful silence. Her expression grew grave when Mairelon described the trap that had caught him during Lady Greythorne's musicale, but it was not until he reached the previous evening and Lord Gideon Starnes's tale of the treasure vault in France that the duchesse was betrayed into exclamation.

"But that is absurd!" she said. "Or rather— No, go on. I will know the whole of it, before I take my turn."

"There's not much more to tell," Mairelon said. "Starnes mentioned that his compatriot had said something about setting footpads on Prince Durmontov, and we thought it best to warn him. When we got to the George, he'd already been and gone, so we went after him."

"And arrived in a most timely fashion," the prince put in. "I thought it wise to tell you at once, since it seems connected with that peculiar message my Aunt Jeannette received. And then during the ride here came another of these scrying spells, and only Miss Merrill's prompt action kept me from falling into the same trap as Mr. Merrill."

"Very good," the duchesse said, nodding approval at Kim. "I, too, am in your debt. I would not like anything unfortunate to happen to Jeannette's nephew, though he is in general quite capable of taking care of himself."

"And that," said Mairelon, "is all. If you can shed any light on the matter . . ."

"I do not know that I can," the duchesse said slowly. "You see—no, I shall begin at the beginning." She eyed Mairelon apologetically. "It is no great matter, you understand, only that it is a little uncomfortable to admit the follies of one's youth."

"I am all attention," Mairelon said. His tone was polite, but the tension in the set of his shoulders had returned.

The duchesse sighed. "It was twenty-six . . . no, twenty-seven years ago. Things had been growing more and more difficult in France, and it was plain to all of us that some sort of upheaval was soon to come. And it was likewise clear that the nobility and the wizards would have the worst of it. And since the seven of us were all wizards and all French aristocrats—"

"Except for M. Karolyi," the prince put in. "He is Hungarian."

"*Very* Hungarian," the duchesse agreed with a smile. "He is, however, a wizard and a dear friend of the Vicomte de Bragelonne, and as such, we expected that he would fare no better than the rest of us. So the seven of us came together and placed our most precious possessions in a vault—actually, it was a very large room in Marie's cellar. Well, it had to be, with all the books."

"Books?" Mairelon said with interest.

The duchesse nodded. "Marie stored almost her entire magical library, as well as her silver and most of her jewels, and Eustacie had at least as many, and Henri and Jeannette, also. And there was my library, too. We were days hauling it all down. László put in only those things he had with him in France, of course, which was not quite so much. When we finished, the seven of us worked a spell to seal the room completely. It was a very good job, I think. The *sans-culottes* could have burned the house overhead, and the fire would have stopped at the ceiling boards. Not so much as a speck of ash would penetrate."

"That sounds . . . thorough."

"Marie and I were worried about mice getting at the books," the duchesse said placidly. "When one stores such things in a cellar, and there are no cats about, it is a reasonable concern."

"So the treasure vault is real," Mairelon said thoughtfully. "And the seven *livres de mémoire* are the key?"

The duchesse shook her head. "But no! That would have been folly. We did not know, of course, that poor Henri's ship would go down so soon after we left France, but with the times so unsettled we could not be sure that all seven of us would be able to return to open the vault, or even send a key with someone else. And to make the key a book, which is so vulnerable to fire and damp . . . no. That is why I said this Lord Starnes's story was quite absurd."

"Then how *did* you reopen the vault?"

"The key is quite a simple spell, very easy to remember," the duchesse replied. "I don't believe any of us even wrote it down in our *livres de mémoire*. But we never went back to reopen the vault. The Terror . . . was worse than we expected anything to be, and lasted longer, and after that came Bonaparte. By the time he relented somewhat toward wizards, we had all made our lives elsewhere, and we did not feel the risk was worth it." She smiled slightly. "As long as we left everything there, you see, it was quite safe, but it would be easy enough to confiscate it once the spell had been removed. And transporting all those things out of France without attracting attention . . ." She shook her head.

"You mean it's all *still there?*" Kim said. "The silver and the jewels and everything?"

"It is the books I regret most," the duchesse said.

"My aunt, also," said Prince Durmontov, nodding.

Kim blinked at them both in disbelief and shook her head. She saw the corners of Mairelon's mouth twitch in amusement. *Toffs!* she thought. *I'll never understand them.*

"I'm surprised Mme. de Cambriol's husband didn't return, even if none of the rest of you did," Mairelon said. "From what we know, he had a thin time after she died."

"He considered it," the duchesse said. "But he was not himself a wizard; one of us would have had to accompany him to cast the spell to open the vault. He would not ask us to take the risk. Besides, he was always quite certain that his next hand of cards or the next horse race would render the trip unnecessary, and his luck did indeed run well now and then."

"Gamesters often feel so," Mairelon said. "Then as far as you know, the vault is untouched?"

The duchesse nodded. "That is why Louis and Eustacie have returned to France: to open the vault and retrieve our belongings at last. I do not know what we shall do with Henri's and Marie's portions. They have no living relatives I know of."

Mairelon raised a hand to rub his temples. "So we might just as well have given Lord Starnes the de Cambriol book and wished him godspeed that first night," he said bitterly. "He and Mannering are chasing a will-o'-the-wisp; even if they get hold of all seven books, they won't be able to open the vault in France, and even if they could, they'll find it empty by the time they get there. And none of the rest of this would have happened."

"*If* the treasure is all they want," Kim said.

Mairelon looked at her.

"I never knew Mannering much," Kim went on, "but people said he was a fly cove and right knowing. And anyone can see that that Lord Starnes is as cork-brained as they come, even when he's not bosky. *I* wouldn't tell Starnes anything important, and I'm nothing like as downy as Mannering."

"True." Mairelon's expression brightened briefly, then he shook his head and said in a tired voice, "But in that case, we're no further along than we were before."

The duchesse made a hesitant gesture. "There is one more thing, of a sort. I would not have thought of it, only you said that it was Henri's *livre de mémoire* these people have, and Henri—" She smiled reminiscently and shook her head. "Henri d'Armand was a most unusual person. Things that came easily to the rest of us were most difficult for him, and things most persons find greatly difficult were for him very simple. He was in many ways a brilliant wizard, but he never truly believed that."

"I am afraid I don't understand," Mairelon said.

"I explain very badly," the duchesse told him. She thought for a moment. "A *livre de mémoire* is for writing down things that one is most likely to forget. For most of us, that is the unusual—the word that must be changed for a spell to work *so* and not *so*, the one corner of a diagram that must be circled instead of crossed, the ingredient one always forgets. For Henri, it was otherwise."

"But what else—" Prince Durmontov began, then stopped, frowning.

"Henri remembered changes easily enough," the duchesse said, nodding. "It was the original spell itself he sometimes had difficulty in recalling. So his *livre de mémoire* was full of spells, like a true grimoire, except that most of them did not work correctly because he had not yet worked out the necessary changes. We used to laugh with him about it."

"So d'Armand's *livre de mémoire* looks useful, but isn't quite," Mairelon said thoughtfully. "Do you think that Mannering is after the other books in order to correct the spells in the one he's got?"

"That would be of little use," the prince said. "Without knowing the wizards, he could not know which spells the bits and pieces in the other *livres de mémoire* refer to."

"Bits and pieces." Mairelon's eyes widened. "All his spells are bits and pieces, strung together. . . ."

"This is all very possible," the duchesse said. "But it is still not quite what I wished to say." She hesitated, then went on slowly, "Your description of this . . . this trap, M. Merrill, sounds familiar—very like something that happened once by accident when the seven of us were constructing a new spell. If you do not object, I would like to examine the remnant that you say still affects you. I think perhaps, if I am right, I may be able to offer some suggestions."

"I am at your disposal, Your Grace," Mairelon said instantly. "So long as you are quite certain your examination will not expose you to the same . . . misfortune."

"If it is as I suspect, I can assure you it will not." The duchesse rose and nodded to Kim and the prince. "I trust you will excuse us. My workroom is not large enough for so many. I do not expect that we will be long. M. Merrill? This way."

TWENTY-TWO

K im could not help fidgeting in Mairelon's absence, but he was not gone long. In less than half an hour, he and the duchesse returned. The duchesse looked grave; Mairelon seemed in a state of suppressed excitement. "I will let you know as soon as I am certain," the duchesse said to Mairelon. "I cannot promise anything yet, you understand, but the basis is plainly Henri's spell for sharing *la puissance*. I do not see how this wizard has— But it may be clearer after I check some of my reference books."

"I sincerely hope so, Your Grace," Mairelon said.

"You understand the risk?"

Mairelon's jaw tightened. "Thoroughly. I will . . . consider the matter carefully."

Kim gave him an inquiring look, but neither he nor the Duchesse seemed inclined to explain.

They took their leave soon after. Mairelon spent the journey back to London in a brown study. Prince Durmontov, after one or two unsuccessful attempts to rouse him, beguiled the time by telling Kim about his family in Russia. It was very interesting, and she was almost sorry when they let him off at his new lodgings.

"Prince Durmontov," Mairelon said as the prince climbed out of the coach. "From what the Duchesse Delagardie has said, we may need more than one wizard to . . . remedy the current situation. As you are already somewhat involved—"

"You may depend on me," the prince replied.

Mairelon relapsed into reverie as soon as the coach pulled away, and remained so until they reached Grosvenor Square. There he roused himself to send Hunch off with messages for Lord Kerring, Lord Shoreham, and Renée D'Auber. Kim knew better than to insist on touchy explanations in front of the grooms and footmen, but by the time they entered the house, she was bursting with impatience.

"Is my mother in?" Mairelon demanded of the footman. "Well, when she arrives, tell her I would like to speak with her. I'll be in the library."

"Mairelon," Kim said as they climbed the stairs, "what did that duchesse tell you? And what did she mean about risks?"

"Hmm? Oh, I thought that she'd made that clear." Mairelon turned in at the library door and began scanning the shelves.

Kim followed him in and shut the door behind them. "She maybe made it clear to you, but I wasn't there," she said. "What did she say?"

"The magic-draining enchantment does seem to be based on an early version of a spell the duchesse is familiar with," Mairelon said without looking at Kim. "*Les Griffonais* invented it for their own use, years ago. Unfortunately, that particular spell was flawed to begin with, and the version that's affecting me has some unusual variations."

"The duchesse can still get rid of it though, can't she?"

"Possibly. She suggested casting the spell afresh, properly, and then disassembling it. The odds are good that doing so would take this other enchantment with it." He frowned suddenly and turned. "I have covered that with you, haven't I?"

"It was in that first book you gave me," Kim said. "The one with all the Greek."

"And?"

This is not *the time I'd pick for lessons.* But she could see that Mairelon wouldn't tell her any more until she answered. She thought for a moment, trying to remember what the book had said. "The easiest way to correct a flawed spell is to cast it a second time and do it right. The structure of the new spell is stronger, and . . . and it sort of takes over the one with the mistake in it."

Mairelon smiled suddenly. "Not quite the way Cornelius phrased it, but correct in its essentials. D'Armand's spell was meant to be cast by himself and his six friends, as a way of sharing their magical abilities during major projects. They used it only for short periods; keeping it going for more than a few days was, er, uncomfortable for everyone, and they suspected that long-term maintenance would have . . . unpleasant consequences."

Ma Yanger, Kim thought. "Does that mean that whoever is keeping this spell on you is uncomfortable?"

"I devoutly hope so," Mairelon said. "But according to the duchesse, the early versions of the spell were unstable—they fell apart after a few minutes, or hours at most. Our mystery wizard seems to have found some way of stabilizing the spell without correcting any of the other fundamental flaws." He frowned again. "He also seems to have altered the spell a bit."

"Altered it?" Kim said. "Why would he change the spell and not fix any of it?"

Mairelon shrugged. "The flaws have to do with the way

magical power is shared among the seven participants. Our mystery wizard has found a way to use it to strip away power, rather than share it. Possibly he didn't think it necessary to fix the parts he didn't need. But because of the changes he made, we can't be perfectly certain that recasting the spell will work the way it's supposed to."

"Is that what the duchesse meant when she talked about risks?" Kim said, frowning.

"Partly." Mairelon went back to scanning the shelves; after a moment, he pulled out a thick brown book and carried it to the library table.

"What's the other part?" Kim said, her stomach knotting. Mairelon only got like this when he was about to do something dangerously goose-witted—and knew it.

"Other part of what?" Mairelon said.

"The risk."

Mairelon looked at her, then looked away. "There's a distinct possibility that if this doesn't work, I'll lose my magical abilities permanently. You don't have to be concerned about your training," he added hastily. "Kerring will be happy to take you on, if . . . But it's not likely to be necessary."

"The training ain't what I'm nattered about!"

"Isn't what you're upset about," Mairelon corrected, then added in a low voice. "I appreciate your concern."

It ain't just concern! "Mairelon . . ." Kim hesitated. "Is it worth it?"

"It will settle matters, one way or another. And the risk isn't great." But his eyes did not meet hers, and she knew he was not as certain as he pretended. She could also see that he had made up his mind, and, having done so, was not about to change it.

"Of all the buffle-headed things to say!" she said angrily. "Next you'll be telling me that gallivanting around France with the whole army after you wasn't dangerous. Have a little sense!"

Mairelon looked at her and smiled crookedly. "Why should I start now?"

The library door opened and Lady Wendall entered. "You wished to see me, Richard? Good heavens, look at the pair of you! I can see you have a great deal to tell me."

"More than you realize," Mairelon said. "We may have found a way of removing this antimagic spell or whatever it is. It'll take six wizards besides me; I trust you'll be one of them?"

"Of course, dear. Who are the others?"

"Kerring, Shoreham, and Renée, if they agree; Prince Durmontov already has, and the Duchesse Delagardie will be directing the spellcasting. We'll need to clear out the ballroom; the library isn't large enough for the floor diagrams."

"Very well," Lady Wendall said, stripping off her gloves. "But you appear to be leaving out a good deal, and you *did* promise to tell me all about it when you returned."

"Did I?" Mairelon said. "Well, I suppose it is only fair."

As Lady Wendall and Mairelon settled in to talk, Kim stole quietly out of the library, her emotions in turmoil. Mairelon's choices for the other six wizards to cast the spell that would—they hoped—return his magic to him were logical ones; all six were either trusted friends, like Kerring and Shoreham, or wizards already involved in the matter, like the duchesse and Prince Durmontov, or both. But though she knew it made no sense for him to include a mere apprentice in the spellworking, she could not help feeling hurt and left out because there was no place for her.

She did not have much time to indulge in hurt feelings; less than half an hour later, Lord Franton arrived and requested the favor of a private word with her. Kim swallowed hard when the message was brought to her; in the excitement of the morning, she had forgotten—or allowed herself to forget—that she could expect a visit from him. *Well, at least I'll get it over with.*

Lord Franton was waiting for her in the drawing room. He looked up and smiled as she entered. Kim swallowed again, and he must have seen something in her expression, for his smile became uncertain at the edges. "Miss Merrill—"

"Mairelon told me—I mean, I—" Kim's face grew warm and she stuttered to a stop, unable to think of a way to phrase what she wanted to say. She should have just let him speak, instead of trying to refuse him before he'd even begun.

The marquis looked at her. His eyebrows flew up and his expression stiffened slightly. "Am I to understand that you are aware of my intentions, but are not willing to entertain my offer?"

"That's it," Kim said with relief.

There was a pause. "May I inquire as to the reason?"

Kim hesitated, searching for a way of expressing her difficulties that would be neither insulting nor wounding. "We'd both end up being miserable. I'm no wife for a gentry cove."

"Is it your background, then?" Lord Franton smiled and shook his head. "That need not worry you. You're a wizard now; what you were before does not matter to me."

"Yes, it does," Kim said softly. "Because part of the time you're sorry about it, and part of the time you think it makes me interesting, and part of the time you ignore it. But you never *forget* it." Mairelon was the only toff who truly didn't care that she'd been a street thief . . . but she'd best not think of him just now.

"I do not—" Lord Franton cut off his automatic denial before it was well-launched. He considered for a moment, his lips pressed tightly together, then looked at Kim once more. "I think I see what you are getting at," he said with reluctance.

"You never really forget it," Kim repeated. "And I don't think you ever would."

"I could try," he offered tentatively. "That is, if your sentiments are such that you would reconsider . . . ?"

Kim could only shake her head wordlessly.

"I see," Lord Franton said after a moment. "I . . . honor your frankness, and I wish you well. Give you good day."

He bowed and left. Kim stood staring at the door for a long time afterward, wondering why she did not feel more relieved and hoping she had not just made the biggest mistake of her life.

By evening, preparations for the spell to disenchant Mairelon were well underway and Kim felt more excluded than ever. A message from the duchesse arrived late in the day, and was apparently very promising, for it set off another round of notes and letters to the proposed participants. Mairelon spent the remainder of the evening shut up with his books, and the following morning conferring with his mother; then Renée D'Auber and Prince Durmontov arrived, and the four of them went into the ballroom to prepare for the casting ritual.

Under other circumstances, the activity would have been fascinating, for Kim had not previously seen a major ritual spellcasting requiring several wizards. All of the participants, however, were too occupied with learning the parts required of them, and with making certain that every aspect of the spell was precise to a fault, to explain anything to Kim. Nor could she bring herself to distract any of them with questions—not when Mairelon's magic depended on their getting everything exactly right.

So she ran whatever mysterious errands anyone thought to ask of her, supplied the wizards in the ballroom with new grapes, sour wine, and powdered pearls on request, and concealed her fears as best she could. Lord Kerring and Lord Shoreham turned up shortly after the preparations had begun and went instantly to join the others, leaving only the duchesse still unaccounted-for.

Mrs. Lowe was somewhat disturbed to learn that callers other than the participating wizards were to be denied, but after expressing her opinion of the imprudence of such a move and of the folly of suddenly determining to perform a major spellcasting at the height of the Season, she retired to her rooms and did not reappear. Consequently, it was Kim, waiting impatiently in the drawing room for the duchesse to arrive, who heard the commotion from the front hall. Slightly puzzled, she hurried out into the hallway and down the stairs.

"Don't go gammoning me!" a young voice said belligerently as she made her way downward. "I come for the frog-maker. I got a message, and I ain't givin' it to nobody else. So you just hop to it and tell him so, see?"

"Mr. Merrill is not at home to callers," the butler said with the air of someone repeating himself.

"That's nothing to me," the belligerent young voice said. "I got a message for that Kim, and I'll see him straight and no bobbery."

"I'm Kim," said Kim, coming around the last turn. "What do you—Matt!"

The dark-haired youth who had somehow insinuated his way into the front hall turned and gaped at her. "Garn!" he said after a moment. "I knew you was a frogmaker, but—" His

Adam's apple bobbed as he swallowed hard and shook his head. "Well, I'm scunnered, that's all," he announced.

"You said you have a message for me?" Kim said sedately, imitating as best she could Lady Wendall's calm, matter-of-fact responses to startling announcements and events. Tom Correy's nephew could think what he liked; she owed him no explanations. Tom would be another matter.

"Tom needs to see you, right away," Matt said, confirming her misgivings. Well, she'd known she was going to have to face Tom sooner or later and tell him the truth about her sex; she just hadn't expected it to be this soon.

"Tell him I'll come by this evening," she said. They'd have finished reworking the spell on Mairelon by then, and they'd know the results. One way, or another.

"No," Matt said with considerable force. "Right now! You got to come back with me."

Kim frowned. "Something's happened?"

"Yes–no— You just got to come," Matt said desperately. "Tom'll explain."

"Oh?" Kim's eyes narrowed. Matt was Jack Stower's nephew, as well as Tom Correy's. But Jack was safe in Shoreham's hands, and had been since yesterday morning. Still . . . "How do I know Tom sent you?"

"He said to tell you to mind when the rattling cove took you for a mumper, and the old fussock rang a peal over him to get you off."

Kim nodded, satisfied. No one but Tom and Mother Tibb knew about that incident, and Mother Tibb was dead.

"You'll come?" Matt said anxiously.

"Let me think a minute," Kim said. There was nothing for her to do here but fret; running off to see Tom would at least occupy her while the spellcasting went forward. It felt like abandoning Mairelon—but she couldn't help him, and if she *could* help Tom, shouldn't she do it? She'd known Tom Correy longer, and she owed him a good deal. "I'll be back in a minute," she told Matt, and ran upstairs to the ballroom.

The wizards had finished the preliminaries, and were standing in a clump near the door. In the center of the ballroom floor, two overlapping triangles had been drawn by carefully spreading wet rowan-ash in straight lines, forming a six-pointed star. A small table had been placed just outside each point to hold the various items the wizards would need for their parts in the spellcasting.

"We'll begin as soon as the duchesse arrives and checks everything over," Mairelon was saying as Kim entered. "It shouldn't be— Kim! Has the Duchesse Delagardie come?"

"Not yet," Kim said. "They'll bring her up as soon as she gets here, though. I got to go down to see Tom Correy; something's happened."

Mairelon frowned. "You're sure—no, of course you are. But . . . Now?" He glanced at the windows, alight with the afternoon sun.

Kim shrugged. "Tom's got to find out I'm a girl sometime."

"All right. But take Hunch."

Kim nodded, swallowing a small lump of disappointment. She had, she realized, been hoping he would tell her to stay. Well, that was Mairelon for you. She hurried back toward the stairs, and nearly ran into Mrs. Lowe.

"Kim! Really, you must not race about like that."

"Sorry," Kim said, intent on getting past her.

Mrs. Lowe grasped Kim's arm and gave it a gentle shake. "Whatever is your hurry?"

"I'm going out," Kim said. "Excuse me, I have to go."

"Without your abigail?" Mrs. Lowe said, maintaining her grip on Kim's arm.

"It's . . . wizard business; Mairelon knows all about it." At least, he knew as much as she did. "And I'm taking Hunch."

Mrs. Lowe considered. "Hunch is no doubt very useful, in his way, but it is hardly proper for you to wander about the city in his company, even if it is on *wizard business.*" She sniffed. "I shall come with you myself."

"No! I mean, I don't think—"

"I was under the impression you were in a hurry," Mrs. Lowe said. "Shall we go?"

"It isn't anywhere proper," Kim said. "You won't like it."

"I had already formed that conclusion," Mrs. Lowe replied. "I may also add that I am neither blind, nor deaf, nor foolish, and if you think I am unaware that something is very wrong and has been for some time, you are very much mistaken."

Kim could only stare at her in consternation.

"It is not my place to pry into matters which my nephew plainly does not wish to confide in me," Mrs. Lowe went on. "I can, however, make sure that his ward does nothing disgraceful while he is otherwise occupied. And I intend to do so."

"It isn't disgraceful. And I told you, he knows about it already."

"Richard," said Mrs. Lowe austerely, "is frequently oblivious to the social niceties." She paused. "Should you wish to continue this discussion, I suggest we do so in the carriage. That is, if you are in fact in so much of a hurry as you at first appeared."

"Oh, I am," Kim muttered, and started down the stairs, wondering what Tom would make of this.

TWENTY-THREE

Matt was eloquent in his disapproval of Mrs. Lowe's presence; fortunately, he expressed himself in terms utterly unintelligible to her. He was somewhat mollified when he realized that they were to travel in a bang-up gentry coach. Mrs. Lowe ignored him. Hunch, on seeing the oddly assorted group, blinked and began chewing on his mustache. Kim felt entirely in sympathy with him.

As they drove off, they passed the Duchesse Delagardie pulling up in a landau. *That means they'll be starting the counterspell soon,* Kim thought, and shivered. Such a complex spell would take considerable time to cast, but even so, everything would probably be finished by the time she returned. *One way or another.*

Possibly because he was feeling the same anxiety as Kim regarding Mairelon's welfare, Hunch not only took the most direct route to Tom's but also drove the horses rather faster than was either wise or required. Matt was much impressed, and said so at some length until Kim advised him to stubble it. Somewhat sulkily, he did so.

When they pulled up outside Tom's shop at last, Kim descended and hurried inside without waiting for Mrs. Lowe or Matt. Tom was sorting through a pile of old clothes on one of the tables, but he looked up when he heard the door. His eyes widened in startlement, and he said, " 'Morning, miss. Anything I can do for you?"

"You're the one that sent Matt to get me," Kim said, half enjoying his bafflement, half fearing his reaction when he finally realized who she was.

"I sent—" Tom stared at her and his jaw dropped. *"Kim?"*

"Matt said you wanted to see me right away," Kim said nervously. "And I didn't think I'd pass for a boy in daylight, and I thought it was time I told you anyway, and— What was it you wanted?"

"Kim." Tom's astonished expression slowly gave way to something very like horror. "I never knew. I wouldn't of done it if—I mean, I thought—I—you—"

"What's the matter?" Kim said, frowning. "Why'd you want to see me?"

"He didn't," said a deep voice from behind Tom. "I did." The owner of the voice moved out of the shadows as he spoke. He was not much taller than Kim, but broad and square and as solidly built as the cargo-handlers on the London docks. His clothes, however, proclaimed him no dockworker; they were the neat and well-tailored wear of a respectable businessman who might be expected, on occasion, to deal with members of the *ton*. Though "respectable" was not the usual term employed to describe the sort of business Kim knew he engaged in.

"Mannering!" she said in disgust, and looked at Tom reproachfully. She was more annoyed than frightened, even when a second man with the look of a bully hector about him joined Mannering. She was considerably nearer the door than they were, and the carriage was no more than two feet beyond that; if anything looked like trouble, she could pike off in a twinkling long before it came near.

"I'm sorry, Kim," Tom said. "But he—I wouldn't of done it if I'd known you—I'm sorry."

Kim shook her head. Tom's betrayal had surprised her, but only a little. Kim knew well enough the pressure that someone like Mannering could apply to compel coopera- tion, and the sort of loyalty that could stand up under such an assault was a rare commodity. Or at least, rare in the rookeries, tenements, and stews; she was quite sure that no threat could have persuaded Mairelon to bend to Manner- ing's schemes.

"Hold your tongue!" Mannering said to Tom. "Your young friend and I have business."

"Indeed?" said Mrs. Lowe from behind Kim. "Then I sug- gest you execute it so that we may be on our way. This is *not* the sort of establishment at which I wish to linger."

"What? Who's this?" Mannering demanded.

"I do not desire to be presented to this individual," Mrs. Lowe informed Kim. "You will oblige me by not doing so."

Kim nodded and looked at Mannering. Swallowing seven or eight questions that she wanted to ask immediately, she settled for a cautious, "What is it you want?"

"This is *private* business," Mannering said with a significant look first at Tom, then at Mrs. Lowe.

With evident reluctance, and a worried look at Kim, Tom vanished through the rear door. Mannering jerked his head at his henchman and said, "Watch him."

The henchman started to follow Tom out, then hesitated, eyeing Kim. Mannering scowled. "I said, watch the togs-man," he repeated. "I can deal with a couple of women my-self."

The henchman nodded and left at last. Mannering looked pointedly at Mrs. Lowe. Mrs. Lowe, however, was unmoved. "I told you, this business is private," Mannering said pointedly after a moment.

"I am not in the least hard of hearing," Mrs. Lowe replied. "However, if you think that I propose to leave my nephew's ward alone with a person such as yourself, you are quite mis-taken."

"Madam," said Mannering in a threatening tone, "I am a wizard!"

"What has that to do with the matter?" Mrs. Lowe re-turned imperturbably. "The social niceties, as I have repeat-edly pointed out, must be observed." She paused. "You will not, I hope, pretend to offer either of us a mischief—not in broad daylight with two grooms and a coachman just out-side."

Mannering looked from Kim to Mrs. Lowe, plainly off balance.

"If you have something to say to me, you'd better say it," Kim told him.

"And you had best say it quickly," Mrs. Lowe said. "Per-haps I should also mention that before I came in, I sent that singularly impenetrable young man—the one who brought your message—in search of a constable. While he did not im-press me as being particularly reliable as a general matter, I think that in this instance he can be depended upon to fulfill his commission."

"You're lying!"

"Care to wager on it?" Kim said. Though it wasn't likely to do much actual good; in this part of town, Matt could be hours finding anyone. "Pay or play; I got business elsewhere."

"This is more important," Mannering said, still eyeing Mrs. Lowe doubtfully.

Frowning slightly, Kim glanced at Mrs. Lowe herself. Mairelon's aunt stood in front of the grimy windows of Tom's shop, looking enormously proper, entirely sure of herself, and totally out of place. Kim blinked, then suppressed a grin. *Mannering's dealt with gentry before, but I'll wager he's never dealt with one who didn't want to borrow money—and for sure he's never had to face a respectable lady before. No wonder he's nattered.* Anything that made Mannering uncomfortable was a good notion as far as Kim was concerned; she looked back at Mannering and said, "What's so important? That de Cambriol book?"

"You've got it," Mannering said, leaning forward. His eyes glittered, and he seemed to have suddenly forgotten Mrs. Lowe's presence entirely. "My clerk said you showed it to him. I'll pay a round sum for it."

"How much?" Kim said, hoping Mrs. Lowe would have sense enough to keep her comments and opinions, whatever they were, to herself. If she could get him talking . . .

Mannering stepped forward. "How does fifty pounds sound?" he said in a voice just above a whisper.

Kim's eyebrows flew up. Fifty pounds was an undreamed-of fortune, by the standards of her old life. Coming from a usurer accustomed to dealing with the gentry, however, it was nothing short of an insult. "I ain't no gull," she said scornfully. "Mairelon gives me more than that for pin-money. Make a serious offer, or I'm leaving."

"I'm serious." Mannering stepped forward again, and Kim felt a twinge of fear. "Oh, I'm very serious. You have no idea how serious I am. Give me that book!"

"I think not," Mrs. Lowe put in calmly. "Kim, am I correct in guessing that this . . . person is responsible for that outrageous disruption in the library two weeks ago?"

Kim turned a little to answer, and took the opportunity to put a little more space between herself and Mannering. She was still well out of his reach, but a little caution never hurt anybody. "He was behind it," she told Mrs. Lowe.

Mrs. Lowe's head moved a fraction of an inch, shifting her attention to Mannering. Mannering fell back a step. Mrs. Lowe continued to study him for a moment; finally, she said in tones of icy reproof, "I take leave to tell you, sir, that you are unprincipled, presumptuous, and criminally self-serving; moreover, I must assume from your behavior that you lack both manners and wit into the bargain."

Mannering stared at Mrs. Lowe as if he could not believe his ears. Kim wondered whether he had ever before had his character so thoroughly cut up in quite such a formal and cold-blooded manner; somehow, she doubted it. "Wit?" he said in a strangled voice. "You think I lack wit?"

"It is the obvious conclusion," Mrs. Lowe said. "For even if one sets aside the illegal aspects of pilfering a book from my nephew's library, a more poorly conceived and badly executed endeavor than your attempt would be difficult to imagine. Nor has my opinion of your civility or intelligence been improved by your actions since our arrival today."

"I am a genius!" Mannering's eyes widened in passion and he raised a beefy fist for emphasis.

Mrs. Lowe was unimpressed. "I have seen no sign of it."

"I am a wizard!"

"So is my nephew," Mrs. Lowe said. "And while I do not by any means consider him unintelligent, he is certainly no genius."

"Ah, but he was born a wizard," Mannering said. "I made myself a wizard! No one else has ever done that."

"Indeed?" Mrs. Lowe said in tones of polite disbelief.

Mannering flung his arms out and gave an unintelligible

roar. Magic exploded into the shop with such force that Kim's skin stung. The pile of clothes in front of her shivered and rose into the air. It hovered for a moment, then began to spin. Tattered shirts, worn breeches, several mufflers, and a jacket with a hole in the left elbow went flying in all directions. Kim dodged one of the shirts and two mufflers, keeping her eyes on Mannering all the while. She hadn't really believed, until this minute, that Mannering could be a wizard.

As suddenly as it had begun, the spell stopped. The flying clothes plowed into walls with the last of their momentum and slid down into limp heaps. "There, you see?" Mannering said.

"That is precisely the sort of display I was referring to earlier," Mrs. Lowe said. "You would have made a more favorable impression had you chosen to *reduce* the mess in this room, rather than to increase it."

"How *did* you make yourself a wizard?" Kim put in quickly, before Mannering took a notion to blow the whole shop up just to prove his genius to Mrs. Lowe.

"You'd like to know that, wouldn't you?" Mannering said. "You and your toff friends don't want anyone doing real magic but you. That's why you won't give me the book, isn't it?"

Kim blinked, startled by this leap of logic. "We haven't agreed on a price yet," she pointed out cautiously.

"Hang the price! I want the book. Now."

"What, you think I'm a flat?" Kim shook her head and snorted. "I don't cart it around with me everywhere I go. What do you want it for, anyways?"

Mannering smiled. In a calm, too-reasonable voice, he said, "Why, to make it hold on steady-like."

"To make *what* hold on?"

"The spell." Mannering rocked forward on the balls of his feet. "It keeps wobbling," he said in a confidential tone. "And it takes more magic to straighten it out every time. I have to keep finding new magic to keep it from collapsing. If I had the right book, I wouldn't have to work so hard to keep them in line."

A chill ran up Kim's spine; she wasn't quite sure what Mannering was getting at, but she was positive that she wasn't going to like it one bit once she figured it out. And she didn't like his erratic behavior. Still, his mercurial changes of mood had kept him talking so far; if he continued, she might find out something useful. "Keep who in line?"

"My wizards," Mannering said. "Some of them used to be your friends. You used to like Wags, didn't you? And Bright Bess, I know you got on with her. You don't want them to end up like that Yanger woman, do you?"

The image of Ma's slack-jawed, drooling face rose in Kim's mind. Kim's stomach tightened. "What did you do to Ma Yanger?"

"I didn't do anything," Mannering said, still in the same much-too-reasonable voice. "Not really. She could even have had her magic back, if she'd been willing to go along like the rest of them. Some of her magic, anyway. It was your toff friends who destroyed her, and now you're going to do the same to the others."

"Gammon!" Kim said. "I ain't doing nothing."

"I believe that in this instance, doing nothing is indubitably the wisest course," Mrs. Lowe commented. "I must deplore your manner of expression, however, no matter how appropriate it may be under these circumstances."

Mannering turned on her in sudden fury. "Interfering harpy! If you were a wizard, I'd do you like Yanger!"

"So you *were* behind it!" Kim said.

"No, I told you, it was your toff friends," Mannering said,

abruptly reasonable once more. "They unbalanced the spell, and . . ." He shrugged.

Kim frowned. "You still aren't making sense." She was beginning to think he never would. *One thing at a time.* "What has this got to do with the de Cambriol book?"

"It has the rest of the spell in it," Mannering said. "It has to, or they wouldn't be trying so hard to keep me from getting it." He rocked back on his heels. "The comte's book only had a few words, and the Russian's was no help at all."

"The rest of the spell that lets wizards share their power?" Kim guessed.

"You know it!" Mannering rocked forward, eyes glittering feverishly. "You've read the de Cambriol book, haven't you?"

"I've heard talk," Kim said cautiously. "Is that how you made yourself a wizard—by getting somebody to share his power with you?"

"Of course. He didn't know I wouldn't have to give it back as long as I kept the spell going."

"Kept it going?" Kim stared, then shook her head, remembering what Mairelon had told her. "You gudgeon! That spell was never meant to last more than a day or two!"

In the doorway, Mrs. Lowe pursed her lips and gave Kim a reproving glance, but said nothing.

"That's what they want you to think," Mannering said, and smiled slyly. "I've kept it up for months now. It just takes adding another wizard's power now and then, to keep up the level of magic in the spell."

"You cast the whole spell again every couple of weeks?" Kim said, thinking of the elaborate preparations in the ballroom at Grosvenor Square.

"No, of course not!" Mannering said. "Just the last bit, that links a wizard in with the main spell. I thought of that myself," he added with pride. "And I don't even have to do that very often, because the spell absorbs the magic whenever someone attacks me."

Not just when someone attacks, Kim thought. Mairelon's spell had been intended just to trace Mannering's scrying spell, but all his magic had been swallowed up by this . . . this enchantment of Mannering's. The thought made her feel ill.

"It's getting harder to keep it balanced, though," Mannering went on. "I need more power, but if I get too much at once it starts to burn out the spell. That's what did for Ma Yanger—when those wizard friends of yours attacked me just for looking at them at that opera, it was too much for my sharing-spell to handle all at once."

Mairelon's first tracing spell, Kim thought, feeling even sicker than before. They'd found Ma the day after the incident with the flying book, and they'd known she couldn't have been incapacitated for very long, but they'd never connected the two.

"The wobble hurt everybody else in the link, too," Mannering went on, "but it burned the Yanger woman's mind out completely." He laughed suddenly, a harsh, half-mad sound. "Serves her right for being so uncooperative."

"Uncooperative?"

"She wouldn't work for me," Mannering said in the pouting tone of a child complaining that he had been denied a sweet. "I'd have let her have a little magic, if she had agreed, but she wouldn't." He frowned and added fretfully, "The spell's been unbalanced ever since. I thought it would settle after I added that Russian's magic, but it's worse than ever. I'm going to need a new wizard soon. I suppose I'll have to take Starnes after all, but I wanted to have everything steadied down before I started on wizards with real training."

And in another minute or two, it might occur to him that he had a wizard right in front of him who was barely started on her "real training," and therefore much safer to steal magic from than Lord Starnes was likely to be. Surreptitiously, behind a fold of her skirt, Kim made the one-handed gesture Shoreham had shown her and murmured the activating word of the spell in a voice too low for Mannering to hear. If he had all the skills of a real wizard, and not just the borrowed power, he'd feel the refuge spell go up, but by then it would be too late for him to stop it. From what Shoreham had said . . .

Mannering's head jerked back as if he had been struck. "What are you doing?" he demanded. "You're trying to trick me, like those others, like that Russian. Well, I'll stop that! *I hold yours, to me thy power comes!*"

The air crackled with the power of Mannering's final words, and Kim felt his spell strike her shield. The force behind the blow was enormous; had the shield been meant to withstand it, force for force and power for power, Kim knew it would have failed. But Gerard's Refuge didn't block or absorb or resist attacks—it "sort of shoves them to one side where they can go off without doing any harm," Shoreham had said. Mannering's spell slid sideways and whizzed invisibly past Kim's ear.

Kim stared at him in shock. "You cast that spell in *English!*"

"Of course! I am an English wizard," Mannering said proudly. His expression changed. "You— How are you keeping your magic? I should have it by now!" He raised his hands. "*I hold yours, to me—*"

"That is *quite* enough of that!" Mrs. Lowe said, and stepped in front of Kim.

"*—your power comes!*" Mannering finished. Kim flinched, but Mrs. Lowe did not seem to feel a thing as the spell hit her. Mannering, however, groaned and clutched his head.

"What did you do?" Kim asked, staring at Mannering.

"Nothing whatever. Nothing was all that was necessary."

Mrs. Lowe gave a small, wintry smile. "While I did not entirely comprehend what this . . . person was saying, it seemed clear from his remarks that whatever spell he was casting was meant to affect another wizard's magical powers. As I am no wizard and have no such abilities, the spell could not affect me. I presume it recoiled on him, and though I understand that spell recoils can be quite painful, I must say that I think he deserves it."

Kim found herself heartily in agreement with this sentiment. "How did you guess it would work that way?"

"My dear Kim, I have not spent years as a member of a family rife with wizards without learning some of the basic principles involved in magic! One need not have the ability in order to understand the theory, after all." With a brisk nod, she resumed her place in the outer doorway, watching Mannering.

Mannering looked up, panting, and took a deep breath. "You're keeping me from your magic. How are you keeping me from getting your magic? That Russian taught you, didn't he?"

"Prince Durmontov?" Kim said.

"I got his magic, all of it, but he still cast a spell at my men when they went to bring him here. How could he do that?"

So Mannering didn't know which wizard's magic he'd stolen on the night of the musicale. Well, she certainly wasn't going to straighten him out. "Why did you want to talk to the prince?" Kim asked.

"He's got training," Mannering said patiently. "I'd have given him back a bit of his magic, just like all the others, in exchange for his help holding the spell together."

"If you think anyone would help you under such circumstances, you have even less intelligence than I had given you credit for," Mrs. Lowe commented. "Why should he help you keep hold of his power?"

"He wouldn't want to end up like the Yanger woman,

would he? That's what will happen if the spell breaks apart. They all know it, too, all my wizards." Mannering frowned. "But I forgot; he still has magic. Maybe he wouldn't end up a Bedlamite like the rest of them."

But it wasn't Prince Durmontov's magic that Mannering had stolen; it was Mairelon's. And from the sound of it, Mannering's spell had worked exactly the same way on Mairelon as it had on the lesser wizards whose power he had stolen. *Which means that if Mannering's spell breaks apart or goes unstable, Mairelon's likely to end up just as witless as Ma Yanger did.* Kim swallowed hard, hoping her face didn't show what she was thinking. "If you're having trouble keeping the spell stable, why don't you just let it go and start over?" she suggested in what she hoped was a casual tone.

"I can't do that," Mannering said patiently. "If I let it go, I won't be a wizard any more, and none of them would ever let me try again. And they'd all be angry, and if I wasn't a wizard anymore, how could I protect myself? No, what I need is—" Mannering stopped abruptly, and his eyes widened in terror. In a voice that was almost a squeak he said, "What are you doing? Stop—stop it!"

"Stop what?" Kim said, frowning.

"You can't—you don't want this!" Mannering said in tones of desperation. "You won't just destroy me; you'll destroy every wizard in the link!"

No! Mairelon's in the link! thought Kim, and suddenly realized what was happening. The wizards in Grosvenor Square had started recasting the power-sharing spell, and Mannering could feel the beginnings of it because he was linked to Mairelon's magic. Her eyes widened as she remembered her conversation with Mairelon. The duchesse and Lord Kerring and the others thought that Mairelon had been stripped of his magic; they didn't realize that he was somehow part of Mannering's linkage. When they brought Mairelon into their newly cast spell, they'd be bringing in Mannering's entire network of spell-linked wizards as well—and they wouldn't be expecting it. The duchesse's spell was supposed to be the final, unflawed version of the one Mannering had cast, and therefore able to absorb and overpower it, but the duchesse's spell was designed for only seven wizards, not a dozen or more. And on top of that— "Did you cast that power-sharing spell in English, too?" Kim demanded urgently.

"I cast all my spells in English," Mannering said with dignity. "I am an English wizard. I had the others use English, too; I'm not such a flat as to let someone cast a spell on me when I can't understand what he's saying."

"You are a blithering idiot," Kim snarled. *Casting a spell in a foreign language keeps power from spilling into it uncontrollably.* And uncontrolled power was unpredictable; it could make spells stronger, but it also could change their effects. Her own experiment with working magic in English was still vividly clear in her memory; she could practically see the spots dance in front of her eyes. If Mannering had persuaded one of the untrained wizards from the rookery to cast d'Armand's already-flawed power-sharing spell—and to cast it in English—then it was no wonder the spell didn't behave anything like the way it was supposed to.

Kim stared blindly at Mannering, thinking furiously. What would happen when the duchesse's spell linked the magic of six fully trained wizards to Mairelon . . . and through Mairelon, to Mannering's warped version of the same power-sharing spell? More than likely, the two spells would merge, flooding Mannering's network with power. And if absorbing Mairelon's spell had been enough to destroy Ma Yanger's mind, the unexpected addition of six wizards' worth of magic at once would probably burn out the mind of every wizard in the link, just as Mannering claimed. Jemmy and Wags and Bright Bess would turn into vacant-eyed, mindless husks . . . and so would Mairelon.

On top of that, the duchesse and Lady Wendall and Lord Shoreham and the others who were trying to help Mairelon would also be linked into Mannering's network as soon as the spells merged. At best, they would probably lose their magic to his twisted version of the power-sharing spell; at worst, their minds might be burned out as well. Who could tell what effect the uncontrolled power in Mannering's spell might have?

"We got to get back and stop them!" Kim gasped, and started for the door.

"No!" Mannering said, darting forward and grabbing at her left arm. "You have to stay— You have to give me— You have to tell me—"

Kim let his grasp swing her around. As she turned in to face him, she brought her free arm up hard and fast. The heel of her open palm connected cleanly with the bottom of Mannering's chin, snapping his head up and back. He let go of her and staggered backward, off-balance. His head hit the jamb of the rear door, and he went down in a dazed heap.

"Get Hunch!" Kim said over her shoulder to Mrs. Lowe, and started forward. They would have to take Mannering with them; left to himself, there was no knowing what he'd do or whether they'd be able to find him again. And if the duchesse and Kerring and Shoreham had Mannering himself to interrogate, they might be able to figure out a safe way of removing his spell from Mairelon. *If* they got back to Grosvenor Square before the current spellcasting was finished . . .

"Not just yet, I think," Mrs. Lowe murmured. Stepping forward, she jabbed Mannering with the point of her sunshade. Mannering yelped and fell sideways. Mrs. Lowe picked up the thick wooden shaft he had been lying on and barred the rear door.

A moment later, the door rattled as if someone were trying to enter. "Mr. Mannering?" said a muffled voice. "Is everything all right?"

Mannering was shaking his head and trying to rise; Kim knocked him back against the door jamb once more with a well-placed kick. "Get Hunch," she repeated.

Mrs. Lowe pursed her lips disapprovingly, crossed to the outer door, and vanished outside.

I got to get Mairelon to teach me some spells for this kind of thing, Kim thought as she grabbed a linen shirt from the nearest pile of clothes. Keeping a wary eye on Mannering, she yanked at the tough fabric.

The outer door opened again and Hunch and one of the grooms entered. "Now what 'ave you gotten into?" Hunch growled.

"Mr. Mannering?" The barred door rattled again.

"We got to get back to Grosvenor Square as fast as we can, or it's all up with Mairelon," Kim told Hunch, ripping a strip from the shirt as she spoke. "The bully-boy in back don't matter, but we got to take this cove with—" she nodded at Mannering "—and he's a weird sort of frogmaker. If we tie his hands and gag him—"

"I know 'ow to 'andle 'is kind," Hunch said. "I've 'ad to do it for Master Richard a time or two." His hands were busy with the linen strips as he spoke, and in a few seconds he had Mannering expertly bound and gagged. With the groom's help, they loaded him into the coach.

As she climbed in beside Mannering and Mrs. Lowe, Kim heard loud thumping noises from the interior of the shop; apparently Mannering's henchman was trying to break down the door instead of going out the back way and nipping around to the front entrance. She spared a fleeting thought to wonder how much trouble Mannering's bully-boy would make for Tom once he finally got into the front room and found Mannering gone. Well, it was Tom's problem, and with luck Matt would have gotten back with a constable by then. She leaned out the coach window. "Spring 'em," she said to Hunch.

TWENTY-FOUR

The trip back to Grosvenor Square seemed to take forever, though Hunch urged the horses to a speed far greater than was really safe on the crowded streets. Mrs. Lowe sat stiff as a poker beside Kim, radiating disapproval but not saying anything. Mannering had recovered from his daze and alternated between glaring balefully at Kim over his gag and making terrified whimpering noises. On the whole, Kim preferred the glares; as long as he was sane enough to glare, she knew that the wizards in Grosvenor Square hadn't completed their spell.

It's a complicated spell, it'll take a long time. But would it take long enough? The picture of Mairelon turned empty-eyed, grunting, and helpless haunted her. *Faster,* she thought at the horses. *Hurry faster.*

At last they pulled up in front of the door. Kim was out of the coach almost before it stopped moving, and banging the knocker long before any of the grooms reached the door. When it opened at last, an interminable time later, she darted past the startled footman and ran up the stairs to the ballroom. As she tore down the hall, she heard a muffled feminine voice rising toward a climax, but she couldn't tell whether it was Lady Wendall's or the duchesse's. The duchesse was supposed to be last. . . . She flung herself through the ballroom door.

The air inside the ballroom was heavy with power; the sharp, glittering structure of the spell nearly complete. The Duchesse Delagardie stood in one of the triangular points of the star that Kim had watched the wizards preparing. Lady Wendall, Lord Shoreham, Lord Kerring, Renée D'Auber, and Prince Durmontov occupied the other points, and Mairelon himself stood in the center of the star. The duchesse had her back to the door, and her arms were raised in the final invocation.

Kim hesitated. To interrupt now would shatter the spell, and the enormous power that had already been poured into it would recoil on the wizards, doing nearly as much damage as Mannering's spell would. To let them continue would destroy Mairelon's mind as soon as he was linked into the duchesse's spell, not to mention the minds of the other wizards whose magic Mannering had taken, and quite possibly the six spellcasters themselves into the bargain. As soon as Mairelon was linked to the duchesse's spell . . . but if the duchesse linked her spell to *someone else*, instead of Mairelon . . .

Without pausing to think further, Kim picked up her skirts once more and ran forward. Mairelon saw her and took a half-step to meet her, then stopped, plainly realizing that to move any farther he would have to step outside the star. Renée and Lord Shoreham saw her next and frowned; then the other wizards—all but the duchesse. As Kim reached the edge of the star, she realized that the duchesse had closed her eyes to speak the closing words, and a tiny corner of Kim's mind sighed in relief. At least she wouldn't accidentally distract the duchesse and cause the spell to shatter.

Kim made an urgent shooing motion at Mairelon and pointed emphatically to the floor outside the star. *If only he doesn't take a notion to get stubborn . . .* Mairelon hesitated and glanced at the duchesse; he knew, even better than Kim did, the possible consequences of miscasting a major enchantment. Frantically, Kim gestured again for him to move.

On the far side of the diagram, Shoreham frowned and shook his head, but Mairelon's gaze was fixed on Kim's face, and he didn't notice Shoreham's gesture. *Move, move, get out of the star!* And finally, his eyes alight with questions, Mairelon nodded and stepped sideways out of the diagram. As he did, Kim stepped into it, taking his place.

Mairelon turned, an expression of horrified comprehension dawning on his face. He reached for Kim, but he was an instant too late. The duchesse spoke the final syllable and brought her arms down in a decisive movement, finishing the spell.

Power crashed down on Kim, filling her to bursting and beyond, burning through her mind. *Is this what it felt like to Ma Yanger?* The room went dark and she felt herself away. Far away, a babble of voices broke out, but the only one she could decipher was Mairelon's: "Duchesse! The counterspell, quickly!"

Three words blazed across Kim's mind like lightning bolts across a darkened summer sky, and then the storm of uncontrollable power passed. Almost gratefully, she started to collapse. Arms caught her as she fell; she struggled mindlessly until she heard Mairelon's voice by her ear and realized the arms were his. Then she relaxed into unconsciousness.

Her insensibility could not have lasted more than a moment or two, for the first thing she noticed when she began to recover was Mairelon's almost panic-stricken voice in her ears: "Kim! Kim?"

"Mairelon?" she said hazily through a pounding headache. "Oh, good, it worked."

"Thank God!" he said, and kissed her.

Kissing Mairelon was much nicer than she had ever dared to imagine, despite the headache. After much too short a time, he pulled away. "Kim, I—"

"I see you have decided to take my advice after all, Richard," Lady Wendall's amused voice said from somewhere above and behind him. "Marrying your ward is *exactly* the sort of usual scandal I had in mind; I wonder it didn't occur to me before."

"However, it is quite unnecessary for him to add to the talk by kissing her in public," Mrs. Lowe put in. "If he *must* indulge in vulgar behavior, it would be far better done after the notice of his engagement has appeared in the *Gazette*. And in private."

Mairelon looked up, plainly startled, and Kim's heart sank. Then his face went stiff, and her heart sank even further. "It was a momentary aberration, Aunt," he said in a colorless voice. "It won't happen again."

"I should like to think not," Mrs. Lowe said. "It is, perhaps, too much to hope that once you are married you will settle down, but Kim appears to have had at least a little success in keeping you out of trouble. Which is more than can be said for anyone else."

"You don't understand," Mairelon said dully. "Kim doesn't want to marry a toff."

Was that *what was bothering him?* "Well, of all the bacon-brained, sapskulled, squirish, buffle-headed nodcocks!" Kim said with as much indignation as she could muster. "I was talking about the *marquis*, not about *you!*"

Mairelon's eyes kindled. "Then you would?"

"You've whiddled it," Kim informed him.

As he kissed her again, she heard Mrs. Lowe murmur, "Mind your language, Kim," and Shoreham say in an amused tone, "Yes, Your Grace, I believe that was an affirmative answer."

"I'll send the notice to the *Gazette* tomorrow," Mairelon said when he finally came up for air. "No, today. Where's Hunch?"

Kim, feeling rather light-headed, leaned back on Mairelon's shoulder and looked around. Lady Wendall and Renée D'Auber were watching them with expressions that could only be described as smug; Prince Durmontov looked mildly bemused; the Duchesse Delagardie was smiling like a gleeful pixy; and the Lords Shoreham and Kerring were exchanging glances of enormous amusement. No one seemed to be either surprised of disapproving, not even Mrs. Lowe.

"In a minute, dear," Lady Wendall said to Mairelon. "And now that *that* is settled, perhaps you will let Kim explain the necessity for this interesting interruption. I confess, I do not understand it at all."

"Mannering!" Kim said. She tried to struggle to a sitting position, but gave up when her head began to swim. Apparently, the light-headedness hadn't just been an effect of kissing Mairelon. "He ain't piked off, has he?"

"Mannering?" Lord Shoreham frowned. "You don't mean to say you've located the confounded fellow! Where is he?"

"I believe he is currently on the lower stairs," Mrs. Lowe said. "Richard's man has him in charge, and I expect they will arrive momentarily."

"Aunt Agatha, you amaze me," Mairelon said. "How did you come to be, er, involved?"

"If you will assist Kim to one of the sofas, where she may

be more comfortable, I am sure she will explain everything," Mrs. Lowe replied.

Mairelon promptly picked Kim up and carried her to the nearest seat. She did not protest; the headache was beginning to recede, but she still felt shaky and weak. Mairelon took the seat next to her so that he could put his arm around her, and she leaned gratefully into his shoulder. Lord Shoreham, Lord Kerring, and Prince Durmontov pulled up chairs for themselves and the ladies, and they all sat down and looked at Kim expectantly.

"Um," said Kim, trying to decide where to begin.

The doors at the far end opened and Hunch entered, dragging the still-bound-and-gagged Mannering. "Now what?" Lord Shoreham said.

"This 'ere is that Mannering fellow you been a-wanting," Hunch said, looking at Mairelon. "Kim says 'e's some kind of wizard. Where do you want me to put 'im?"

"The far corner will do nicely for the time being, Hunch," Lady Wendall said. "And perhaps you would remain to keep an eye on him for a few minutes? Thank you."

"Mannering." Lord Shoreham shook his head and looked back at Kim. "Where did you find him? And how?"

"I didn't," Kim said. "He found me. He got Tom Correy to send Matt with a message, and—"

"That message was from Mannering?" Mairelon's arm tightened around Kim.

Kim nodded. "He wanted me to nobble the de Cambriol book for him—at least, that's what he started with."

"Wait a minute," Lord Kerring said. "Who is this Mannering person? Yes, yes, I know he's tied up in the corner, but what does he have to do with this interruption? That's what I want to know."

"He's a moneylender, and he's the one behind the magic-draining spell on Mairelon," Kim said. "Only it isn't really a magic-draining spell; it's that one for sharing power, and he's kept it up for months."

"*C'est impossible!*" the duchesse exclaimed.

Renée D'Auber tilted her head to one side. "I think, me, that it will be altogether better if Mademoiselle Kim begins with the beginning and goes on without the interruptions. Or we will very likely still be sitting here tomorrow morning." Beside her, the prince nodded emphatically.

Shoreham laughed. "You are quite right, Mlle. D'Auber. Miss Merrill, if you would proceed?"

"I think it starts with Mannering and Lord Starnes," Kim said after considering for a moment. Taking a deep breath, she plunged into the story: how Starnes had offered Henri d'Armand's *livre de mémoire* to Mannering as part of his collateral for a loan; how Mannering must have found the power-sharing spell and persuaded one of the rookery hedge-wizards to cast it in English; how he had kept the spell going by continually adding new wizards to the linkage.

"Only he must have been running out of wizards," Kim said. "There aren't many real magicians in St. Giles or Covent Gardens. He'd have to find some new wizards to steal power from, or figure out some other way to keep the spell stable. That's why he was trying to steal the rest of the memory books—he thought one of them would tell him how to make the spell permanent."

"Why didn't he just release—oh, of course," Lord Shoreham said. "The rookery wizards would have torn him limb from limb the minute they got their magic back, if he'd tried to release the spell and start over."

Kim nodded. "And without the power-sharing spell, he isn't a wizard at all. He *couldn't* start over."

"And how did you come to learn all this?" Lord Shoreham asked mildly.

"He told me a lot of it himself." As rapidly as she could, Kim laid out the particulars of her visit with Mannering, and the conclusions she had drawn from his ramblings and boasts and threats. It took longer than she had expected, but eventually she finished.

"You took a terrible chance, taking Richard's place in the spell like that," Lady Wendall said. "Without preparation, and barely a year into your apprenticeship—the possible consequences don't bear thinking of."

"Well, it worked," Kim said practically as Mairelon's arm tightened around her once again. "And there wasn't time for anything else." She looked at Mairelon. "I'm just glad you didn't give me any real argument about getting out of the diagram."

Mairelon shrugged. "You'd obviously found out something new, and equally obviously thought it was urgent enough to interrupt. I trusted your judgment—though I might not have if I'd known you intended to take my place in the star!"

"Just as well you didn't, then," Kim said gruffly. Nobody had ever trusted her like that before . . . but then, Mairelon wasn't like anybody else.

"It certainly is," Lord Shoreham agreed. "We owe you rather a lot, Miss Merrill."

Kim's face grew hot, and she shook her head, unable to find words.

"Yes, of course," Lord Kerring said. "But now let's have a look at this Mannering fellow. I confess to a certain curiosity, after all the trouble he's caused." From the expression on his face, Lord Kerring expected his curiosity to be satisfied, one way or another, and he didn't much care what happened to Mannering in the process.

"Yes," said Renée. "That seems to me a most excellent idea."

But when the gag was removed from Mannering's mouth, it quickly became clear that he was wandering mentally in some other realm, where he ruled all wizards with an absolute power and even the King asked for his advice and help. After several fruitless efforts to get something sensible out of him, it was agreed that Lord Kerring and Lord Shoreham would convey him to the Royal College of Wizards, where Lord Shoreham could see that he was properly guarded while Lord Kerring and the duchesse studied the spell that linked him to Mairelon and the other wizards, in hopes of finding a way to undo it.

For the next two days, Mairelon paced the floor, waiting for news. Only the duchesse's strict instruction that he was not to interrupt—and the determined efforts of Lady Wendall and Kim—kept him at home. On the third day, Lord Kerring arrived without warning and carried Mairelon off, leaving Kim to be the one pacing and fretting.

But when Mairelon returned two hours later, it was plain from his expression that the duchesse and Kerring had succeeded in their efforts to return his magic, even before he bounded up the stairs and swung Kim off her feet in his exuberance.

"Put me down!" Kim said, grinning in spite of herself. "You want to break both our necks?"

"Nonsense!" Mairelon said, but he set her on her feet.

"I take it everything worked fine?" Kim asked, just to make him say it straight out.

"Perfectly," Mairelon assured her, and to prove it, he muttered a rapid phrase and made a string of bobbing fairy lights appear and circle their heads briefly.

"Good!" Kim said. She hesitated, then added, "What about Jemmy and Wags and the others? Are they going to be . . . all right, too?"

Mairelon's expression sobered. "Probably, but it will be a tricky business seeing to it. Kerring's been comparing Mannering's spell to a pile of jackstraws; they have to take it apart in exactly the right order, or the whole thing will collapse and damage everyone involved."

"How much time do they have to do the taking apart?"

"No more than a few weeks; if it isn't done by then, the spell will get so unstable that it will collapse anyway." Mairelon's expression was grim. "Shoreham is trying to round up as many of the rookery magicians as possible—dismantling the spell will be quicker and easier if they are present, and we don't want any more like Ma Yanger if we can help it."

Kim nodded soberly. Shoreham's men had found Ma the day before, in a back room at one of Mannering's warehouses. After a careful examination, all of the wizards had agreed that returning her magic to her would do nothing to restore her mind, nor were there other methods that might help her. Shoreham had set one of his men to arranging for her care; the costs would come out of Mannering's property.

"Shoreham will be by later this evening to see you," Mairelon added, studying his hands with an innocent air.

"To see me?" Kim looked at him suspiciously. "What for?"

"I believe he wants to offer you a job, of sorts."

"What sorts?"

"Much the same as the one I've been doing from time to time," Mairelon replied. "He, er, admires your initiative. And this is the second time you've gotten mixed up in some of his doings; I believe he'd be more comfortable if it were official."

Kim snorted. "That business with the Saltash Set was your doings, not Shoreham's, and so was this."

"Yes, well, Shoreham doesn't see it that way. But you needn't agree, if you'd rather not."

Kim paused, considering. "It sounds a lot more interesting than balls and teas and morning calls." Another thought struck her, and she looked at Mairelon. "Am I done with those, now that we're engaged?"

"The Season's only half over," Mairelon said. "But I suppose that if you'd really rather not—"

"Good!" Kim said emphatically. "Let's go tell your mother, quick, before she finishes that note she's writing to Renée D'Auber about going shopping tomorrow."

Mairelon looked suddenly wary. "I, er, believe she has something else in mind."

"No, she said I needed more gowns." Kim shook her head. "I have a wardrobe full of gowns already; what do I need more for?"

Mairelon pursed his lips and said nothing.

"Mairelon . . ."

"Well," he said in an apologetic tone, though his eyes were dancing, "we *are* getting married, you know."

"Oh, Lord," Kim said, appalled. "Bride-clothes! I'll be stuck at the dressmaker's *forever!*"

"Better you than me," said her unsympathetic bridegroom, and offered her his arm to escort her down to dinner.